Yesterday

A Coventry Childhood in Peace and War

Pat Watson

MERTON PRIORY PRESS

First published 2002

Published by Merton Priory Press
67 Merthyr Road, Whitchurch
Cardiff CF1 1DD

ISBN 1 898937 53 2

© Pat Watson 2002

The right of Pat Watson to be identified as author
of this work has been asserted in accordance
with Sections 77 and 78 of the
Copyright, Designs and Patents Act 1988

The cover illustration is from *Bishop Street, Coventry, 1929*,
by Joan Murphy (1900–86), reproduced by kind permission
of the Herbert Art Gallery & Museum.
© The estate of the late Joan Murphy 2002

For Jack and Freya, Tom and Alice,
and remembering Michelle

All the characters in this book are
fictitious and are not intended to represent
any actual persons living or dead.

Printed by
Dinefwr Press Ltd
Rawlings Road, Llandybie
Carmarthenshire SA18 3YD

Contents

	Foreword Dr Carl Chinn MBE, University of Birmingham	5
1	A Lovely Day	7
2	A Gift from Fatty Arbuckle	18
3	Princess Patty and the Jolly Joker	28
4	Queen Squeak	40
5	Joey and the Christmas Fairies	52
6	A Little Spot of Bother	64
7	Miss Bellamy's Burglar	76
8	An Angel Unawares	88
9	Fatty Patty and the World Walker	99
10	Meeting Madame Fallova	109
11	The Silver Dancing Shoe	120
12	Lottie Craxton's Crowning Glory	130

13	Judgement Day	141
14	Miss Miranda and the Ring o'Bells Romance	152
15	A Good Send-Off	164

Foreword

For some people, history is about amassing as many facts and figures as possible in a vain attempt to put forward as objective a view of the past as can be achieved. In this way, history becomes a mass of dates, leading figures and major events that have become almost sterile and from which all emotion has been stripped.

But history is much more than facts and figures. It is about hopes, dreams and aspirations. It is about a smell that pulls you back into a cherished thought; it is about a sound that calls you into days gone by; it is about the feel of something that makes you aware of touches almost but not quite forgotten; it is about a look or a sight that leads you to a place hidden for too long from view; and it is about a taste that arouses you to bring to the fore a savouring of something deep within you.

That is the joy of *Yesterday's Child* by Pat Watson. She has evoked her childhood and brought it to life through her skilful alertness to the importance of using our senses when we head back into our past. Through her we too see Blackie, the dray horse stamping his shaggy feet restlessly; we too feel the rag doll that had fallen into the water butt so that its sawdust had swollen, bursting the red seams and loosening the glue that held the head in place; we too hear the taunt of Fatty Arbuckle thrown at Pat because she was picked on as such a clever dick; we too taste the milk, all creamy and foaming, as it is poured from the milkman's churn to the enamel jug; and we too can smell the dusty disorder of Em Todd's shop where she sold wool, bolts of lace curtain material, household linens and haberdashery.

Pat Watson has done something special. She has taken us with her on a journey into her past and through her words and her powerful awareness of senses she has made her past familiar to us. At the same time, her ability as a writer ensures that she also leads us into sensing our own past. This is a book to be savoured.

1

A Lovely Day

'A bad omen that is, if ever there was one.'

Mrs Peake's watery red eyes gazed at us dolefully from behind her thick glasses. Mrs Peake was very keen on omens, and was able to spot them miles away, especially by hindsight. We shared a yard with the Peakes, who kept a general grocery shop in their front room, with skips of vegetables on the pavement outside. A covered entry separated our two houses, and every night we heard old Mr Peake cursing to himself as he dragged the skips along it and into the yard, to be guarded by Dinkie, his black and white three-legged mongrel. I was playing with Dinkie now, as far as he could play, chained up to his kennel. My mother was washing up at the sink and talking to Mrs Peake through the open door.

'Fell off into the gutter, it did,' Mrs Peake continued. She folded back her newspaper to show us the photograph of the old king's coffin, draped in the Royal Standard. The Imperial Crown had been fixed to the coffin and, it seemed, the Maltese cross on top of it had jolted loose and bounced off into the road during the procession, to the dismay of the onlookers. My mother glanced at the newspaper and nodded. She had too many worries of her own to bother much about the Royal Family and their problems. I rolled the old tennis ball to Dinkie again, and he pounced on it like a puppy. Born on a farm, he had lost his hind leg in a harvesting accident, and had been sold cheap to the Peakes. 'He'll do. I wants him for barking not for running,' Mr Peake had said, as he grudgingly paid over the money. Dinkie had stayed chained up in the yard more or less ever since, but he was still bright-eyed and as lively as ever. He was good company for me. I was an only child, with no-one else to play with.

Funerals seemed to be in fashion that year. After the king's funeral, everyone wanted to go in for the huge wreaths, the long veils and the elaborate mourning. I saw a funeral nearly every week, the big black cars and the crowds of people like a flock of crows round the newly-turned earth. Going to the cemetery was my mother's favourite outing. After a row with my father—and they took place nearly every week, too—she wanted to pour out her woes by her aunt's graveside. I knew Aunt Marie only from a severe sepia portrait in the front room, but years ago she had brought up my mother and her sister Madge, keeping house for her widowed brother and fighting off any would-be stepmothers who came along. Kneeling by the grassy mound, weeping and complaining, was the highspot of my mother's week, and she rose refreshed to face the battles ahead. I enjoyed myself too. I thought the cemetery was a lovely place to play.

So when, a few weeks later, we went over to Miss Plumb's for tea, the scraps of black crepe and purple satin she had waiting for me gave me an idea for a new game. Miss Plumb lived round the corner from us in a block of old watchmakers' cottages, tiny houses with an upper storey of 'top shops' with huge windows, where once clocks and watches had been made. Miss Plumb's father had been a watchmaker, and she still lived in the dark, poky little house where she had been brought up with her five older brothers. A tiny, gentle little grey mouse of a woman, she gave us fish-paste sandwiches for tea and always had a pile of scraps of material for dolls' clothes put aside for me. She scraped a living from dressmaking and alterations for her neighbours, and from the look of it she had recently been working for a family in mourning.

While my mother and Miss Plumb settled down by the kitchen range after tea to go over the local gossip, I brought out my two new dolls. One of the pleasures of going to see Miss Plumb was that on the way we passed a little back-street toyshop, a treasure cave of cheap foreign toys where, if I saved up my pocket-money, I could buy tiny dolls with china heads and feet and bodies made of red rag filled with sawdust, exactly the right size for my doll's house. Now, seeing the satin and the crepe, I knew just the game to play with my new twins, Eric and Una. Eric's china face wore a serene expression which could easily be mistaken for that of a relative stunned by grief, and though Una appeared to be in the best of spirits, her veil would hide her cheerful smile. To my surprise, when I explained all this to Miss Plumb, a look of horror came over her face.

'Funerals? Playing at funerals?' she repeated, looking down at me and my dolls in dismay. 'Well, I'm not sure that's a very nice game for a little girl to be playing at, Patty. I don't know what your mother will say ... .' She broke off, and whispered urgently to my mother as she poured her out a second cup of tea.

To my relief, my mother brushed her objections briskly aside. 'Morbid? Oh no, I don't think so, Louisa. It's just another game to her. She loves coming up to the cemetery with me—plays all sorts of games there, she does. She's very imaginative for her age, you know. Her teacher says so. Now, young lady,' she went on, turning to me. 'Get your things together. We'll have to be off home soon, or I'll have nothing ready for your father when he comes in, and your Aunt Madge will be home from work before long, too.'

I said my thank-you gratefully. The sandwiches had been bloater-paste, my favourite, and I was delighted with my new dolls and the outfits I had made for them. I carried them carefully back in a brown paper bag and several times that week held rehearsals with them under the kitchen table. But I knew to play the game properly I would have to wait till we went to the cemetery again, and I had a feeling we would soon be doing just that.

Sure enough the following day I heard shouting in the scullery, and my father barged angrily through the kitchen as I sat at the table doing a jig-saw puzzle. He stamped upstairs, swearing under his breath, and I heard the bedroom door slam behind him. At first glance my father, stocky and bluff with a weather-beaten face, looked jolly and good-natured, until you noticed his hard little blue eyes watching you suspiciously and weighing you up to make sure he could get the better of you. He was a man who always had to be 'top dog', and though he never actually hit me, he often made an unpleasant pantomime of taking off his belt to thrash me. We were all afraid of him, and sometimes I was pushed in front of him when he was going to hit my mother.

'Look at little Patty,' she and my Aunt Madge would shriek. 'You're frightening little Patty.' And true enough, he was.

Now, though, once he was safely out of the way upstairs, my mother came in, carrying a bunch of daffodils. She put them down on the sideboard while she dabbed her cheeks with Icilma cream rouge to hide the tear-stains, her mouth set in a grim line. Not yet forty, she was already going grey and her face was worn and lined, though in photographs I had seen of her as a girl, she was pretty, dark haired and dark eyed.

'Come along, Patty,' she said, sniffing. 'I'm taking these daffs up to Aunt Marie's grave. Put your jig-saw away and if we're quick we'll be in time to meet Madge out of work. You'd like that, wouldn't you?'

A double treat! Not only a trip to the cemetery, but a visit to the box-factory as well! I might even be allowed to feed Blackie, the dray-horse. I scooped up my jig-saw into its box and put Eric and Una, resplendent in their black and purple, into my pocket. Then I skipped along at my mother's side as she set off down the road.

Soon we entered the cemetery, going first through high iron gates with a lodge at one side. With its arched windows and stunted spire, I took it for a miniature church. Then we swung along a wide drive, the gravel crunching under our feet, with on one side a section of graves fenced off by themselves. Years later I found out that these were reserved for Jewish burials. They looked forgotten now, and neglected, the railings by the roadside broken down in places and rusty. In front of us all I could see stretching away in the distance were monuments and headstones, sparkling in the early spring sunshine. On some, angels pointed optimistically to heaven, and I looked at these with envy, hoping I would have a similar one when I came to live in the cemetery like Aunt Marie. Before long we turned down a narrow path with on either side glass globes of wax flowers, marble vases and fancy headstones, some shaped like open books, others like Greek columns or scrolls of parchment. In spring and summer wildflowers grew thickly between the grassy hillocks, moon-daisies, buttercups, sorrel, ladysmock and clover. The yellow pollen dappled my shoes and I enjoyed the fresh air and the warmth of the sun. It was a pleasant change from our dark, damp terraced house and the dingy backyard. In our neglected strip of garden no flowers grew and it ended in a high brick wall crowned with jagged shards of broken glass set in cement. No wonder I preferred the cemetery.

When we arrived at Aunt Marie's grave I settled down silently to my new game. I took Eric and Una out of my pocket and tidied their clothes, making sure Una's veil came well down over her face. Then I made three wreaths, one for each of us, out of wildflowers, and started the procession. My mother was used to me wandering off, and took no notice. Holding Una and Eric by the hand, their wreaths for convenience slung around their necks, I put on a solemn expression and walked slowly along the path. Determined to find the perfect setting, I went further than I intended, but at last I came to a grave that had everything—a weeping angel, wax flowers and a heart-shaped head-stone with gold lettering. I arranged Eric and Una side by side, their wreaths in front of them. They lolled against each other but I pretended that was because they were overcome with grief. I intended to start the ceremony with a hymn, but here I hit a snag. The only song I knew really well was 'Twinkle, twinkle little star'. Finally I decided if I sang it sadly and solemnly, it would do. My voice wavered a little, and I wished the twins were capable of joining in, but at last I got to the end and laid my wreath at the foot of the grave. I helped the dolls to lay their wreaths, and wondered what to do next. Some way off, one of the cemetery attendants was pushing along a wheelbarrow full of discarded flowers, and he seemed to be watching us suspiciously. Anyway, by now I was getting bored with the whole idea of funerals. They weren't nearly as much fun as I had expected.

'Stay here and pray quietly,' I instructed Eric and Una. 'I'll be back in a minute to fetch you. Don't go away.'

Guided by my mother's kneeling figure in the distance, I made my way back to Aunt Marie's grave and began another game, an old favourite this time. I borrowed a handful of marble chippings from a nearby monument and picked the heads off the buttercups and daisies growing close at hand. These I arranged on dock-leaves like a little shop, helping myself to some crumpled newspaper out of the waste-bin to wrap them up in as imaginary customers came and went. Out of the corner of my eye I could see my mother still whispering bitterly about my father to her aunt, but soon I became absorbed in my game. It came as a shock when at last she scrambled to her feet.

'Come along, Patty.' Her eye fell on the newspaper parcels and she added crossly, 'Where did you get all that rubbish? Throw it away—you don't know where it's been!'

I knew exactly where it had been, of course—in the waste-bin where now I put it back, but I didn't argue. I was too worried about Eric and Una, marooned at the distant grave. In alarm I realised that now I had no idea where I had left them.

'My dollies—I've lost them.' I tried to explain but my mother took no notice. Already she was hurrying along the path to the gate.

'Come along, there's a good girl. We'll be late for Aunt Madge,' she called over her shoulder. 'If you've left anything behind, you can get it next time. We can't stop any longer now.'

The box factory where Aunt Madge worked was on the other side of town, but as usual we took a short cut along the canal bank, arriving at the factory gate just before it was time for her to come out. Conscious of her swollen eyes, my mother stayed out of sight round the corner of the building, and sent me on alone to meet Aunt Madge.

'You wait by the gate, Patty,' she said. 'You'll spot Madge easy as winking when she comes out. Stand over on the other side of the bay where Blackie is. He won't hurt you—he's as gentle as a lamb.'

In the cobbled stall strewn with straw and smelling strongly of ammonia, Blackie the dray-horse was stamping his shaggy feet restlessly, as he waited to be led back for the night to his stable across the factory yard, his delivery round over for the day. Billy Weatherby, his driver, was taking the chance of a quiet smoke, but his round red face broke into smiles when I appeared and he stubbed out his Woodbine on the wall behind him. Like Aunt Madge, he had worked at the factory for years, and had known me as a baby, brought up first in my high pram and then in my push-chair to meet Aunt Madge out of work. As soon as he saw me, he fumbled in the pocket of his overalls and pulled out some dry crusts.

'Come to feed ole Blackie then, have you, my little lass?' he beamed. Taking my hand, he straightened the fingers and laid the crusts on my palm, lifting up my arm so that the huge cart-horse could catch the scent of the bread. 'Now you keep your fingers flat like that, there's a good girl, or Blackie'll tek 'em off for you by accident, see? Hold your hand still and you'll be just fine.'

Half fascinated, half afraid, I waited while the velvet muzzle descended on to my palm and the big yellow teeth crunched up the stale bread. Not daring to move, I endured the tickling sensation as the crusts disappeared into Blackie's moist pink mouth, and then wiped my sticky hand on the skirt of my coat, relieved I had escaped with all my fingers intact. Just then a hooter sounded, signalling the end of the day's work, and footsteps began to clatter down the stone stairs inside the building. A few minutes later I caught sight of my aunt, her shabby coat buttoned and belted over her print overall and her brown felt hat pulled down low over her ears. Unlike my mother, Aunt Madge had never been pretty, and now, at the end of the day at work, she looked worn out and weary. I waved eagerly and, immediately on the alert for trouble, she pushed her way anxiously through the crowd towards me.

'I fed Blackie, Auntie Madge,' I boasted, but for once she cut through my chatter impatiently.

'Where's your mother? Has there been a row?' Not waiting for an answer, she darted along to the corner and soon she and my mother were walking down the street, their heads together, with me scurrying behind them, trying in vain to keep up. I imagined Blackie going back to his stable now, and wondered if he remembered my feeding him. I thought of Eric and Una, left alone in the cemetery as darkness fell. I remembered the grandly dressed people in the big black cars I had seen at the real funerals. Perhaps they would find the twins and take them home with them to live in a wonderful enormous dolls' house, but it didn't seem very likely. If anyone was going to rescue Una and Eric, it would have to be me.

'Aunt Madge,' I began when we arrived back home, to find the house empty and my father gone out to sulk elsewhere, 'I lost my dollies in the cemetery. Do you think we could ... '

'Oh, you don't want to worry about them,' she broke in, starting to unbutton my coat. 'The fairies will find them and take them back to fairyland. They'll be fine, they will—have a lovely time dancing with the fairies. Now change into your slippers, my duck, and I'll make you a nice cup of cocoa.'

Unconvinced, I sat gloomily by the fire drinking my cocoa, and a few minutes later I heard Mr Peake bringing in the skips of vegetables with his usual grunts and groans. Catching sight of my mother at our coalhouse, he paused for a moment to shout something to her about the weather.

'Yes, going to be a wet one by the look of it,' my mother agreed, and my eyes widened in alarm. I knew only too well what getting wet would do to Eric and Una. Once before I had accidentally let one of my small rag dolls fall into the water-butt, and though I had snatched it out at once, the results has been horrific. The sawdust had swollen up in no time, bursting the red rag seams, and the damp had loosened the glue that held the head in place so that it fell off and was smashed to pieces. If the twins got wet, they would be ruined, even if I was ever lucky enough to find them again.

Suddenly, I knew what I must do. Somehow I had to go back to the cemetery now, before the rain came, and find the dolls and bring them safely home. I knew I was hardly ever allowed out alone, so I had to go secretly, but today was Friday, and on Friday Aunt Madge always went to see her workmate Eileen Wimbush at the cookshop on the corner, and they often went to the pictures together. I knew Eileen, a plump, friendly girl who helped her mother in the shop on Saturdays when Mrs Wimbush was rushed off her feet serving the pork batches for which she was famous all over the neighbourhood. Every Saturday a big joint of pork, straight from the oven and kept warm on a chafing dish, was brought into the shop and placed in the window, surrounded by the roast potatoes that had cooked alongside it. Fresh bread rolls, soft inside and crusty out, were cut through and dipped in gravy. Then a thick slice of the hot roast pork, with a generous dab of sage and onion stuffing, went inside, with—if you were lucky—a crunchy chunk of crackling from the top side of the roast. Pork batches and a basin of roast potatoes made Saturday dinner-time a special treat, and I envied Eileen having it every Saturday of her life. Now, though, I was grateful to her, for getting Aunt Madge out of the way. With my father already gone, only my mother remained in the house, and she almost always fell asleep by the fire over the latest copy of *Peg's Paper*. If she woke up, she would think I had got bored and gone to meet Aunt Madge or perhaps had run around to

Miss Plumb's to beg some more scraps for my dolls. But if she did fall asleep on cue, dare I go alone on my search? Outside the kitchen window I heard Dinkie dragging his chain, scratching for fleas. That was it—I would take Dinkie with me! I settled down quietly with a comic to read till the coast was clear.

The fresh air that afternoon must have made my mother sleepy, for she nodded off earlier than usual and didn't stir as I slipped on my coat and crept out to the scullery, clutching my skipping-rope. I tied one end of it to Dinkie's collar and, praying he wouldn't bark, set off down the entry. I knew the way to the cemetery well, and with Dinkie running along smartly on his three legs, soon came to the gates—only to find they were shut fast. My heart sank and I thought at first that all my efforts had been in vain, but then I remembered the broken railings by the road that led into the Jewish cemetery. With Dinkie at my heels, I slipped through and crept along the path that led up to the big gravel drive. Soon we were trotting along in the gathering darkness, and I realised now that at night the cemetery was a very different place from when I played there so happily in the sunshine. A chilly mist swirled in the hollows and the wind made the branches creak eerily. Even the angels seemed sinister, looming at me in silent menace. Dinkie was subdued, and whined to himself as we hurried along.

Angels! At last I remembered the weeping angel at the grave where I had left Eric and Una. If I could find that, my search was over. I paused to peer through the gloom, and Dinkie looked up at me anxiously. A light rain had started to fall, but ahead of me I could see three pale circles on the ground. It was the three wreaths, with the angel bending above them. I gave a gasp of relief as I bent down and gathered up the twins. I checked to see they had come to no harm, and then put them carefully into my pocket before I turned to retrace my steps.

But now disasters came thick and fast. I lost my way back to the main path and wasted precious minutes going the long way round. Dinkie, keen to get home out of the rain, began to tug on the lead and ended by pulling me over on the gravel, grazing my knee. Then, as we scrambled down the sloping bank of the Jewish cemetery, a loose stone turned under my foot, so that I slid the rest of the way, tumbled through the broken railings and ended up in a heap on the pavement outside.

'Ay-up! What's the matter wi'ee, my lass?' A burly man on a bicycle ground to a halt in the gutter and came towards me in concern. Dinkie growled at the sight of a stranger, but it was no stranger to me. Hardly able to believe my eyes, I saw it was none other than Billy Weatherby, riding home after giving Blackie his supper. Seeing me lying there on the ground, he gave a whistle of astonishment.

'Well, bless my soul if it isn't little Patty Palmer,' he exclaimed. 'Whatever are you a-doing here at this time of night? Well, never mind that now, my pigeon. Us'd better get you home to your ma and your auntie. Good job I stayed be'ind to muck out ole Blackie's stable or I'd been gone back to my supper long ago.' He helped me gently to my feet. 'Can you stand, then? There's a brave lass. But you shall ride home on my cross-bar, that you shall, and us'll tie your ole pal here to the carrier so's he can run along be'ind.'

On Billy's bike it seemed next to no time before we were home, and I managed to convince him there was no need to see me safe inside the door. Quickly I put Dinkie back on his chain, and crept silently into the kitchen where my mother was still asleep over her magazine. But I had only just enough time to hang my coat up before Aunt Madge's footsteps came tapping down the entry, waking her up with a start. Luckily when Aunt Madge came into the kitchen, she looked puzzled and flustered.

'Why, Madge, what's up with you? You look as if you'd seen a ghost!' my mother said in surprise. My aunt frowned, shaking her head.

'I can't understand it, Annie,' she replied thoughtfully. 'Do you know, I could have sworn I saw Billy Weatherby riding off on his bike just now from outside our house. But what on earth would he be doing round here at this time? It seems very peculiar.'

'Perhaps he was hanging about hoping to bump into you, Madge,' replied my mother with a smirk. 'I always did think he was a bit sweet on you, you know—I've said so more than once'.

Aunt Madge bridled coyly, her sallow cheeks flushing.

'Billy Weatherby? As if I'd take any notice of him,' she answered huffily. 'I should hope I could do better than that, if I wanted to try. Not that he isn't a good-hearted soul, I'll grant you that. But I don't fancy him as a husband—nor anyone else, neither,' she added hastily, as the entry door banged and my father tramped in at the kitchen door. 'Husbands? No thank you—not for me!'

Unseen by Aunt Madge, my mother gave a sarcastic smile as she put a plate of cold meat down in front of my father. We had all eaten earlier—one of his regular complaints was that we ate in shifts, 'like a model lodging house,' he said—and I began to get ready for bed. I smuggled Eric and Una upstairs with me, hiding them safely under my pillow for the night. Tired out by the fresh air and all the walking, I soon drifted off to sleep, thinking happily of the games I had played in the cemetery, of Blackie's soft muzzle on my hand as I fed him, and of my ride home on Billy Weatherby's bicycle. It had been a lovely day, I thought, and before long in my dreams I was serving stone angels with plates of buttercup and daisy stew.

2

A Gift from Fatty Arbuckle

'We call you Fatty Arbuckle! You didn't know that, did you, for all you're such a clever-dick?'

I flinched back as Maggie O'Shea spat the words into my face, and banged my leg on the dustbins behind me. Her stubby finger stabbed painfully at my shoulder.

'Did you hear me now? Fatty Arbuckle—that's what we call you,' she repeated, grinning unpleasantly.

The spiteful nickname came as a shock. Maggie was supposed to be my best friend, and though I knew nothing then about the podgy Hollywood film star, disgraced years ago by an unsavoury scandal, that didn't stop her meaning from being clear enough. I hesitated, while Maggie watched me with a kind of jeering curiosity, her eyes narrowed in her red, sweaty face, enjoying my dismay. Then I turned and fled down the garden path to lock myself in the lavatory that the O'Sheas shared with their neighbour, old Mrs Cass. I sank down breathless on the scrubbed wooden bench with the hole in the middle, and wondered what to do next.

It was quiet and cool in the dark, white-washed shed, festooned with spiders' webs, a bunch of newspaper squares hanging from a rusty nail. Miserably I rubbed at my sore shoulder—Maggie's finger had come sharp—and tried to decide whether to tell my mother. Would that make me a tell tale? The playground rhyme ran through my head:

'Tell-tale-tit, your tongue shall be slit,
And all the doggies in the town shall have a little bit ... '

I shuddered at the hideous picture this brought to mind. Then, too, Maggie's mother, Aunt Molly, was my own mother's closest friend—'Thick as thieves,' my father was fond of saying—and somehow I knew she'd pretend it didn't matter, that it was all a silly joke and Maggie didn't mean it, that it wasn't even true. And I would have to pretend to believe her. Everything would go on as usual, but nothing would be the same. I would know, and Maggie would know I knew, that to her, to Aunt Molly, and to Maggie's father, Uncle Joe—kind, gentle Uncle Joe!—I was 'Fatty Arbuckle'.

I had played with Maggie O'Shea ever since, as heavyweight toddlers, we had creaked up and down on the seesaw in the park. In those early years we had seen a lot of Aunt Molly, since we lived in Shelley Street opposite the Catholic church, and she was forever popping in and out of it. I thought it was the Cat-lick Church, the way she pronounced it, for her Irish brogue got stronger the minute she stepped over our threshold. She knew my mother was a soft touch for anyone from 'the ould country'—her long-dead mother had been Irish.

'Can ye be after lending me a few coppers till pay-day, Annie, me darlint?' she'd ask. 'Another collection for the priest's vestments, would ye believe? That's the Cat-lick Church all over!'

A thin, rattling, bony woman with bright red cheeks and what my father called 'a cherry nose', she was as noisy as Uncle Joe was quiet. He worked at a factory on the other side of town, cycling there in all weathers, a shy, patient man, the exact opposite of my bullyragging father, who could only go out window-cleaning when the sun shone, and not always then. When Aunt Molly and Uncle Joe came round at Christmas, my father used to pretend to believe her nose was red from the drink, making her screech with laughter.

'To be sure, 'tis from the wants of it,' she would protest, sipping gingerly at a glass of port and lemon or some of my mother's home-made elderberry wine. She was a martyr, she said, to indigestion, and always carried peppermints in her pocket.

When we were old enough, Maggie was sent to the Catholic school next to the church, and I went off to the ordinary school at the end of the road, past Salters' second-hand shop with the parrot in the window and the Ring o' Bells pub on the corner. Looking back, I think this was when a tinge of jealousy began to sour the friendship between the families. I was considered to be clever, with from the first a good chance of a scholarship, while Maggie, grown into a stolid, suet-pudding child, was docile and good but not particularly bright—to be honest, not bright at all. Aunt Molly used to come and sit with my mother in the afternoon till it was time to fetch us from school. Sometimes we all went back to our house and sometimes we went with Maggie and Aunt Molly to their house, through a warren of backstreets, alleys and jetties and across the park where we had first met. It was in Maggie's yard that suddenly, without any warning, she came out with the words she'd obviously bottled up for weeks. Perhaps I'd been boasting of my successes in the classroom that day, perhaps I'd beaten her once too often in the game we were playing. Whatever it was, all at once she thrust her malicious face into mine and hissed, 'We call you Fatty Arbuckle!'

And now I was cowering in the lavatory, shocked to realise I had been discussed, not affectionately or admiringly, but mockingly, derisively discussed, behind my back. At any moment Mrs Cass might start rattling at the latch, muttering and glaring at me as I came out. The children in Maggie's street said she was a witch, and I believed them. Tall as a man, with her stringy grey hair and long, dusty black skirts, she certainly looked like one, and I'd heard Aunt Molly telling my mother that she'd seen her at the end of the garden at night, dancing and bowing to the new moon. A sudden thought struck me—did Mrs Cass know what I was called by the O'Sheas? Did everybody know?

It was at that moment I heard my mother calling me from Aunt Molly's back door. To my relief I realised I had no need to face Maggie again—it was time to go home. I pulled hard on the lavatory chain to cover my tracks and unlocked the door. Maggie was lurking behind Aunt Molly in the kitchen doorway, and I avoided her eye. My mother bundled me into my coat and wound my scarf round my neck.

'Look at you, Patty—you're all over cobwebs!' She brushed at my hair impatiently with her hand. 'Whatever have you been doing to yourself? Come on, now—your dad will be home and waiting for his tea.'

She turned to have a last word with Aunt Molly, and in those few minutes I made up my mind. I could never tell her about

Maggie's unkindness. Not because she wouldn't believe me, not because I was afraid of being branded as a tell-tale, but because if she did believe me, there might be a row, perhaps between my father and my mother—'I told you not to take up with them Micks!'—or perhaps between my mother and my real aunt, Aunt Madge, who lived with us—'Like I said before, Annie, it's best to keep yourself to yourself. Molly O'Shea does nothing but sponge off you!'—and in either case my mother would be spending the next few days lying down in a darkened room with a vinegar-rag on her forehead, suffering, yet again, from her 'nerves'.

Next day we saw nothing of Aunt Molly, and I thought, of course, that Maggie had confessed to her mother and they were both too ashamed to come near us. But when another day went by without a word, my mother began to feel uneasy, and after school took me round to the O'Sheas' house to find out what was wrong. I half-expected to see Maggie or her mother peeping guiltily at us from behind the curtains, but instead the curtains were drawn upstairs and down, something unheard of in the daytime unless there was a funeral in the street. There was no answer to our knock at first. Not till my mother had knocked three times did a curtain twitch, and then it was at Mrs Cass's window. When she recognised us, she swiftly appeared at her own front door, and stared grimly at us with raised eyebrows.

'They didn't tell you either, then? And you such pals of theirs. Well, you do surprise me. I made sure you'd know all about it, if anybody did,' she said sarcastically, as my mother shook her head in bewilderment.

'Tell us what?' she asked nervously. 'What was there to tell? We haven't seen them since the day before yesterday ... .'

'And neither's nobody!' Mrs Cass interrupted triumphantly. 'A midnight flit, that's what they've done. They've cleared off back to Ireland most likely, and good riddance to them, that's for sure, if you ask me!'

'A midnight flit?' My mother looked aghast. 'But why? Whatever made them do such a thing? And not to say a word to us—does anybody know why?'

I do, I thought. Maggie told them what she said to me, and they've run away. They just packed up and went, because she was so rude to me. I'll never see them again, and I'm glad!'

But Mrs Cass soon disillusioned me. Maggie's rudeness, it seemed, was the least of their problems.

'Anybody know why?' she snorted. 'Just about everybody around here knows well enough, all the shopkeepers, all the tallymen, all the pub landlords and the bookies, they owed money right, left and centre, the O'Sheas did, what with him gambling every last penny he could lay his hands on and her drinking it all away. They were in debt up to their eyebrows and when they'd borrowed money from everybody daft enough to lend it to them'—here she shot my mother a shrewd glance—'they packed up and went, in the middle of the night before last.'

'Gambling? Drinking?' queried my mother faintly. 'But Molly didn't drink, hardly at all, and Joe wouldn't even buy a ticket for the Irish Sweepstake. And as for buying things on credit from the tallyman, she always said she'd sooner do without than be in debt.'

'Maybe that's what she told you, but actions speak louder than words,' retorted Mrs Cass. 'Living next door to them, I knew what they were really like. It's been nothing but folks banging on my door ever since they've been gone, trying to track them down. You saw what they chose to let you see. If you were taken in, it's no fault of mine.'

With that, she stepped back inside and closed the door, leaving us standing in the gathering dusk. Her mouth tightly pursed and with a furious glint in her eye, my mother set off down the road so fast I could hardly keep up with her, and by the time we reached home I was panting for breath. Aunt Madge by now was back from the box factory, and my father sat by the fire reading the paper and waiting for his tea. They both looked up as we came in, but a warning glance from my mother kept them quiet. I had already heard more than enough from Mrs Cass.

Bundled off to bed early after a boiled egg and some toast, I lay awake in the bedroom I shared with Aunt Madge and tried to make sense of what had been said. Downstairs I could hear my mother pouring out the whole story, followed by a babble of recriminations, weeping and swearing, this last from my father who felt he'd been made a fool of, especially by Molly and her 'cherry nose'. I realised that because we didn't drink, gamble or get into debt,

Molly and Joe had pretended they didn't, either, in order to take what advantage they could of our friendship. Because they had got into such a mess, they had had to make a run for it, unable even to risk saying goodbye. Maggie, I suspected, had been in on the secret. Freed by the knowledge that in a few hours she would be on the other side of the Irish Sea, she'd been able to pay me back for being 'a clever-dick' by taunting me with my ugly nickname. I sat up in the darkness, hugging my knees to my chest, enjoying the drama going on downstairs and knowing that an army of angry creditors would keep Maggie safely out of my life for ever.

The O'Sheas' midnight flit, like all neighbourhood scandals, was a nine days' wonder, and since it appeared that we were far from being the only victims my mother soon overcame her 'nerves' sufficiently to join in the gossip and deplore the way Molly and Joe had lived their double life. Gradually the memory faded of Aunt Molly's daily visits, and I played solitary games in our own backyard, free from the shadow of Mrs Cass. Wary of being taken in again, my mother heeded Aunt Madge's advice to keep herself to herself, and if she missed the soft, Irish voice wheedling a few coppers out of her every week, she didn't say so. If the O'Sheas were mentioned, she would sniff and mutter something about 'the priest's vestments, indeed!' while my father would growl, 'Indigestion, my foot! No wonder she was always sucking those damn peppermints!'

By the time some months later that a tear-stained letter of apology and explanation arrived, anger and indignation had faded, and the result in the end was a pen-friendship that went on for years. It was almost as if my mother preferred having friends in Ireland to having Irish friends living in her pocket, and her obsession with 'the ould country' became stronger than ever. She started taking an Irish newspaper and began to collect ornaments carved out of Irish bogwood, a tiny cauldron, a little harp and a miniature Celtic cross. The one I liked best had a realistic figure of a farmer with a pig tethered by a string. The motto on the base read, 'Now, don't be r'adin' milestones!' I spend hours arranging all the pieces on my mother's bedroom mantelpiece, with the farmer in the middle.

Every week my mother wrote to Aunt Molly with news of my

progress at school and all the local gossip, receiving in return news of Joe's job as a council road-sweeper, Maggie's life as a pupil of the holy sisters and Molly's own busy days in the village and up in the hills where her brother Daniel had a smallholding. At Christmas a goose came, plucked and ready for the oven, followed on St Patrick's Day by a green and gold box filled with shamrock, carefully packed in damp moss. In return we sent presents and sticks of rock from the seaside. The only thing my mother could never bring herself to mention was the Georgian silver teapot.

This had been kept with our other family treasures—a photograph album with brass clasps, an ivory carving and a mottled glass rolling-pin—in the cupboard of the mahogany chiffonnière in the front room. Round about the time of the O'Sheas' midnight flit, we discovered that the teapot had disappeared. Nobody could remember when they saw it last. After all, the front door was never locked in the daytime—the baker opened it to put in the loaf out of the dust of the street, and if we didn't hear the milkman's can on the doorstep, he would open the door to give us a call.

'Harry Edwards was here last Monday,' Aunt Madge remarked thoughtfully. She had never liked my father's shifty side-kick who helped him with the window-cleaning round. 'He came again on Thursday—or was it Friday?'

'I'm almost sure I saw it on Saturday when I went in there to get the rent-book,' said my mother. 'And the baker's got a new lad helping him ... .' her voice trailed off uncertainly.

Hanging in the air unspoken was the thought that, though either Harry Edwards or the baker's boy might be the culprit, there were other suspects as well, now too far away to question. In the end, after a lot of speculation, nothing was said to anybody about the missing teapot, for fear of 'giving offence'. The photograph album, the carving and the glass rolling-pin were taken upstairs and hidden on top of the wardrobe inside an old suitcase, where they remained for years. The teapot, eventually, was forgotten.

Over the years, my mother and Aunt Molly kept in touch. Photographs came of Maggie, dressed like a miniature bride to make her First Communion—'All bought on tick, I'll bet a pound to a penny!' snorted Aunt Madge—then in her uniform for High School, and later driving a pony-trap with her Uncle Daniel by her side and Aunt Molly peeping from the cottage doorway. Soon she was starting work, at first as a hotel receptionist in the nearby town and before long promoted to a similar job in Dublin. The next photo, brightly tinted, showed her with an elaborate hairstyle and too much jewellery. Beside her now stood a shock-headed young man in a gangster-style navy suit with sharp lapels and wide shoulders. Aunt Madge tittered and my mother sniffed but said nothing. I was still at school, in the sixth form, and the last thing they wanted was ideas put into my head by Maggie's nonsense. It was while she was working away from home that Uncle Joe died—an accident in the peat-bogs, Aunt Molly wrote, and she herself was moving from the village to keep house for Daniel, since they were both on their own now. My mother, then not long widowed, wrote back that I'd be leaving home soon, too, to go to college. Everything was changing so fast, it was hard to keep up with it. Before we knew it, it would be Christmas again, and it didn't seem five minutes since last year, when we'd had that lovely goose from them as usual ... .

Sure enough, Christmas came and went, and the goose with it, but the following spring a letter arrived addressed in an unfamiliar hand, and Maggie wrote to say Aunt Molly's last illness had been sudden and swift. The parish priest had found lodgings for Uncle Daniel, too feeble now to keep up the smallholding on his own, and she herself would be married soon and living in Dublin for good. She wrote again occasionally over the next few months, but finally, too busy perhaps with wedding plans, her letters ceased.

'Not even a Christmas card!' my mother complained bitterly that year. For me the ghost of Fatty Arbuckle came, and went.

We hardly mentioned the O'Sheas in the years that followed, and once my mother and aunt died, I moved away in my own turn, travelling where my work took me. Not till the early Eighties, when I came back to sort out some paperwork to do with my pension, did I see Shelley Street again. Hardly any of the old landmarks remained, swept away by the Blitz and the post-war reconstruction. The old warren of alleys and backstreets was gone and in its place stood a gleaming shopping precinct and a modern block of council offices. Though Shelley Street remained, it had been gentrified out of all recognition, the Ring o'Bells a bistro with tables outside on the pavement and a delicatessen where Chalmers' grocery had been. I noticed, though, that Salters' second-hand shop was still there, empty and with a tattered 'To Let' sign in the window where once the parrot had squawked obscenities. On either side the artisans' cottages, bright with fresh paint, window-boxes and brass knockers, looked attractive—and affluent. A half-formed plan came back into my head. Why not? I thought. After I'd sorted out my pension papers ready for an early retirement, I went to visit an estate agent.

Luckily, I had judged right—the area was on its way up, and soon Salters' Antique Gallery, as I called it, took off. What I had picked up as a hobby over the years stood me in good stead, and with my pension behind me I could afford to sit out the quiet times and adopt the laid-back attitude essential to dealing with an up-market clientele. With thick carpets, gleaming glass cabinets to house the stock, and flowers on the counter and on the tables round the showroom, the atmosphere was hushed and expensive. No parrot squawked in the window now—it held a few choice pieces displayed on black velvet. Gold-leaf lettering on the glass read, 'Quality Antiques Bought and Sold', and a discreet buzzer warned me when the door was opened. I spent the day happily checking out the trade papers and combing the auction catalogues for useful stock.

I had just ringed lot number 147—'Pair of pewter Art Nouveau vases with green glass liners, made for Liberty by Archibald Knox'—when the buzzer sounded late one autumn afternoon. It was getting dark outside and for a moment I couldn't see clearly the figure by the door. Then, as she made her way nervously between the showcases of figurines and porcelain, I saw it was a woman of about my own age, shabbily dressed and carrying a rexine shopping-bag. She looked round uncertainly before she spoke to me. Did we buy silver? Yes, we did. She fumbled in the bag and brought out a Georgian silver teapot, one I had last seen resting between an ivory carving and a glass rolling-pin more than half a century ago. But now I knew more than enough about silver and Sheffield plate and the difference between them. Turning the teapot over in my hands, I noted in places the warm gleam of copper below the thin coating of silver plate, and looked up at

Maggie O'Shea. It was clear she had no idea we had once played together in her back garden. She was anxious, trembling, humble.

'What do you want for it?' I asked, keeping my voice steady and even.

'My God, missus, I don't know … I had it from my mother. She thought it was worth a bit. My husband's been working over here, but now he's gone and I'm on my own, I'm going back to my children in Ireland. I'd like to take a bit of money with me.'

Her shabby clothes, her resignation, told the whole story. Widowed, she was going home and the teapot, stolen but for some reason of sentiment or caution never pawned or sold, would pay her fare and perhaps something over. A shade rose between us, not of merry Aunt Molly or gentle Uncle Joe, not even of my own foolish, easily deceived mother, but of a fat, long-forgotten film star. His name on her lips had been my first betrayal, still echoing down the years. But somehow I couldn't bear to turn her away with the £20 which was the going rate for her pathetic treasure. And these days I could afford to be generous, after all. I looked down at the battered heirloom, phoney as our early friendship, and took out a roll of notes from the till. Counting out six fifties, I pushed them over the counter to her. She gave a little gasp of relief and thrust them quickly into her purse.

'Thank you, missus.'

She turned and scuttled out of the shop as if she thought I might change my mind. Looking down at the teapot again, I smiled sadly.

'Don't thank me, Maggie O'Shea,' I said softly, as she closed the door and disappeared down Shelley Street. 'Don't thank me, Maggie—thank Fatty Arbuckle.'

3

Princess Patty and the Jolly Joker

'Milko!'

There was the rattle of a churn on the doorstep as the milkman, Sam Chinn, opened the front door and gave us a shout to let us know he was waiting. Carrying our enamel jug I hurried through from the scullery and watched while he dipped his pint measure into the churn and poured the milk, all creamy and foaming, into the jug. Pixie, his horse, waited patiently in the sunshine, tossing her head to keep off the flies. The milk float, smart with maroon paint and gold lines, had a spray of purple rhododendron tucked into one of the brass loops that held the traces, and Sam wore a wallflower in the buttonhole of his khaki cow-gown. Of all the tradesmen who called—the baker with his bread-cart, the coalman with his sacks, the Friday fishmonger and the paper-boy—Sam was the dandy, with his ready smile and his eye for the ladies. He saw me looking at the flower in his buttonhole, plucked it out and with a wink and a flourish, presented it to me as he turned to go.

'There you are, duchess,' he grinned, putting the lid back on the churn with a clatter. 'Though I bet you're never a wallflower yourself at the parties, are you? All the boys want to dance with you, I'll be bound!'

Before I could answer, he was gone, leaving me standing there on the step with the jug in one hand and the sweet-smelling flower in the other. Somehow I knew, without knowing how I knew, that Sam's chatter was just nonsense. I was far too young for dances and boys, and I didn't really understand what he meant by being a wallflower. But even so, his words hit home. I'd never been to a party. I hardly ever played with other children anyway, except at school, and nobody we knew had money to spare for parties. I'd read about them in books, of course, but that was different.

I took the milk into the pantry and put it on the thrall, the stone slab that kept our eggs and butter fresh, draping over the top of the jug the circle of muslin edged with coloured glass beads to keep out the flies and the flakes of whitewash that floated down from the damp walls. Then I went to show my mother the flower Sam had given me, telling her what he had said. She sniffed and poked the wallflower impatiently into an eggcup on the windowsill which already held some buttercups and daises I had picked in the park. I looked at it wistfully, remembering Sam's teasing words. Somehow the velvety petals and the fragrant smell spoke of a different, extravagant life-style, where parties happened all the time and children laughed and shouted and had fun.

I had left the doors open behind me, having both hands full, so I went back now to close them. I stood for a moment on the front doorstep, looking up and down the sunny street. At this time in the morning, it was almost empty, Sam's milk-float long since gone and hardly any other traffic around at all. Apart from the battered old vans used by the Salters for their second-hand business, only two people in the street had motor-cars. One was the local bookmaker, who drove a flashy eau de nil sports car with a leaping silver horse and jockey for a mascot. Known to have a red-haired girlfriend and a wife who drank, he was considered beyond the pale. The other car belonged to Mr Sephton, who had an office and a builder's yard fronting on Shelley Street. He lived in a big house on the other side of the park, surrounded by lawns and flowerbeds. We saw him driving home in the evening in his gleaming black Rover, back to his frail grey-haired wife and their three pretty daughters. Once he had been the city's mayor, and we had all basked in his reflected glory.

Just then, the gate of the priests' house opposite opened, and young Father Con came out, carrying a big cardboard box. I watched curiously, and when he caught sight of me his face lit up and he came hurrying over the road, beaming in delight. We didn't go to his church, but he knew he could rely on us when he had a favour to ask. My mother liked to keep in with the priests, partly by way of hedging her religious bets and partly because they sometimes gave my father useful odd jobs to do.

'Ah, Patty, just the very girl I was wanting to see!' Father Con set down his box on the pavement and I saw inside a pile of cardboard trays and collecting-boxes. 'Could you be asking your mother to spare me a moment? The flag day for Father Hudson's Homes has come round again. Sure, you'd never be thinking a whole year's gone by since the last one, would you? Say I won't keep her a minute, there's a good girl.'

'Yes, Father.' I ran eagerly back into the house to fetch my mother, excited to know it was time for us to sell flags again. Every year we stood on our doorstep on a Saturday morning asking passers-by to give a few coppers to the children's homes run by the Catholic church, fielding the ones who tried to get out of giving by crossing the road when they saw one of the priests standing by the gate with their own collecting-box. I always enjoyed handing out the little paper flags in return for the donations—it made me feel important to be part of something going on all over the city that day. I liked, too, to listen to my mother's scathing comments to Aunt Madge, who sat darning stockings on the front room sofa to keep us company.

'Thank you, Mrs Reilly ... wouldn't hurt her to give more than that, she's always got plenty when it comes to a bottle of port ... Thank you, Mr Benson, yes, I think it will rain later myself ... trust him to look on the black side ... Spare a copper for the poor children ... didn't even look at me and dolled up to the nines ... Good morning, Mrs Cass ... couldn't be bothered to answer, she couldn't ... Oh, thank you, Bunty. Give my regards to your mother, won't you?'

Saturday morning was shopping morning for most of our neighbours, and on flag-day I could be sure of seeing nearly everybody I knew.

Now my mother came from the kitchen, wiping her hands on her apron, to see Father Con, and soon the tray, the flags and the collecting-box were ready on the sideboard for Saturday morning. Over the next few days I watched the weather anxiously, afraid it would rain and spoil my treat, but the sunshine held and I finally decided that with the priests all interceding for a fine day, we weren't likely to be disappointed after all.

When Saturday came my mother took off her apron, tidied her

hair and put on her hat. Though she was only going to be standing on the doorstep, she wouldn't be seen in the street without it. I hung the flag-tray round my neck by its string, decorating the front edge with a row of flags pinned into the cardboard. A small poster explaining the purpose of the collection hung down from the tray, fluttering against my knees in the breeze, and I wished my teacher at school could see me all decked out. She would be sure to tell the class about it—she might even tell Mrs Pugh, the headmistress, and Mrs Pugh would be so pleased she'd have me out in front of the whole school at assembly and she'd say ... .

'Wake up, Patty!'

A sharp nudge from my mother's elbow jolted me out of my daydream and I realised with a start that our first customer was waiting to be given his flag. In my confusion I almost upset the tray, but I just managed to stop it tipping over in time. Feeling hot and flustered, I handed a flag to the elderly man waiting patiently on the pavement, smiling kindly down at me.

'Patty? Why, Mrs Palmer, what a big girl she's getting!' Looking up I realised that it was Mr Sephton who was pinning the flag on to his jacket. 'I remember you being born, young lady. Your father was cleaning our windows at the office and your auntie came running up the street to fetch him.' He turned to my mother. 'Now I come to think of it, our grandson John was born round about the same time. And he's going away to school in a few weeks—how time flies! His mother's having a little farewell party for him soon. I'll see Patty gets an invitation. She'd like that, wouldn't she?'

An invitation—to a party! Hardly able to speak for excitement, I looked up at my mother to see if she realised what Mr Sephton had said. But already she had gone back into the front room to tell Aunt Madge about it, leaving me marooned on the doorstep with my flags.

'Mr Sephton, Madge. Nice old man, he is—reckons he's going to invite Patty to a party they're having for their John before he goes to boarding school. Doubt if anything will come of it, but you never know. Though they're a stuck-up lot, the Sephton girls.'

Several days passed, and my hopes had begun to fade when one evening Mr Sephton's car drew up on his way home and he stepped across the pavement to poke an envelope through our letter-box. Hearing it drop on the lino I rushed in and picked it up. 'Miss Patty Palmer', it said on the front, but I knew better than to open it myself. I took it through to the kitchen where my mother was doing the ironing, and put it down on the table. To my mother, ironing was a serious business.

Now, holding the handle of the flat-iron in a flannel pad, she turned it up to her face a few inches from her cheek, to test the heat. In winter she warmed it on a trivet in front of the range, but in summer it was heated up on the gas-stove. Too hot, and it would scorch the clothes, too cool and it wouldn't get the creases out. Frowning, she spat on the hot surface and the spittle bounced off with a hiss. Satisfied, she got on with her work. I waited impatiently till she had finished what she was doing and the iron was heating up again.

'What's this, then? 'Miss Patty Palmer'?' She took up the thick square envelope and opened it carefully. Inside was a card, decorated with a colourful picture of balloons and streamers. 'You are invited,' she read, ' ... Saturday 17th. Oh, it's this Saturday then.' A look of annoyance crossed her face. 'But you won't be able to go, Patty—it's not at Mr Sephton's house, it's at his daughter's place in the country. We can't get you there, my duck. You'll have to write and say you can't go. That's put the lid on it, that has.'

With a heavy heart, I picked up the pretty card while she got on again with the ironing. Sadly I admired the neat copper-plate handwriting of my name, the date and the address where the party was to be held. I turned the card over, intending to put it back into the envelope and it was then I saw that on the back of the card were a few scribbled words. I couldn't read them—Miss Liddle's best reader I might be, but joined-up writing defeated me. Hardly daring to hope, I held out the card to my mother. Her eyes widened with astonishment as she read.

'Why, you lucky girl! It says, 'I will pick Patty up at three on Saturday, and bring her home after the party' and it's signed by Mr Sephton. He's going to take you in his car, after he finishes at the office on Saturday. Well, that's a different kettle of fish, if you like. Taken quite a fancy to you, he must have done. Now we'll have to think what you're going to wear!'

It was soon clear that I had nothing already that would do for a party, and that anything ready-made would be too expensive by far. But Aunt Madge came to the rescue, finding a length of green satin in her wardrobe drawer that Miss Plumb round the corner could cut up and turn into a dress that would make me the belle of the ball. The next few days were taken up with fitting and measuring, and at last my party dress was ready. Standing on Aunt Madge's bed in our bedroom so that I could see myself in the dressing-table mirror, the transformation was so complete I could hardly recognise myself.

Gazing into the mirror, I could see it was a party dress all right, but somehow there seemed to be too much of it. Afraid of making it too short, Miss Plumb had made it too long. Knowing, too, that to put it kindly, I was on the plump side, she had been afraid of making it too tight, and had made it too loose. Frills had been mentioned, so she had added them everywhere she could—to the hem, to the sleeves, to the collar and on each side down the front of the bodice. Bunches of small rosebuds nestled coyly at the waist, while a broad sash was tied in an awkward bow in the middle of my back, ready to be squashed the moment I sat down. The shiny satin cast a greenish glow over my face, giving it an eerie pallor, and altogether I looked rather like a wedding-cake on legs. Perhaps, I thought, this was how you were supposed to look at a party—how would I know? But even so, I wasn't at all too sure.

My mother and Aunt Madge, though, had no such misgivings. They looked at me in admiration. I was wearing a party dress, so naturally I looked different from my everyday self. I had some new, clean white socks to wear and my father had polished up my shoes specially for me. A large tin of toffees was bought and wrapped up in fancy paper to give to John, together with a bunch of flowers for his mother. So as far as they were concerned, everything was ready for the great day. My party dress was taken off carefully and hung up on a hanger, and I was given an extra-strong cup of cocoa that night, in case excitement about the party kept me awake. Even so, it was a long time before I dropped off to sleep. It had finally dawned on me that I had no idea how to behave at a party.

When Saturday came, I was dressed and ready by two o'clock.

As a finishing touch, my hair had been Marcel-waved by Mr Niblett, our local barber, who had a ladies' salon at the back of his shop, and now it hung in the rigid waves and curls created by his hot curling-tongs. My head was sore where he had accidentally burnt my scalp, but I hadn't complained. I sat in the front room and waited nervously for Mr Sephton's car to arrive. When he finally drew up, just after three, he was in a hurry and in no time I was settled in splendid isolation on the back seat with my gifts. He exchanged a few words with my mother, Aunt Madge peeping from behind the front room curtains to wave as we set off. I had never felt so lonely in my life.

The unfamiliar sensation of riding in a motor-car took my mind off my worries for a while, and soon we were driving down country lanes and the scent of hawthorn blossom drifted in through the open window. We turned in at large gates—the eldest Sephton girl had married well—and followed a gravel drive up to a big house with wisteria growing round the mullioned windows. The front door was open and Mr Sephton helped me out and up the steps.

A maid in uniform was waiting in the hall, and he handed me over to her, saying he had to move his car out of the way of the other visitors. I could hear a lively tune being played on the piano as I followed the maid down the corridor. She left me standing on the threshold of a large room with french windows open on to the garden. Inside the room the party was already in full swing. Children—there seemed to be dozens of them—were rushing about chasing balloons, bursting them with screams of delight when they caught them. Over on the far side, a group of smartly-dressed women sat chatting, mothers, I presumed, though they looked nothing like my own mother, while in a corner by the door were several other women each wearing a uniform, navy or fawn, who must be nannies or nursery-maids. They were talking quietly while carefully watching the children playing.

'Now, Master Nigel, I saw that—what have I told you about playing fair?' one called out as a small, red-faced boy tripped over another in his efforts to grab a balloon. 'A right chip off the old block, he is,' she continued quietly to the nanny next to her. 'Hard work as threshing it is to get any manners into him, I can tell you.'

By now the mothers opposite had seen me standing in the doorway, and a tall, dark-haired woman came forward towards me. She looked at me with a frown and finally spoke.

'Ah, you must be the little girl my father invited—Patty, isn't it? What? You've brought John a present?'—as I offered it—'How kind, but there was no need. This isn't a birthday party, you know. And some flowers for me? Lovely!' She took the parcel and the flowers and pushed them carelessly into the hands of the maid, who was passing. 'Thompson, see to these, will you?' Then, turning to me she added, 'Just stand there for a moment. This game's nearly over, and then you can join in.' She exchanged a wry smile over her shoulder with the other mothers. 'Such a pretty dress—did you have it made specially or was it from Harrod's?' I saw them titter, and somehow I knew that all the time she meant the opposite of what she was saying.

I saw now that the games were being organised by a thin, bony woman with a loud, braying laugh, who was chivvying the children into dashing about in pursuit of the balloons. As John's mother rejoined her friends, I heard her say languidly, 'Isn't it lucky for me Cousin Edith is so frightfully good with kiddies? Frankly, I'm just hopeless myself,' and to my alarm I realised that Cousin Edith was about to pounce on me as the last balloon was popped. Flashing a toothy smile, she bore down and swept me into the crowd. I could see now what was wrong with my dress—it was too fussy and too shiny. The other girls were wearing simple dresses in pale colours, with hardly a frill in sight. Miserably I tried to edge away, but Cousin Edith was having none of it.

'Come on, young woman, can't have you loafing on the sidelines,' she roared. 'What's your name? Matty? Oh, Patty, I see! Now then, everybody, this is Patty and she's going to join in our next game, which is Musical Chairs. Thompson's going to put out the chairs for us'—the maid dragged a row of chairs into the centre of the room, helped by one of the nannies—'jolly good show, Thompson!—and off we go!'

She grabbed my hand and before I knew where I was she was dragging me round the chairs in time to the piano, played by a pale girl who seemed to be some sort of governess. When the music broke off, I stood still, not knowing what to do. Cousin Edith pushed me none too gently towards a chair, but a small girl in a blue dress slipped in front of me.

'Oh, you muffed it!' Cousin Edith gave a mock groan. 'You let Felicity beat you to it, old girl. Never mind, you can stay in the game just this once, and next time you jolly well push the others out of the way, d'you see?'

But next time, too, I held back, conscious that my mother and Aunt Madge would think it was rude to push. 'Blind Man's Buff' followed, when it was fairly easy for me to keep to the back of the crowd, but for 'Pinning the Donkey's Tail On' there was no escape and I soon found myself almost at the head of the queue. Any minute I would have to stand out in front of everybody and Cousin Edith would tie the scarf round my eyes and twirl me round with shouts of glee. I knew I could never pin the tail into the right place on the picture of the tail-less donkey on the wall. I was hot and sticky, my hair was falling out of Mr Niblett's careful arrangement and I just wanted to get away by myself for a moment.

Muttering an excuse to the child behind me, I slipped unseen out of the room.

Out in the hall I held my breath, but no-one came after me. Through an open door opposite, I saw a table set with a magnificent party tea—jellies, blancmange, cakes, chocolate biscuits, iced sponges—my eyes widened in delight. I decided I would find somewhere to hide and then, when the games were over and the children went into the other room for their tea, I would slip out again and join the crowd. That way, it seemed to me, I would get the best of both worlds.

Luckily the first door I opened led into a sort of dark little cloak-room, with a deep sink holding glass vases and water-jugs. There was an old tin trunk in the corner, and hanging over it several mud-stained mackintoshes and coats. Careless now of my party dress, I curled up on top of the trunk and pulled the coats and mackintoshes like a curtain in front of me. I would be invisible, I felt sure, to anyone coming in at the door. Anyway, who would come in? Everybody was busy at the party.

But I was wrong. I had been there only a few minutes when the door opened and a man came into the washroom carrying a large suitcase. Peeping through the coats I could see big coloured letters on the side of the case—'The Jolly Joker'. The man took off his jacket and put on instead a red and yellow tabard, lettered like the case. Then looking in the mirror he began to make up his face with greasepaint—a red nose, a big smiling mouth, a pair of dark, arched eyebrows. He had just finished when the door opened again, and in came the maid, Thompson. To my surprise, the Joker seemed to be expecting her.

'Cor, Henry, I'd have never known you,' she gasped, looking at his face. From under her apron she took out a flat oval case. 'Here's the pearls—she won't be wearing 'em till the county ball at the end of next month, and we'll be miles away by then. I'll put the box back in the safe and nobody'll guess it's empty. Where are you going to put the pearls? You've got your act to do in five minutes.'

The man grinned. 'Leave that to me, Daisy. I know what I'm doing. Let's get this over with, shall we? You just go and tell madam that the Jolly Joker's ready.' He picked up a top hat and set it jauntily on his head. 'Be in clover, we shall, when we've pulled this one off,' he added.

Thompson set off obediently and a moment later the Joker picked up the suitcase and followed her out. It all happened so quickly I had no idea what he had done with the pearls, but I knew that somehow I had to find out. In the uproar of getting the children seated for the entertainment I slipped back unnoticed into the room, just as the Jolly Joker started his patter.

'Good afternoon, my little princes and princesses,' he began. 'Now I'm called the Jolly Joker 'cos I've come here to tell you some jolly jokes and to show you some clever tricks.' As he rambled on, he was setting up his props on a card-table at the side of the room, and I watched him like a hawk. There was a large dice with big coloured spots, a velvet bag, a pile of hoops, a hat-box and a silk cushion. With them he put his top hat, doffing it with a low bow to the mothers, who all tittered girlishly. I looked at the props in dismay—he could have hidden the pearls anywhere. Somehow I had to get a closer look at them. Just then the Jolly Joker turned to his audience and spoke in a confidential whisper.

'Now, princesses and princes, I need a helper,' he began. 'would anyone like to ... .'

'Me! Me!' At once there was a clamour of voices, but I was leaving nothing to chance. I shot to my feet and pushing everyone else out of the way, I landed firmly beside the Jolly Joker and looked up at him with a guileless expression on my face. Taken aback, he looked down at me.

'Well, well, well, here's a keen little lady,' he said, smiling at the mothers. 'What's your name, then, princess? Patty? Well, we'll let Princess Patty help me for our first trick, and then we'll give someone else a turn.'

I had, I realised, no time to lose. The Jolly Joker, talking all the while, held out the top hat to me. Instantly I turned it upside down, scattering out of it the coloured scarves hidden in the double lining. The Jolly Joker, with his wand raised, let out a snarl of annoyance which he tried to turn into a unconvincing chuckle.

'Now, Princess Patty,' he began, but already I was rummaging in the velvet bag and hat-box. Both empty! Frantically I seized the dice and shook it hard, but it was too light to be hiding anything inside it. By now, of course, there were cries of outrage from the audience.

'The poor kid's gone potty,' shouted Cousin Edith. 'Stop her, somebody! She's ruining the show!'

'Thompson, take that wretched child away,' John's mother called angrily. 'What are you waiting for? Remove her at once!'

But at last I had realised where the pearls must be—in the one thing the Jolly Joker had never put down—his magic wand. Evading Thompson, I hurled myself at him and grabbed hold of the end of the wand. Sure enough, it was hollow and it came apart in two pieces. Out of it cascaded the long, elegant string of gleaming pearls. Cousin Edith gave a gasp of astonishment.

'Caroline—look! The rotter's got your pearls! What's going on?'

Pandemonium broke out as the Jolly Joker fled through the open french windows followed by Thompson, who sent Cousin Edith flying with a vicious push. I picked up the pearls and gave them back to John's mother, while someone else phoned for the police. Eventually everything was sorted out and the party tea took place at last.

When Mr Sephton drove me home, with a bag full of chocolate biscuits as a reward for my cleverness, he told my mother and

Aunt Madge all about it, and they could hardly believe their ears.

'Quick thinking it was, and no mistake,' he declared. 'How Patty guessed that Joker johnnie had the pearls hidden in his wand I can't imagine. But she gave him his comeuppance right enough. Seems Thompson was in it with him, too. Good job we asked Patty to the party, wasn't it? Just shows, you never know how things are going to turn out.'

Later on, as I sat up in bed drinking my cocoa and munching a chocolate biscuit, I thought about my exciting day. Like most days, there had been good bits—the party tea and the ride in Mr Sephton's motor-car—and bad bits—Cousin Edith and her awful games—but on the whole I'd enjoyed it. I hadn't exactly been the belle of the ball, but nor had I been a wallflower, either. My first party had been quite different from what I had expected, thanks to the Jolly Joker.

4

Queen Squeak

I looked at the shoes, and I couldn't believe they were for me. I always had clumpy brown leather shoes with a broad strap over the instep and a buckle at the side, hard-wearing, dull shoes, each new pair exactly like the old ones. But these shoes, nestling in white tissue paper in a neat little box, were made of gleaming black patent leather, fastened with a dainty ankle-strap, party shoes almost, and like nothing I'd ever had before. I couldn't help feeling there had been some mistake. Aunt Madge was looking on with a sour expression on her face and my mother wore a nervous smile, but my father was grinning in delight at my surprise. He took the shoes carefully out of the shoebox and set them down on the rag rug in front of the kitchen range.

'Go on, my duck,' he said encouragingly. 'Try them on. They're your size. Mrs Black got them from the warehouse for us.' He turned to my mother, ignoring my aunt's frown. 'Ever so much cheaper, they were. She's done us a good turn and no mistake. Wipe 'em over with a drop of milk, she says, to stop them from cracking, and they'll last for ages. Best quality, they are, a proper bargain.'

I realised now what had happened. Mrs Black was one of my father's window-cleaning customers, and she kept a children's outfitters near the cemetery. She sold socks and vests, fleecy Liberty bodices and long woollen stockings. Life-size dummies of children stood stiffly in her window, dressed in tweed coats with neat little velvet collars, soft leather gaiters clasped tightly round their legs. Her shop was too expensive for us to buy from as a rule—our shopping was done nearer to home, in the Gosford Street Emporium—but for some reason she had done my father a favour, getting him shoes for me at cost price. I could just imagine the wheedling and flattery that had gone on, and now, though the shoes were the wrong sort, showy and unsuitable for school, we couldn't afford to offend her by returning them. Suppressing my excitement, I kicked off my shabby old slippers and pushed my feet in their darned white cotton socks into the hard, shiny black toes of the new shoes. I wriggled my heels into place and with trembling fingers hooked the long, unfamiliar straps around my ankles. They fastened with awkward, tiny gilt buttons, and for once in my life I wouldn't have changed places with anybody on earth—not even Shirley Temple.

I realised immediately, of course, that they were too tight, but nothing would have made me say so. Modelled on a more fashionable last, the new shoes lacked the ample 'growing-room' of my familiar brown school shoes, but this, it seemed to me, was a small price to pay for the glory of black patent and ankle-straps. My father pinched the glossy toes and nodded in satisfaction.

'They're fine—fit her a treat, they do. That's got her set up for her new class, hasn't it, Patty? Tek them off now, so's you don't spoil them. You can wear your old ones till you go back to school next week. Mrs Black was pleased as Punch to help us out. Not as black as she's painted arter all, is she?' he chortled, delighted at his own wit. Aunt Madge gave him a scornful glare, and behind his back my mother sniffed crossly.

I was well aware why my mother and my aunt disliked my wonderful new shoes. To them, anything bright and shining was 'common', and they spent good money only on long-lasting, hard-wearing clothes in dark, dull colours. But I was looking forward to appearing in the playground in shoes to boast about. I had been at school a year now, and while I was usually 'top' in the classroom, my standing in the playground remained low. I couldn't run fast, or I got out of breath, I couldn't climb on the railings for fear of getting my dress dirty, I never had sweets to share out because 'they rot your teeth'. But all this would be forgotten when I turned up on Monday morning in my black patent-leather ankle-strap shoes ... .

I was used now to the kaleidoscope of noise that had frightened me so much at first, after the quiet kitchen where I read my books and played silently with my dolls. I was looking forward to going back to the jangling bell, the headmistress's loud, bossy voice, the perky piano that marched us line by line in and out of the hall for prayers. I would be going up out of Miss Liddle's reception class into Miss Priddy's Class Two. I liked Miss Liddle, pretty, smiling and gentle as she was, but even so, I still remembered my first day in her class with a shudder. When we arrived, she had given out the boxes we were to keep on the ledge under our desks. A cardboard Woodbine box, made to contain paper packets of cheap cigarettes, it was exactly the right size to hold four small tins, the sort that had once each held six Oxo cubes. While Miss Liddle was busy with a latecomer, I peeped inside my four tins in turn. A few pieces of white chalk in one, with a small, square blackboard rubber, then coloured cardboard counters in the next, and then a handful of broken wax crayons—all that was fine, what I expected. But in the last tin—I caught back a cry of horror—a heap of dead worms! What could they be for? Oily and brown, they were coiled loosely together, and I quickly shut the lid on them with shaking hands. Only much later, when Miss Liddle said, 'Take out your plasticine, everyone,' did I realise my mistake ... .

As time went by, I learned to count with my counters and to copy with my chalks on to my small blackboard the letters Miss Liddle wrote up on her big board at the front of the room.

'Poor tired mother says "huh", and there's a chair for her to sit down on,' she said, tracing the small letter 'h' slowly and sounding it carefully. 'And father puffs his pipe, look, here it is,' as she wrote up a 'p'. Every letter had a story—'l' was a tall lady, little 'i' was throwing his cap in the air, 's' was a hissing snake, and so on.

Before long, I was reading about Bess, Tess and Jess, who seemed to spend most of their time in a gig with, for some reason, a pig. Sometimes, on clean writing paper with faint blue lines, we recorded in pencil the adventures of the Little Red Hen and her narrow escape from the Sly Old Fox. Stories—this was what I enjoyed most of all at school. I remembered them word for word, and repeated them endlessly to my dolls when I got home. I loved writing them out, too, and while the others sat chewing the end of their pencils, I worked steadily on, line after line. 'Once upon a time,' I wrote happily, as the milk monitors dragged in the crates of little bottles, and the sweet, milky smell mingled with the fumes from our damp coats drying on the radiator, 'there was a Little Red Hen ... .'

Every day my mother, along with all the other mothers of reception class children, made five journeys to and from the school. It was in a busy part of the city, just beyond the end of Shelley Street, and there were no crossing wardens then to see us safety across the road. She waited with me till the bell rang, and returned at morning playtime, bringing a jug of cocoa or Oxo in the winter to warm me up and keep out the cold. A buttered bun or a 'piece'—a hunk of bread spread with jam or dripping—was thrust through the railings, like feeding animals in a zoo, I thought. This was to keep us from starvation till we were fetched home for midday dinner. Then we trudged back for afternoon school till hometime, signalled in Miss Liddle's by a plaintive song:

> Our day at school is o-o-o-ver,
> And we are going home.
> Goodbye, goodbye, be always kind and true,
> Goodbye, goodbye, we will be kind and true ... .

Now I was to go up into Miss Priddy's class. Miss Priddy, a plain, sardonic woman with severely cropped grey hair, was said to be strict—no buns at playtime for her class!—and given to keeping her pupils in late if they offended against her rules. But I was sure now that, dazzling her with my black patent ankle-strap shoes, I would be able to get on the right side of her at once. I looked forward to Monday morning with an unfamiliar sensation in the pit of my stomach, which I finally recognised as excitement.

I went to sleep on Sunday night with my clothes for school laid out neatly on the chair at the foot of my bed, my underclothes, my socks and a clean handkerchief ready to tuck into the pocket on the leg of my navy knickers. My plaid dress, let down from last winter, was hanging with its crisp box pleats on the door of the wardrobe, hiding the mirror. Aunt Madge was not fond of mirrors, and those in the bedroom we shared were usually covered by clothes on hangers. Years in childhood of being taunted as 'ugly' by her pretty little sister—my mother—had made my aunt avoid her reflection whenever possible. My new shoes waited, gleaming, in their box on the floor below the chair.

When Aunt Madge came up to bed, I pretended to be asleep. Only after she had drunk her Ovaltine and blown out the candle did I open my eyes on the darkness. Soon, I thought, it would be morning, and I would be setting off for school. I imagined the scene in the playground, the girls crowding round me to look at my shoes, the boys pretending not to notice but watching from the playground railings. The girls would want to try them on—'Go on, Patty, please!' they begged in my fantasy—but I would fall back on the excuse that 'my mother said I mustn't'. They would invite me to play with them at playtime, and I would be the best and the cleverest at all the games, Farmer's in his Den, Grandmother's Footsteps, Oranges and Lemons. I would be the most popular girl in the class, in the school ... I would be chosen to be the May Queen when we did the maypole dances ... while the crown of flowers was being placed on my head, my mousy pump-water hair magically transformed into a gleaming mass of blonde ringlets, I drifted off to sleep, and the next thing I knew Aunt Madge was shaking me awake.

'Come on, lazybones, get up now. Don't want to be late for Miss Priddy, do you?' She had on her hat and coat, ready for the box factory, and I felt a kiss hovering in the air, but as usual the moment passed.

I dressed quickly and with my shoes in my hand went downstairs to wash in the enamel bowl at the stone sink in the back kitchen. I was determined not to put on my new shoes till the last moment, for fear of splashing them. After breakfast—my favourite, toast and dripping, as a special treat—I had my hair brushed smooth, put on my coat and hat and then, finally, squeezed my feet into my precious shoes. Luckily, it was a fine day.

By clenching my toes and adopting a rolling gait, I managed—just—to keep up with my mother as she hurried along. Shelley Street was noisy at that time in the morning, busy with office-workers heading for the factories in Alba Street and Winchester Road. We passed the parrot in the window of Salters' second-hand shop, the Ring o'Bells pub, the row of shops by the traffic-lights, and then we crossed to the Royal Victorola Picture Palace, better known as the Flea Pit, which was next to the school gates. Slowed down by my shoes, we were hardly inside the playground when the bell rang and I had to scurry to my line. No chance for me to show off my shoes now—that would have to wait till playtime.

As usual on the first day of term, we all went straight into the hall before joining our new classes. Mrs Pugh, the headmistress, a tall, dignified woman dressed in black, was on the platform, waiting for us. Her hair, as always after a holiday, shone bright gold in the light from the tall hall windows. It would gradually fade as the weeks went by, only to blaze out again after our next school holiday. Mrs Pugh was a widow from Wales—in those days, women left teaching when they married, returning only if their husbands died. My mother, who could 'never stand the Welsh', was incensed when Mrs Pugh taught us a few words of her native language in order to hear us sing 'Land of my Fathers', regarding it as little short of treason.

'To Cymru my heart shall be true!' we roared in an orgy of emotion at the school concert, while my mother sniffed furiously on the back row.

Today, though, Miss Salaman, Mrs Pugh's deputy, played us loudly into the hall with the tune we knew as 'Cat's got the Measles'. Some of the older boys, wild from weeks of freedom on the streets, incautiously sang the words softly under their breath.

Cat's got the measles, the measles, the measles,
Cat's got the measles, the measle's got the cat!

But not softly enough. With a cry of fury, Mrs Pugh banged her hymn book down on the table in front of her, and brought the jaunty music to a halt.

'You stupid boys,' she shouted, as Miss Salaman's fingers skittered to a stop. 'How many times have I to tell you? I will not have that dreadful nonsense sung in my school. Look you, nobody would keep an animal in that condition, would they?' She glared round the hall. 'Well, would they?' she repeated angrily.

'No, Mrs Pugh,' we chanted, stifling our giggles at the thought of the unfortunate cat.

'Very well then. Now we'll get on and sing, 'God whose name is Love'—and I want fairy voices from everybody,' she added swiftly, as Miss Salaman started to play, 'or there'll be some people staying in at playtime to practice, won't there, you boys at the back?'

It took three repeats of the hymn to satisfy Mrs Pugh, but at last we arrived in Miss Priddy's classroom. Neat piles of exercise books were waiting for us in our places, and I found I was to sit next to Peggy Bowles, a pale, thin girl who was so shy she never spoke above a whisper. Probably Miss Liddle had given us both a good report, saying we could be trusted to sit together quietly and get on with our work. I flexed my sore toes in relief and watched to see if Peggy cast any envious glances at my gleaming shoes, but she was too busy looking at her books—squared paper for sums, wide lines for copy writing, plain paper for spelling tests and a large blank drawing-book. Miss Priddy called the register, and then looked thoughtfully around the room. We didn't need to be told—we knew at once that she was choosing a monitor to take the register to Mrs Pugh's office, and a forest of hands shot up. Miss Priddy raised an eyebrow.

'Let me see now ... .' She watched as we stretched our hands even further towards the ceiling. 'Yes, I think I remember Miss Liddle saying that Patty Palmer could be trusted to go on messages. We'll give her a try.'

She held the register out to me, and bursting with pride I rose and hurried forward while Peggy and the rest watched jealously. Now, I thought happily, now they'll all see my new shoes and—

But I had hardly gone a step when, 'Squeak!'

In the silent room, it rang out like a pistol shot.

'Squeak!' again.

There was a burst of sniggers from behind me. Miss Priddy's face was inscrutable.

'Squeak—squeak—squeak!' I had reached her desk. She handed me the register without a flicker.

Scarlet with mortification, I attempted to explain.

'Please, Miss Priddy, it's my new ... '

'Never mind that now, child, run along to Mrs Pugh's office, or we'll all be in trouble.' Miss Priddy waved me away and picked up her chalk.

With a barrage of squeaks I headed for the door and closed it behind me on the grinning class. As I squeaked my way down the empty corridor, my mind worked furiously. The noise of the traffic must have drowned my squeaks as we came along the street to school, and the loud piano had muffled them in the hall. Only now, when everyone was settled down to work in silence, could my shoes make themselves heard. Treading as lightly as I could, I crept through the open door of Mrs Pugh's office and slid the register on to the pile by her desk. Not till I was almost out of the door again did my treacherous shoes suddenly betray me.

'Squeak!'

I sensed rather than saw Mrs Pugh look up from her desk in astonishment, but before she could speak I was gone, squeaking back down the corridor as hard as I could go.

Miss Priddy carefully took no notice of me as I made my way back to my seat—squeak, squeak, squeak—and got on with my work. I saw the boys nudge each other, grinning, and the girls smirking behind their hands. No longer did I expect envy and admiration at playtime, and when the bell went I ran out and hid in the lavatories, where I lurked till it was time to go in again. Then I miserably squeaked my way back to my desk and thankfully sank down in blessed silence to get on with the exercises Miss Priddy had written up on the blackboard.

But my relief was short-lived. For some extraordinary reason, Miss Priddy seemed to want a monitor constantly that morning. I was asked to take Miss Liddle a pile of reading books, to remind Miss Minchin about the Boot Fund accounts, to ask Miss Salaman for the list of hymns for the week and finally to visit Mrs Pugh's office again with a copy of our class timetable. Everywhere my squeaks rang out loud and clear, and my cheeks burned. But I performed my errands with dogged desperation, and at the end of the morning Miss Priddy said, with one of her rare smiles,

'Well done, Patty. You know, I think you deserve a special title—we'll have to call you Queen Squeak in future!'

Not till years later did I realise that in the staffroom at playtime she had agreed to send me on my rounds so that the rest of the teachers could share the joke. A comical figure I must have been, with my prim and proper manners, red as a beetroot, squeaking my way around the school.

My mother met me at dinner time, waiting now I was in Class Two by the Royal Victorola instead of by the school gate. Seeing my flushed, glum face she hurried forward in alarm, but when I poured out my story she ignored my complaints, seeming thrilled instead that Miss Priddy had made me her monitor, and given me a special nickname.

'Queen Squeak!' she said in delight. 'Well, well, Queen Squeak indeed. Wait till your dad and Aunt Madge hear about this. Queen Squeak!'

'Don't rub it in,' I wanted to say, but I knew it was no use. My mother had seized on the idea with enthusiasm, and while I was eating my shepherd's pie she found a long strip of cardboard to cut the top edge into points, colouring it yellow with my crayons and sticking on to it 'jewels' from a broken bracelet. Just as the crown was completed, my father came home for his dinner—Aunt Madge had sandwiches at work—and the whole story had to be told over again. My mother ended by wedging the crown firmly on my head. Like the shoes, it was too tight.

With the crown making my head ache and the shoes rubbing my feet into blisters, I miserably made my way back to school. I knew my mother would insist on going with me to the classroom to curry further favour with Miss Priddy, so there was no chance of 'losing' the crown on the way. Sure enough, she came with me right to the door of Class Two, and the uproar we caused brought Miss Priddy hurrying over. Taking in the situation at a glance, and silencing the class with an upraised hand, she gave my mother a polite smile.

'Very nice, Mrs Palmer, just the thing for our Queen Squeak, of course. And it would come in useful for the nativity play at Christmas, if you'll be kind enough to let us keep it, perhaps?'

Somehow, while she was talking, she manoeuvred my mother off down the corridor, and then turned to me.

'Not quite suitable to wear in the classroom, Patty, I think,' she continued, 'so we'll keep it on the windowsill for now.' She twitched the crown off my head as she spoke. 'You can wear it at playtime, of course, if you want to. Off you go to your place now, and get on with your work.'

With the crown safely marooned on the windowsill—'Miss Priddy wants to keep it,' I told my mother at home-time—only the shoes remained, still squeaking as loud as ever. That night, I lay awake again in the darkness, but now I no longer imagined scenes of glory. Instead the shoes, once my pride and joy, now seemed to leer at me malevolently, squeaking and performing a mocking dance of triumph. I tossed and turned, and then, suddenly, I remembered something. When my father had first shown me the shoes, he had mentioned milk—what was it he had said? Perhaps milk was the answer, perhaps milk would stop the shoes from squeaking, or at least quieten them down. It was worth a try. Cautiously I sat up in bed. A few feet away, Aunt Madge snored softly. Hardly daring to breathe, I lowered my feet to the bedroom floor, picked up the shoes in my hand and crept across the ice-cold lino to the bedroom door. To my relief, it was open—Aunt Madge, even asleep, liked to keep an ear on my parents' bedroom for sounds of one of their periodic rows in which she would have to intervene. Soon I was tiptoeing down the stairs and into the back kitchen. A shaft of moonlight through the tiny window shone on my gleaming black shoes, but my heart no longer swelled with pride. Wasting no time, I headed straight for the pantry.

There, on the stone thrall was the jug of milk, covered with its muslin cloth. Taking off the cover, I breathed a thankful sigh—the jug was nearly full. Carefully I lifted it—but how much should I use? Afraid of half-measures, I tilted the jug over each shoe in turn, sloshing in enough to fill it from toe to heel. Then, realising I could never carry the shoes back upstairs full of milk, I hid them behind the legs of the mangle, and filled the jug up again with cold water from the tap before putting it in its place on the thrall. Soon I was back in my warm bed and, feeling I had done all I could, I fell at last into an uneasy sleep.

Next morning my heart sank when I realised what I had done —whatever had made me do such a thing? I dressed quickly and hurried downstairs. Luckily my mother was busy making Aunt Madge's sandwiches, so I slipped out into the back kitchen, poured the milk out of the shoes down the sink and dabbed the damp linings with a towel. When the time came to set off for school, I pushed my feet into the clammy shoes and wriggled my toes cautiously. Yes, they did seem just a little looser. My hopes rose. I took a step, and they sank again—the squeak was as loud as ever, and now it ended in an equally raucous 'Squelch!'

I squeaked and squelched for the rest of the day, but by now the joke was wearing thin, and apart from a few jeers I was left alone in the playground. For the last lesson of the day, country dancing, we joined with Miss Salaman's class and Miss Priddy tactfully suggested I should stand by the piano and turn over the music for Miss Salaman when she gave me the signal. I watched the others spinning merrily round the hall, and glared at my shoes, furious at the way they had let me down. I remembered Aunt Madge once saying, 'Pride goes before a fall.' Now I knew what she meant.

During the day, the milk had dried out of the shoes, but when home-time came I found that instead of squelching, they had a new refrain—they flapped. Due, probably, to their overnight soaking, the soles had worked free from their uppers and as I walked along I could hear, 'Squeak … flap … squeak … flap, flap.' My mother was too taken up with questioning me about Miss Priddy to notice what was going on at ground level, and when we arrived home I hastily put on my slippers. Not till my father came home did the truth come to light. Picking up the shoes to clean them, he gave a bellow of fury.

'Good Lord deliver us! What's happened to these shoes?' he roared, waving them in the air. 'Two days' wear they've had, and they're falling to pieces already!'

Sure enough, the soles of both shoes flapped loose, like grinning mouths, the cobbler's sprigs that had held them on flashing like sharp little teeth. No longer gleaming, the black patent was scuffed and worn, split where I had walked awkwardly on my cramped toes. My mother's mouth dropped open, and Aunt Madge, just arrived back from the box factory, smiled to herself in grim satisfaction. With a snort of disgust, my father threw the battered shoes under the sink.

'She can't wear them again, poor kid,' he declared angrily. 'They smell something awful as well—fish glue, I suppose. She'll have to mek do with her old ones for a bit, that's all, and have a new pair for her birthday or summat. I shan't say nothing to Mrs Black about it—it weren't her fault, neither. Never mind, Patty, I'll polish your old ones up for you as good as new, for the time being.'

Hiding my relief, and hardly knowing whether to feel glad or sorry, I went on playing with my dolls under the table.

'Comes of trying to do things on the cheap,' I heard Aunt Madge say to my mother as she ate her teatime kipper. 'Faulty, I daresay, that's why Mrs Black got them for next to nothing.'

'Can't be helped—no use crying over spilt milk, anyway,' sniffed my mother in reply. 'And talking of milk, just look at the watery stuff the milkman left yesterday. You wouldn't think they'd have the cheek to charge for it, would you?'

So my secret was safe, I thought, and the milkman was getting the blame. Soon my black patent-leather ankle-strap shoes would be forgotten.

And nobody would remember Queen Squeak, either.

Except me ... .

5

Joey and the Christmas Fairies

'Baggy britches! Droopy drawers!'

The jeering cry echoed down the hot, dusty street and was followed by a jumble of curses ending in a high-pitched shriek of laughter. Startled, my aunt pulled up short and looked indignantly round to see who had called after us—a cheeky errand-boy, perhaps, or a bleary-eyed drunk staggering out of the Ring o'Bells opposite. But as usual at this time in the afternoon, the street was deserted. Then suddenly, from the dark doorway of Salters' second-hand shop came a sardonic chuckle and a loud raspberry. Aunt Madge gave a snort of fury.

'That Joey—he wants his neck wringing,' she grumbled. 'Him and his foul language—it's a disgrace.'

I nodded, but secretly I felt relieved it was only Salters' parrot that had mocked us. There was nothing personal about his insults. He would have been just as rude to old Father Desmond from the priests' house, or to any of the saintly widows who lived in the disused convent next to the church. Swearing didn't worry me like it seemed to worry Aunt Madge.

'Nasty, dirty little creature,' she went on crossly. 'Ought not to be allowed. Oh, hello, Ivy,' she broke off, quickly calming down as an untidy young woman appeared in the doorway. 'Come out for a breath of air, have you? It's a warm one today, and no mistake.'

'No, not really, Miss Fennel. I—er—I just popped out to apologise.' Ivy Salter hurriedly threw a heavy plush tablecloth over the parrot-cage in the shop window. 'I said to mother, "There's that wretched bird again, annoying people!" It's our Vernon as teaches him all those dreadful words. It must have given you a proper turn, him squawking out at you like that. Won't you come in and have a cup of tea with us before you go on home? Mother'd be ever so pleased to see you—show there's no hard feelings, like?'

I held my breath. Every day I passed Salters' shop on my way home from school, and to me it was an Aladdin's cave full of treasures. The window was crammed with coloured glass vases, ships in bottles, candlesticks, oil-lamps and tortoiseshell photo-frames, all wedged in around the big parrot-cage and festooned with cobwebs and discarded feathers. What lay further inside I could only imagine, and I longed for Aunt Madge to accept Ivy's invitation so that I could see for myself the crowded rooms full of piled-up furniture and household junk. I hadn't much hope, though, that she would. My aunt's guiding rule was to keep herself to herself, and that meant no hobnobbing with the neighbours. But I knew she was tired. We had been traipsing round town all afternoon, trying to match the pink wool she needed to finish knitting her winter vests. As she said, it was a very hot day, and a cup of tea would be more than welcome. Then again, the Salters, for all they did house clearances, were hard-working business people who had been in the street nearly as long as my aunt's own family. Ivy's parents always treated my mother and Aunt Madge with due respect, knowing they had come down in the world since their father died. To refuse Ivy's offer might cause offence, something to be avoided at all costs. To my delight, my aunt allowed her tired face to relax into a forgiving smile.

'Thank you, Ivy, that's very kind of you,' she replied at last. 'Yes, it was a bit of a shock, but let's say no more about it. A cup of tea would be lovely, if you're sure it's no trouble. Come along, Patty, and mind you don't touch anything in the shop, there's a good girl.'

Hardly able to believe my luck, I followed Aunt Madge through the doorway, cluttered with walking-sticks and umbrellas, old tennis racquets and fire-irons. The shop was double-fronted and in the room on the left chairs were piled up higgledy-piggledy on tables, and cupboards and wardrobes were ranged two deep around the walls. Against them leaned stacks of picture-frames with grimy, broken glass and mirrors chipped and spotted with age. On the other side of the entrance, shelves lined the alcoves, full of dusty books and battered ornaments, with most of the light from the window blocked now by Joey's shrouded cage. There was a peculiar musty smell, a mixture of damp, decay, mildew and birdseed, but I looked eagerly round as we edged through the narrow passage to the door marked 'Private'. The frowsty parrot, the derelict furniture, the muddle of pottery, glass and books on the shelves all fascinated me. Where did it come from? Who had owned it before? Would anyone ever buy it and if so, who and why? I sidled past the bed frames and rocking chairs, the chests of drawers and the dented fenders—there was even an old dolls' house, I saw in excitement—and followed my aunt into the room at the back of the shop. This, too, was full of odds and ends accumulated in the course of Mr Salter's business, but here an attempt had been made to arrange them into the semblance of a cosy parlour. A bunch of faded crepe paper flowers had been thrust awkwardly into a cracked vase on the hearth, and swags of fringed velvet were draped across the mantelpiece. Mrs Salter, a stout, ginger-haired woman in shiny black satin, reclined in a rickety armchair by the window, listlessly turning over the pages of *Home Chat*. She brightened up as we came in.

'Miss Fennel—and little Patty! This is a treat, isn't it, Ivy? Father's out on a call at the moment. He won't half be sorry to have missed you. Sit yourselves down'—she drove a mangy cat off the sofa with a blow from *Home Chat*—'and Ivy'll get some fresh tea made in no time.'

As I perched on the greasy sofa next to Aunt Madge, I looked round the room with its shabby treasures—a grandfather clock, a marble figurine, an ornate brass gong—and wondered what booty Mr Salter would bring home this time. 'Send for Salters' was his slogan, and it appeared in all his newspaper advertisements and on his letter-heading, along with words like 'discreet', 'sympathetic' and 'bereavement'. 'A death in the family? Send for Salters. A prompt and efficient removal? Send for Salters. For a fair and free valuation, send for Salters. Houses cleared for immediate cash settlement'. I didn't know what some of the words meant, but I knew all of it off by heart.

'There's your tea, Patty dear. And you'll have a little slice of sponge cake, won't you?' Ivy was playing hostess while her mother chatted to Aunt Madge. Mrs Slater was clearly torn between a feeling of automatic respect, since a long-established family tailoring business, even a defunct one, ranked considerably higher than a house clearance firm, and the knowledge that she could buy and sell everything my family owned these days with the small change in her handbag. Ivy had tactfully avoided mentioning Joey's outburst, letting it be understood we were 'just passing' and had been persuaded to stay for afternoon tea. Relieved to learn that Mr Salter, a red-faced whiskery little man with a horsy manner, was otherwise engaged and the loutish Vernon with him, Aunt Madge balanced her cup genteelly on her knee and tried to relax. She herself was divided between the fear that she was letting herself down by condescending to social inferiors and the hope that, as wealthy neighbours, the Salters might one day prove to be worth cultivating.

Just as we were about to go, there was a clatter outside the door and Mrs Salter looked up sharply.

''s too early for Ted,' she said, frowning. 'Must be our Bunty back from her dancing class. Hang on and have a word with her, Miss Fennel, won't you? She'll love to see your Patty, Bunty will. She's that fond of kiddies!'

Bunty Salter came in at the door, her curly blonde hair a frizzy halo round her head like thistledown. A few years younger than Ivy with her rigid Marcelled waves and print overall, Bunty seemed out of place in the dingy, crowded room with her pale blue silk dress and her satin dancing pumps. She gave me a brilliant smile, shook hands politely with Aunt Madge and then swooped down on the last slice of sponge cake.

'Oooh, I'm starvin'!' She flashed a pert grin round the room. 'Takes it out of you, dancing does, I can tell you. I'm doing acro, ballet and tap now, Miss Fennel,' she went on, turning to Aunt Madge. 'Miss Rose doesn't 'alf keep you working at it. She's a real slave-driver, she is. But I'm going to be in the panto at the Opera House at Christmas, see, so I've got to be good.'

'Don't start talking about Christmas. It ain't the end of August yet.' Mrs Salter heaved herself up out of her armchair to shuffle after us as we stood up to leave. 'Now you call in again, Miss Fennel, any time you like, and'—her eye fell upon the dolls' house in the corner of the shop—'let your Patty come and visit the girls sometimes. They'd be tickled pink to see her, and she can play with the toys and things.' She put out a thick forefinger and poked the heads of a row of tiny china mandarins on a shelf, setting them all nodding in unison. 'Yes, you come in as much as you like, my duck. Don't you forget, now!'

After that, of course, I took to loitering past the secondhand shop every time my mother sent me out for an errand, and gradually it became established that Ivy and Bunty 'thought the world of me' and liked nothing better than to dust off the furniture in the dolls' house so that I could play with it, or bring down a rusty tricycle from the attic so that I could ride round and round the cobbled yard at the back of the premises. My mother and Aunt Madge agreed between themselves that I could come to no harm from the Salter girls, and they soon gathered that Vernon was too sullen and too shy to address a word to me. His sisters bullied him into hooking up an old swing on a low branch of the apple tree at the end of the yard, so that I could push myself dreamily to and fro on it, but apart from that I saw nothing of Vernon or his father. Mrs Salter dozed over a cup of tea in the parlour, and the two girls put themselves out to amuse me. When school started again after the summer holidays I had to give up my weekday visits, but instead I slipped up there on Saturday mornings, eagerly checking to see what new knick-knacks had come in through the week, and sorting the books into alphabetical order like a proper library.

While the warm weather lasted, Bunty practised her dance routines in the yard, with me as an admiring audience. Wearing a short pleated tunic and red leather tap shoes, she performed quick-fire sequences of steps over and over again, walked on her hands and turned somersaults till she was out of breath. Miss Rose, her teacher, had impressed on her the need to practise hard with the pantomime auditions looming ahead. Bunty was certain of a place in the chorus line, but secretly, I knew, she was hoping for a solo role. As we sat drinking glasses of Tizer on the bench by the garden shed, she told me the story of the pantomime and about the parts that might come her way.

'There's the princess's maid, Rosey Posey, that's a comedy role,' she explained. 'That'd be nearly all tap, with a bit of acro. Or there's Fairy Bluebell, that's all ballet. It's not so much fun, but it'll be the best costume. Or then there's Dandini. He's a sort of second principal boy, but he doesn't have much dancing except for the hunting scene. I'll just have to try for them all and see what I can get. I don't want to end up in the back row of the chorus.'

'Oh, you won't, Bunty!' Since I privately thought she deserved the pick of all the parts, I was sure Bunty was bound to be the star of the show whatever role she was given. Perhaps it would all turn out to be just like one of the Shirley Temple films I saw at the pictures, and Bunty would save the show by stepping into the lead at the last moment. I was hoping Aunt Madge would get tickets for us to go when the time came, but I knew she might think it was a waste of money. I told myself I'd just have to try to catch her in a good mood.

Meanwhile the nights grew darker and soon as I passed Salters' window after school the lights were on inside. Sometimes when I pressed my nose against the glass I would see Mrs Salter feeding Joey with grapes, even, to my horror, putting them between her lips for him to take with his cruel curved beak.

'I don't know how you can, our mother,' I had heard Ivy say with a shudder when she saw Mrs Salter doing this, but she only laughed, teasing Joey by holding the grapes just out of his reach so that he fluttered his wings furiously like a green and red tornado. Though in a way, I knew, I owed my friendship with the Salter girls to Joey, I never really liked him. I hated being there when Mrs Salter took it in her head to open the cage door so that he could fly around the shop. More than once he had landed on my shoulder as I played with the dolls' house, and given my ear a spiteful tweak before I managed to shrug him off. Sometimes, too, when he was free, he would perch high up on the top of a wardrobe or on the antlers of a moth-eaten stag's head over the door, and it would take the combined efforts of Ivy, Bunty, Mrs Salter and me to get him down again and back into his cage. I liked it best when he was safely behind bars.

It was the beginning of October when the pantomime auditions were finally held. The whole of one Saturday was to be given over to them, and I decided to time my visit to the Salters so that I would be there when Bunty came back with her news. In any case I had other errands to do earlier in the day. For one thing I had started going with my father over to the old convent when he went across to collect his window-cleaning money from the elderly widows who lived there now the long-departed nuns were gone. Though we didn't belong to their church—nor to any church, come to that—my father cleaned their windows at a reduced rate, liking to keep on the right side of the priests who would sometimes put useful jobs of work his way. The convent, a shabby warren of passages smelling of beeswax and incense, attracted me by its air of quiet melancholy and remoteness. Plaster statues loomed unexpectedly in dark corners and heavy framed texts hung on the walls. I trotted at my father's heels up and down the bare wooden stairs and hovered while he tapped on doors, touching his cap and collecting coppers. Sometimes he would be asked to step inside and do a little job—knock in a nail to hang up a holy picture, or unscrew a jar of pickles. Then I might be given a peppermint in return, or a religious bookmark decorated in gaudy colours. Often we bumped into one of the priests, pink and white Father Desmond, swarthy Father Murtagh or young Father Con, visiting one of the widows who was sick or reminding them of a special mass to be held later that day. Then I would be told I was getting to be a grand big girl now, and patted on the head.

We usually made our visit to the convent in the morning and then, if the collection had gone well, we went back home to have pork batches for our dinner from the cook shop on the corner. Today I could hardly eat mine for excitement, wondering how Bunty was getting on at the Opera House. I was sure she would get a part, but I knew from the backstage dramas I had seen in films that the way to the top in the theatre was beset with hazards. I hoped anxiously that Bunty would beware of jealous rivals and underhanded plots, and avoid trapdoors and mysterious messages. As soon as my batch was eaten, I tidied away my toys and waited impatiently while my mother wiped my face and brushed my hair. Then, unable to bear the suspense any longer, I scurried off up the street.

Ivy and her mother greeted me absent-mindedly, and it was clear they were as eager as I was to hear Bunty's news. Cups of tea were made and left to get cold, Ivy put a tray of scones in the oven and then forgot them till reminded by the smell of burning. Mrs

Salter covered up Joey's cage, saying he 'got on her nerves', and every time the shop door rattled we all jumped to our feet. At last, though, Bunty burst in, her face radiant.

'I'm going to double!' she announced, hugging her mother and then twirling Ivy round in a jig on the hearth-rug. 'I'm going to be Rosey Posey and Fairy Bluebell as well. They said I was just what they wanted for both parts. Oh, Patty, you were right. I haven't got to be in the back row of the chorus, after all!'

From then on, every spare minute was given up to learning her two parts. Luckily the words she had to speak were in rhyme, and soon I knew them as well as Bunty did. Vernon, grumbling, was set to clear out one of the attics so that she could practice her dances in peace up there, and before long she was perfect in those as well. At home I dropped hints about booking tickets, but all I got from Aunt Madge was, 'We'll see.'

It was a rainy night early in December when, on my way home from school, I stopped as usual to look in Salters' window and realised that Joey was no longer there. Not only that, but his cage was missing, too. I could hardly believe my eyes. The window had been cleaned out, dusted and polished. The candlesticks, photo-frames and lamps were rearranged to form a background and in the centre, where the parrot-cage usually stood, there was a panorama of fairyland. Tiny celluloid dolls, three or four inches high, dressed in crepe paper and tinsel, were set around in the foreground while others hung from loops of cotton overhead. Some wore long, bell-shaped dresses to the ground while the rest had short tutus edged with tinsel or spangles, all in a rainbow of vivid colours. To my delight I saw they had small matching wings fastened to their backs and each held a miniature wand topped by a tiny silver star. Cotton wool carpeted the window like snow and an oil-lamp lit the scene, making the tinsel sparkle and shine. Forgetful of the rain, I stood staring wide-eyed at the transformation. At last I spotted a small, handwritten notice: 'Christmas Tree Fairies—Short Dresses 1s. 0d., Long Dresses 1s. 3d.'.

Luckily it was Friday, so next day I was able to go straight up to Salters' to find out what was going on. Once through the shop door, I saw that Joey had been moved with his cage into the room opposite, and was sitting sulking among the piled-up furniture. In the parlour at the back of the shop I found Ivy, busily cutting out crepe paper skirts and wings, with tinsel in gleaming piles at her elbow and a big cardboard box full of the tiny dolls on the table.

'Oh, Ivy, did you make them? They're lovely!' I looked in admiration at the finished fairies lined up on the sideboard. 'I've never seen anything so pretty. You are clever!'

Ivy gave me a pleased smile. 'Oh, I dunno,' she said modestly. 'Just thought I'd make myself some Christmas pocket-money, that's all. But they're going ever so well,' she added in satisfaction. 'Sold a dozen already, and I've got orders for five more in special colours.' She picked up her needle and began to stitch the tinsel along a hem. 'Bunty's out at rehearsal, Patty, but you can stay and watch me doing this if you want to.'

I settled down and busied myself tidying up Ivy's sewing-box, but I had no sooner finished when Mrs Salter waddled in with Joey perched on her shoulder.

'Pore ole boy,' she crooned to him, stroking his breast feathers with her finger. 'Turned 'im out of his winder, they have, haven't they? Ho, what a shame. And all because of the Christmas fairies!'

'Now, mother, don't bring that bird in here, please.' Ivy looked up in alarm. 'I don't want him messing up my things. I've just spent ages doing these.'

'Oh, all right, then. He'll 'ave to go back in his cage.' Mrs Salter shrugged, making Joey squawk and flutter wildly. 'Seems a shame to shut him up all the same, though. I'll give him a proper fly around when you're finished. Are you off now, my duck?' she added to me as I got up to go. 'Ta-ra then, and give my best respects to Miss Fennel and your mother.'

Avoiding Joey's outstretched beak, I made my escape, and when I got home I discovered that Ivy wasn't the only one who was busy earning extra money for Christmas. My mother every year used her floristry skills to make holly wreaths and crosses for the neighbours to take to their family graves. The twigs of holly were wired on to rough shapes knocked up out of scraps of wood by my father and, thanks to the clever use of variegated leaves and clusters of berries, the home-made wreaths were quite as good, if not better, than those sold at far higher prices in the shops. I loved the fragrant scent of the evergreens, and by the week before Christmas every flat surface in the back kitchen was covered with glossy branches and heaps of moss, turning it into a green grotto smelling of the countryside. For some reason I didn't quite understand, the wreaths were by way of being a family secret, though everyone round about knew that my mother was making them. Perhaps my father, for pride's sake, didn't want it said openly that she was earning money, in case people thought he couldn't provide properly for his family. Married women, except for the poorest, weren't supposed to go out to work. Whatever the cause, the wreaths were only delivered under cover of darkness, when prying eyes would see nothing. My mother had no time to do this herself, so my father took them on his bicycle, hanging them from the handlebars with loops of hairy twine, and swearing about the prickles.

This year the delivery of the last batch of wreaths coincided with Bunty's first night at the pantomime. We still hadn't any tickets, as far as I knew, and I was moping in the kitchen when my mother came in, a large holly wreath in her hands.

'Look at this now, Patty,' she said in exasperation. 'Your father's gone and forgotten Mrs Salter's wreath. It was on the mangle by itself. I promised to let her have it for tomorrow. Do you think you could take it up to her?' Then her face clouded over. 'But whatever you do, don't stop for the money now, or it will look like cadging. She might think we'd sent you with it so's she'd give you some extra cash for yourself. Tell you what, just leave it inside the shop door and come straight back. That'll be the best plan. She can pay me for it later.'

Pleased to have the chance to see Ivy's fairies again, I pulled on my coat and carried the big wreath carefully up the street. It was dark inside the shop but the light was on in the window display and I spent a few minutes looking at the dolls before I noticed that the price-ticket had fallen face down in the cotton wool snow. It needed to be put up again at once, I thought. Nobody would buy the dolls if they didn't know they were for sale. The shop door was unlatched so I slipped quietly in and put the wreath down on a bookcase in the corner. Then I picked my way in the darkness across to the window and leaned carefully in till my fingers reached the price-ticket and I could wedge it upright again. Then I turned to go. But just at that moment the parlour door opened and all the

Salters—except for Bunty, who was at the theatre already—came out, dressed in their best for the pantomime. Remembering my mother's warning about cadging, I kept quiet in the shadows, and only realised too late as I heard the key turn in the lock that I had ended up a prisoner. The back door would be locked too, of course, and I stared round in desperation. My mother wouldn't come to look for me, since she would think I had stayed to chat to the Salters after all. I might easily have to wait there till they all came back from the theatre. It was eerie and frightening in the silent shop. Anything might be lurking in the corners, and I had a job to hold back the tears. Then a strange scratching noise came from the room next door, and I froze in horror.

'Droopy drawers!'

I gave a gasp of relief. It was only Joey after all. But a moment later, strong wings beat through the air above my head, and I froze again. It was Joey, all right, but not Joey safely inside his cage. The bird was loose and flying round the shop. Mrs Salter must have let him out and then, in the excitement of the pantomime, forgotten to shut him up again. I crouched down, hoping he couldn't see me in the darkness. Then there was a scrabbling sound in the window, and peering in cautiously I could see Joey, picking up the dolls one by one in his beak and tossing them over his shoulder with chuckles of glee. Left to his own devices, he was getting his revenge on the Christmas fairies.

Disaster struck when a few minutes later he made a clumsy lurch into the air to try to snatch down the dolls hanging up over his head. His wing caught the lighted oil-lamp a heavy blow, shattering the glass chimney and sending it crashing down on to the cotton wool and the dolls. In seconds the whole window was ablaze, and as the flames billowed towards me I realised I had to act quickly. On the counter behind me was the thick plush tablecloth Ivy used to cover Joey's cage. I seized it and hurled it over the flames, just as there came a crash at the shop door and the lock smashed. Father Con came dashing in, grabbed me and carried me out into the street. In the distance I heard the sound of a fire-engine on its way.

'Father Desmond raised the alarm,' Father Con gasped. 'You're all right now, Patty. We were in the convent sitting with old Mrs

Jenks when we saw the flames start up in the shop window. You were a brave girl, smothering them like you did. Here's your mother now—she'll take care of you. No great harm done, Mrs Palmer, thank the good Lord.'

Next day, no awkward questions were asked. The Salters were only too pleased to find the damage was so light, just a few Christmas fairies burnt to cinders and Joey's singed tail-feathers, after all. Father Con praised me to the skies and I was rewarded with front seats for the pantomime. As for Joey, the shock had quietened him down once and for all. He never spoke again—except to imitate a fire engine ... .

6

A Little Spot of Bother

'Knock, knock,' I said, hugging myself with glee. Aunt Madge smiled indulgently.
'Who's there?' she replied.
'Hark the herald.'
Back came the expected answer.
'Hark the herald who?'
'Hark the herald angel sing, Mrs Simpson's pinched our king!' I shrieked with laughter, and expected Aunt Madge to join in. The 'knock, knock' jokes were all the rage in the playground that year. But all she said was, 'Don't say 'pinched'—I've told you before!' so I was disappointed. Wrong again! So many words were forbidden, it was difficult to keep track of them. I ran through them in my head as I got on with my tea—ain't, chucked, shove, belly, bum and dozens more, apart from the real swear-words like damn and blast, too bad even to be thought of, much less spoken. For me, conversation was a minefield, avoiding the rude words and putting in the polite ones, the pleases and thank-yous. None of the other children at school seemed to bother, but then, they didn't have my mother and Aunt Madge watching every word. Gloomily I gave up on the Mrs Simpson joke. The fun, somehow, had gone out of it.

Mrs Simpson herself, though, remained a puzzle. For some time now I had thought that Aunt Mae, one of my Birmingham aunties, was perhaps the girlfriend of the Prince of Wales. This was because Aunt Mae had once caused considerable comment by turning up to visit us wearing bright red trousers. At that time she was the only woman I had ever seen in trousers, apart from newspaper photographs of Wallis Simpson. Since they were both dark-haired and rake-thin—Aunt Mae from chronic asthma—it seemed possible to me that they were the same person, and the family was keeping quiet about it. Recently I had found out my mistake—as the joke said, Mrs Simpson was going to marry her prince, which for some reason prevented him from becoming our king. Aunt Mae, I knew, couldn't do that, being married already to Uncle Wally, who kept greyhounds. But the topic of Mrs Simpson was being discussed everywhere, not only in the school playground. Every time my father opened a newspaper, he exploded with fury as he spelled out the headlines. To him, the Abdication was a conspiracy of 'the bosses'.

'They never bloody well intended to let him be king—he'd seen too much!' he roared. 'Just another of their dirty, underhanded tricks, this is. A trumped up excuse, arter he'd been to Wales and seen the miners starving. Shoved him off the throne afore he could upset their applecart for 'em. Plain as a pikestaff—anybody with half an eye can see that.'

I listened wide-eyed as the forbidden words came tumbling out, and my mother and Aunt Madge exchanged disgusted glances. They saw Wallis Simpson as the cause of all the trouble—American for a start, divorced, and no better than she should be, trousers or no trousers. They were glad to see the back of the Uncrowned King, with his socialite entourage and his constant scandals. They much preferred the King-to-be, the former Prince Albert, Duke of York, shy, gentle and well-behaved, with his dark-eyed Scottish wife, Elizabeth Bowes-Lyon, and their two pretty princesses, Elizabeth—'Lilibet' in the family—and the sometimes lovably mischievous little Margaret Rose. A respectable, family-man king—that was what the country needed.

Helped by Aunt Madge, I had already built up a collection of photographs of the two princesses, stuck in my scrapbook along with those of Shirley Temple and Jane Withers, the child film stars I was taken to see from time to time at the Royal Victorola. It was Aunt Madge who took me to the cinema, as films made my mother's head ache, unless they starred George Raft or Ronald Colman. The only thing I envied the princesses for was their play-house 'Y Bwthyn Bach', a thatched cottage given to Princess Elizabeth by the people of Wales on her sixth birthday. Set in the grounds of the Royal Lodge in Windsor Great Park, it was large enough for them to entertain other children and even grown-ups to tea.

'Do they do the washing-up themselves?' I asked Aunt Madge enviously. Being 'caggy-handed'—lefthanded and clumsy with it—I was never allowed to help wash up for fear I would break things. I imagined Lilibet happily washing up a china teaset in the miniature kitchen, while her sister dried it on a fine linen teacloth. But Aunt Madge shook her head. 'I shouldn't think so, my duck,' she replied. 'Wouldn't do, would it? Not now she's going to be the heir to the throne.'

Reluctantly, I agreed. So, perhaps, being a princess wasn't all it was cracked up to be. Maybe I was better off as I was, with my cut-out cardboard model of the royal playhouse and my scrapbook full of pictures.

Meanwhile the date of the Coronation drew nearer. It was still to take place on the twelfth of May, despite the change in the leading roles. Celebrations were to be held up and down the land, and every child was to be presented with a souvenir mug or beaker, decorated with a joint portrait of the new king and queen. When we first heard about this, we thought the king himself was coming to give out the mugs personally, perhaps with the queen and the princesses unpacking them and handing them up one by one. In morning prayers, though, Mrs Pugh disillusioned us—they would be given to us instead by the mayor. He would be touring the city schools in the summer term, and we were all to make decorations and learn special songs ready for his visit.

'Stands to reason, my duck,' Aunt Madge explained when I complained bitterly that the king wasn't coming. 'Couldn't travel all over the country, could he, to see everybody? Anyway, he's too busy getting himself crowned in Westminster Abbey. I expect there's plenty to be done, making sure the crown's a good fit for a start. Wouldn't do to have it falling down round his ears because it was too big, or sitting on top of his head like a pea on a drum because it was too small. Don't you worry—you'll see it all in the papers, and it will be on the news at the pictures next time we go, sure to be.'

At school by now we were all in a frenzy of preparations for the mayor's visit. We might not think much of him as a substitute for the new king, but to Mrs Pugh it was a heaven-sent chance to bring herself to the attention of the powers-that-were. If she could impress them by what she could do with the unpromising material they'd given her to work with, maybe there was a slim chance that they would offer her the headship of one of the new, modern schools being built on the city's latest housing estates. With this at the back of her mind, she had us practising 'God Save the King' till our throats were sore, and every scrap of red, white and blue tissue paper in the school was converted into banners and bunting. The reception class made pom-poms by the dozen, Miss Priddy's class painted scores of Union Jacks and Miss Minchin's children made gold-painted models of the crown jewels. In the top class, Miss Salaman's, I helped with the production of cut-out cardboard shields, a bizarre mixture of Scottish lions, Coventry elephants and royal unicorns. Gradually the school hall took on the appearance of a patriotic Christmas grotto.

While all this was going on, my mother took it into her head to come up to the school to see Miss Salaman. I would be going up to the junior school after the summer holiday, and already she was keen to improve my chances of a scholarship to grammar school when the time came. She regarded playtime and PE as a wicked waste of valuable time, and told Miss Salaman so in no uncertain words.

'She isn't going to earn her living kicking her legs about,' she said firmly. 'And she catches cold if she stands around in the playground in all the draughts. You let her stay in the classroom and read a book while the others are out at their physical jerks. Do her a lot more good, that will. And if she stays in at playtime as well, she can do all sorts of jobs for you. She can be handy enough when she puts her mind to it. Wants to be a teacher herself, one day,' she added pointedly.

Miss Salaman tactfully avoided making any direct promises, but from then on she often asked me to stay behind in the classroom when the other children went out to play, to put out the paint trays, the plasticine boards or the cardboard weaving looms. As coronation fever ran higher, she set me to trace off the decorations for the cut-out shields, ready to be painted after play. Usually I was left on my own, but one afternoon I had company. Gwennie Norton was to stay in with me.

The reason was that Gwennie Norton had had her head shaved, by order of the nit-nurse. 'Nit' was another forbidden word, and I shied away from it in my mind as I looked at Gwennie. She was wearing a woollen tam o'shanter pulled down over her ears and under it her face was pale and peaky. But as Miss Salaman gave us our instructions, behind her back Gwennie gave me a wicked wink, and as soon as the door closed on the rest of the class, she tugged off her hat with a sign of relief.

'Cor! That tammy's 'ot,' she said with a grin. 'Thank 'eaven old Aunt Sally let me stay in. Come on now, what've we got to do? You'll have to show me, or I'll get in a right mess.'

Disarmed, I set about explaining how to deal with the assorted templates, trying hard not to stare at the faint, thistledown fuzz that had replaced Gwennie's golden curls. I knew she came from a big, disreputable family spread all through the school, often in trouble with Mrs Pugh and even, it was rumoured, sometimes with the police as well. They lived in one of the courts off Alba Street—courts were squalid yards edged by tumbledown houses, tucked away out of sight down narrow alleys—and I found it hard to imagine how they all found room to fit in. Crowded together like that, no wonder that, often as not, Gwennie fell foul of the nit-nurse. I'd been warned not to play with her, for fear of 'picking something up', but I silenced my conscience by telling myself we weren't playing—we were working, and obeying Miss Salaman's instructions at that. But I secretly decided to say nothing about Gwennie to my mother or Aunt Madge when I got home that night.

With Gwennie's help—and in spite of her fears, she was as sharp as a needle—the work was soon done, and we fell to chatting. Curiosity got the better of me, and I began to ask about her family. Hearing I was an only one, she looked at me incredulously.

'Blimey! There's nine of us,' she gasped. 'There'll be ten when our Maisie has her babby, and that won't be long. You remember Maisie—used to be in the big girls' school upstairs? She left last year, and went to work in the flour mill.'

Thinking back, I remembered Maisie—a plumper, rosier version of Gwennie herself. With the others girls who were leaving the senior school upstairs, she had come down, as the custom was, to say goodbye to the infant teachers at the end of term. Some of the girls had carried large tins of toffees, offering them first to the class teacher and then flinging a lavish handful to the children. Maisie had been in the group, but she hadn't carried any toffees—there was no money to spare in her family for luxuries like that. Now, less than a year later, she was starting a family of her own, but with no husband and no other place to go, she had to stay at home to wait for her baby.

'That bloomin' foreman ... .' Gwennie grumbled. I guessed—wrongly, of course—that she meant the foreman had given Maisie the sack for some reason. Puzzled by what seemed to me an unusual state of affairs, a baby coming to a single girl, I tried to work out what lay behind Gwennie's words, but before I could ask any questions we heard the clatter of footsteps in the corridor, and she snatched up her beret, pulled it down over her ears, and gave me a final friendly wink as she slid nimbly into her own seat on the back row. My encounter with the local underworld was over, or so I thought.

A few days later, Mrs Pugh sent for all of us in the top class to recite to her in the hall. At the time, we had no idea why she wanted to find out if she could hear us speaking from one end of the long, empty room to the other, but she stood whispering with Miss Salaman as we went up one by one on to the platform.

'Just a little poem will do—a nursery rhyme if you don't know anything else,' she told us. 'But I want to hear every word you say, you know, so don't be nervous. I'm not a dragon, though I come from Wales!'

This, intended to put us at our ease, had exactly the opposite effect, so that half the class were too tongue-tied to say a word and the other half collapsed into self-conscious giggles. Luckily, I was used to reciting. I had a whole repertoire of 'pieces' I performed when we had visitors at home—'A wise old owl lived in an oak', 'Under a toadstool crept a wee elf', 'I have a little shadow that goes in and out with me' and so on. When my turn came, I suddenly remembered how I had brought the house down at the school Christmas concert, dressed in a borrowed kimono and a head-dress of artificial chrysanthemums. I marched to the middle of the stage and announced, 'Jappyland.'

Miss Salaman nodded approvingly. She knew what was coming.

'Jappyland's a happy land, the ladies living there,
Have dainty faces, tiny feet, and flowers in their hair ... .'

There were several more stanzas, all in the same vein, and when I came to the end, Mrs Pugh was smiling in delight.

'My word, Patty Palmer, that was lovely!' she beamed. She turned to Miss Salaman. 'I think that settled it, don't you? Stay behind, Patty, and the rest of you back off to your lessons.' She beckoned to me and I trotted obediently down to the other end of the hall. 'You see,' she explained, 'we need a clever little girl with a nice big voice to make a speech of welcome to the mayor when he comes at the end of term to present our coronation mugs. Your teacher will help you write a lovely little speech, I'm sure, and your mother will let you wear your best dress just for that one day, won't she?'

'Yes, Mrs Pugh.' My first delight faded as I imagined what a fuss my mother would make about the whole affair. This would surely be the culmination of all her efforts to curry favour with my teachers. When I got back to the classroom, I found the others busy with a composition lesson, but Miss Salaman set me at once to write my speech, beginning with 'Welcome to our school' and ending with 'God Save the King!' and three loyal cheers.

When the bell went for hometime, she came out with me to the gate and called to my mother, who as usual was waiting for me by the Royal Victorola. They went into a whispered conference while the other mothers stared and the children pointed, and I shuffled my feet and pretended to be reading over my speech, which I had got to learn at home. Afterwards we hurried off, my mother's face, instead of being sallow, now flushed with pride and excitement.

'Wait till your Aunt Madge hears this!' she exclaimed, as she hurried me along. 'Fancy being picked out of the whole school to welcome the mayor! Miss Salaman was ever so pleased with you, too. She said to make sure you got plenty of sleep between now and then, so you're all ready to do your very best. I know what I'll do—I'll make you a nice cup of cocoa every night before bedtime.'

My heart sank—the fuss was starting. But worse was to come—my mother and Aunt Madge decided between them that none of my dresses was suitable for a public performance, and a trip was planned on Saturday to buy me a new one. I thought of the little princesses at the coronation—white lace trimmed with silver bows, silver slippers and purple velvet cloaks edged with ermine—but it seemed unlikely our local shops would have anything to offer on those lines. I was right, of course. As we trudged round the shops everything we saw was too small, too dear or both. Then, hot and tired on the way home, Aunt Madge suddenly remembered Em Todd's shop, tucked away between the undertaker's and the barber's, just round the corner from Shelley Street. Em Todd sold wool, bolts of lace curtain material, household linens and haberdashery, with as a side-line a few children's clothes. Everything was piled in dusty disorder on the shelves behind the counter, while Em Todd lurked in the shadows at the back of the shop, knitting and drinking cups of tea. She had known my mother and my aunt as girls—though it was hard to imagine any of the three as a girl—and she often would reduce their purchases by a penny or two 'for old times' sake'. Now we shuffled into the shop and she came forward with her knitting wool trailing behind her, a gleam in her boot-button black eyes, looking to me like a spider pouncing on a juicy fly that had wandered into its web. After the usual preliminary gossip, my mother explained what we wanted. Em Todd nodded thoughtfully.

'Yes, if I can find it, I've got just what you want. And I can let you have it cheap, too, seeing as it's the last one ... .' She turned to rummage in the drawers behind her. 'Now where is it ... I had my hand on it only the other day. Ah!' She gave a triumphant cry. 'Here it is!' I held my breath.

From the bottom of the drawer she whisked out a creased and crumpled dress and spread it on the counter. I looked at it in dismay, but my mother and Aunt Madge gave little murmurs of delight and approval. In dingy white stockinet, with small red and blue spots, it had a narrow sash and a Peter Pan collar. Long tight sleeves ended in fussy, turned-back cuffs, and round red buttons marched down the front of the bodice. The uneven hem was coming unravelled, giving it a lop-sided appearance. My mother reached out and looked at the tag in the back of the collar.

'It's her size, all right,' she said to Aunt Madge, 'and just the right colours, too. It'd do a treat, I think, don't you?'

'Good quality, that is,' put in Em Todd firmly. 'Lovely bit of stuff. I sold ever so many for the old king's jubilee a couple of years back, and the rest went for the coronation, all except this one. What a stroke of luck for you I've got it left. Wrap it up, shall I? You can soon tack the hem up again, and I'll knock sixpence off, seeing it's you.'

Outside it was dark, and the gas lamps were lit as we made our way home down Shelley Street. In the chip shop next to the Ring o'Bells I saw Gwennie Norton getting the family tea, and waved secretly to her behind Aunt Madge's back. Her hair was starting to grow again now, and out of school she left off her tammy. Seeing her cheered me up for a minute, but then I remembered the dress. When we got home, I would have to try it on.

'It's a bit on the tight side, but it'll look better when it's ironed.' Aunt Madge looked at me thoughtfully as I stood in front of the kitchen range encased in the spotted dress. 'Let's see—a week on Friday she needs it for, doesn't she? Plenty of time to get the hem stitched up, then, Annie. Might be worth giving it a wash through as well, seeing as it's a bit dusty, if you don't think it'll run up?'

Nobody, naturally, asked me what I thought about the dress, and I knew it was no use protesting that I didn't like it. I went to school on Monday morning and told Miss Salaman I had a new dress ready for the mayor's visit, but she was busy collecting the milk money and just gave me a vague smile. Then, at playtime, Gwennie cornered me and told me something that made me forget the dress, at least for a minute. She was grinning all over her face with delight.

'Hey, Patty, know you saw me at the chippy?' she demanded excitedly. 'We was having fish'n'chips to celebrate. Our Maisie's had her baby. Little boy it is, and she's calling 'im Wilfred. Here!'—a sudden thought struck her—''Ow about coming to see 'im arter school? Maisie wouldn't mind, and he's ever so sweet, just like a doll. Go on, will you come?'

'Oh, I'd love to!' My eyes shone at the thought of seeing the tiny baby. Then I remembered. My mother met me out of school and she would never agree to visit Gwennie's home for any reason, far less to see Maisie's baby. There had been harsh comments at home when the news leaked out, about the coming baby and the family in general. But how could I explain to Gwennie without hurting her feelings?

'Maybe later on,' I said hurriedly. 'My mother won't let me do anything till after the mayor's visit. You know what she's like.'

'Yes—sooner you than me, I tell you, chum. Never mind, just say when you want to come. Any time—you'd be welcome, honest.'

Sadly I put the thought of the baby out of my mind, but fate seemed determined to play into my hands. Next day a letter came for my mother. She frowned as she read it.

'Oh, that's a nuisance.' She turned to me. 'Cousin Lottie's coming tomorrow to bring Bert's trousers to be shortened, and she can't get here till four o'clock. That means I can't meet you out of school. Can you come home just this once on your own? If you cross by the traffic lights you'll be safe enough. Don't speak to anyone, mind, and come straight home.'

Careful not to show too much excitement, I nodded, but my heart was beating fast. Here was my chance to call in at Gwennie's on my way home. Next day I saved my playtime chocolate biscuit—a penny Buzz—as a gift for the baby, and when hometime came I set off with Gwennie at top speed.

'I can't stay long—we've got visitors,' I said as we turned up the dark alley that led to the court. But I had reckoned without the fascination of Wilfred himself. As Maisie lifted him proudly out of his cot in the corner of the shabby room, I gazed and gazed at his tiny, perfect hands and feet, the golden mist of fluffy hair and his delicate, rosy face.

'I brought him a biscuit,' I said, holding out the Buzz, and Maisie gave me a loving smile.

'Oh, Patty dear, 'e can't eat that just yet,' she said gently. 'Save it for 'im later on, shall I? You are a good girl to bring it for him. Like to hold him, would you?'

I sat in a rickety armchair with Wilfred on my lap, flattered to see he didn't cry as I settled him gingerly in my arms. Sammy and

Sue, the five-year-old twins, pushed near to look at him, but Mrs Norton shooed them wearily away.

'How many times must I tell you?' she scolded. Then, to me, 'Been orf school they 'ave, poorly, but I'll be that glad when they go back. Now then, Patty, Maisie's got to feed Wilf so you'll 'ave to give 'im back. Like to stay to tea, would you, if your mother won't be worriting?'

My mother! Hurriedly I handed back the baby with a last look at his bright blue eyes. Then I said goodbye and set off for home at a gallop. Luckily my mother took it I had been kept behind to practise my speech, and was too busy boasting to Lottie about it to grumble at me. After tea I got out Primrose, my baby doll, but somehow it wasn't the same. I thought of Maisie tenderly lifting Wilfred up from his cot, and wondered if one day I'd have a real baby of my own. I recited my speech for Cousin Lottie, had my cocoa and went to bed to dream of babies. Next week, I knew, would be here soon enough, and I would have to appear in public in my dreadful red, white and blue dress.

By Monday my throat was sore from practising my speech for Mrs Pugh, for Miss Salaman, for my mother and for Aunt Madge. My mother imagined I was getting a cold and rubbed my chest at night with Vick, so that I swallowed the fumes along with my cocoa. My head ached, and I dreaded Friday coming, and with it the mayor. At last the time came for me to get dressed for the great occasion, and my mother hurried me to school with my finery hidden beneath my coat. The dress, after washing, was tighter than ever, and I felt hot and sticky as we crossed the playground. In the classroom, confusion reigned, as Miss Salaman sorted out the children who were to sing in the choir from those who, being 'growlers', were simply to join in the cheering. Mrs Pugh, meanwhile, was bobbing about in the corridor, her hair newly golden from a visit to the hairdressers, and at the sight of us she seized my mother and hurried her off to the visitors' seats at the back of the hall. Dizzy from all the rushing about, I slipped off my coat and sank down on a chair, while Miss Salaman sent off her groups of children into the hall. Then she turned to me.

'Well now, Patty, let's have a look at you, shall we? H'm, yes, red and blue spots ... very nice.' Then her eyes widened, and she broke off in alarm, putting out a hand under my chin to turn my face to the light of the window. A little cry of dismay broke from her, and she gasped, 'Oh no! Patty, you've got spots on your face and your neck as well—you've got *measles*!'

Rushing back home to go to bed, I put two and two together, but kept quiet about it. The sore throat, the sniffles, the headaches and the dizziness were explained—ever since my secret visit to Maisie and her baby, I'd been coming down with measles, caught from Sammy and Sue. My mother, knowing nothing of this, could hardly blame me, but she pulled my dress off me in furious silence. Too outlandish for everyday wear, it was pushed to the back of a cupboard and, years later, cut up for dusters.

Back at school, the ceremony went ahead without me, and a few days afterwards my coronation beaker was sent home to me by Mrs Pugh. What happened to it, I have no idea. I certainly can't remember drinking out of it. Perhaps my mother put it away out of sight, not wanting to be reminded of our little spot of bother ... .

7

Miss Bellamy's Burglar

'Yore Madge is reely shy, ain't she?'

Aunt Vera had caught a quick glimpse of Aunt Madge as she whisked upstairs the minute my Birmingham aunties came in at the door. Luckily they always assumed it was shyness on her part, when in fact it was a fierce hostility to them and their loud Brummie voices.

'Madge? Oh, she's got some jobs to do,' replied my mother vaguely. 'Now I'll just put the kettle on,' she added, hastily changing the subject. 'You'll want a cup of tea after coming all that way on the bus, I'm sure. Cold, was it?'

Without waiting for an answer, she disappeared into the back kitchen, leaving me alone with the noisy crowd of aunts and uncles. I stood up and put down my doll carefully on my chair. I knew well enough what was coming next.

'And here's little Patty—my, you aren't half getting a big girl!' Auntie Vee, a tall, handsome woman with dark, flashing eyes and the beginnings of a moustache, pounced on me and gave me a prickly kiss. A spinster like Aunt Madge, Vera had stayed at home to look after her widowed father until he died. Now she kept house for Uncle Freddie, a burly, good-natured postman, crammed today into his best blue serge suit. He rumpled my hair with a heavy hand, and then made way for Auntie Mae, the family comedian, thin as a rake with a turned-up nose and frizzy hair. She held me at arm's length and then hugged me close, nearly stifling me in clouds of cheap perfume.

'Why, you are growing up, ducky,' she exclaimed. 'Look, our Gladys, ain't she big for her age? I'd 'ardly have known her, honest!' She handed me on to Auntie Glad as if we were playing a game of 'Pass the Parcel'. Gladys, shabbily dressed and, according to my mother, 'always on the cadge', nodded with a touch of envy.

'There's one as never goes short of a good meal,' she agreed. 'All right for some, ennit?'

Quiet Uncle Ernie, the odd one out, said nothing, patting me gently on the shoulder and then sitting down in a corner. Always edgy and uneasy, he was something of a fish out of water and seldom joined in the chatter. After their last visit I had heard my mother telling Aunt Madge he was a bookies' runner, illegally collecting bets in pubs and on street corners, one jump ahead of the police.

'And Vera reckons he's never been the same since he was in Winson Green for receiving,' she had added in a whisper. 'Vee says his two sons were to blame really, but he got himself sent down instead to protect them. Says now they never go near him, for all that. You don't know what to believe, do you? She's bound to make his own side good.'

Now, as my mother came in with a tray of cups of tea, the clatter of the entry door and the rumble of wheels down the passage at the side of the house announced the arrival of my father, back with his truck and ladders from his window-cleaning round. A moment later there was an uproar of greetings, followed by deafening shrieks of laughter as my father pretended to be bowled over at seeing his brothers and sisters. Though he had lost touch with his family when, aged twelve, he had run away from home to escape his own brutal bully of a father, he had gone back when he was in the Navy and could boast about his days afloat. By then both his parents were dead, but he had kept in touch with his other relations, and I enjoyed their visits like nothing else. With their bright, flashy clothes and their rackety voices, they made my mother and Aunt Madge look paler than ever, and I never knew what they were going to say or do next. 'Common' they might be, in the eyes of my aunt, but for all that they added something—a spice of recklessness, a hint of danger—to our grey, penny-pinching life. For a few hours the house rang with their good-humoured sallies as they gleefully pulled my father's leg and tried in vain to get my mother to join in the fun, while she sat back aloof behind the teapot. Only half-understanding most of what was said, I nevertheless hugged myself with delight to see my father teased unmercifully about scrapes and squabbles long since past and reminded of the days when he, as the eldest, had been the one to get the worst of it in the family battles.

'And what do you think, Patty? Ronnie got blamed for that as well, didn't you, our kid?' hooted Auntie Vee. 'Though it was yore Auntie Mae as stole the sugar from the pantry all along, the little madam! She was a naughty girl, not like you, wasn't you, our Mae? You can't deny it!'

Sheepish and embarrassed, my father tried in vain to shrug off their shrill chaff, turning sulky when they went too far. Then they quickly exchanged warning smirks, and went back to their high tea of tinned salmon and pears and custard, till a chance reminder set them off, noisy as ever.

What made their visits memorable for me, though, was that they always brought presents, probably paid for by Freddie, the wealthy one of the family. These were always the same—cigarettes for my father, Player's Navy Cut because of his time at sea, a big slab of chocolate each for my mother and aunt, and for me a toy or sweets—a monkey on a stick, perhaps, or an enormous packet of jelly babies, bought in Birmingham's Bull Ring as they made their way to the bus station. I imagine they thought I lived a dull life of it, and felt they had to bring something to cheer up 'the pore little kiddie'. There was a sort of ritual about the present-giving, which never took place until just before they were ready to leave. I knew it wasn't polite to appear to be expecting a present, but I couldn't help looking secretly at Auntie Vee's oilcloth shopping-bag, which she always stowed away in a corner on coming into the room. What would it be today? I wondered to myself. Whatever it was, it always carried with it a feeling of foreignness, a touch of the exotic, a tinselly glamour that was a reflection of the givers and their colourful, alien way of life.

When the time came at last, though, I was in for a surprise. Perhaps the aunts and uncles had been late getting into the centre of Birmingham and had needed to dash straight on to the bus, perhaps they had just forgotten altogether about buying presents at the other end, and remembered in dismay during the journey. Whatever the reason, they had clearly bought them this time at the Candy Store, the expensive confectioners by the bus stop in

Coventry, for the name of the shop was printed on the paper bags. They had been able to buy the usual cigarettes and bars of chocolate, of course, but the gift for me had posed a problem. No cheap children's sweets were sold at the Candy Store, and they had obviously panicked. My eyes were wide with astonishment as I looked at what they had brought me—a huge, totally unsuitable presentation box of 'King George' chocolates, decorated with shiny embossed gold lettering and topped by an enormous crisp bow of red satin ribbon. Hardly able to gasp out a 'Thank you!' I clasped the treasure in my arms and lifted my face for the farewell kisses. Never in my life had anyone given me a present like this, a grown-up present, a whole pound box of chocolates all to myself. My mind raced ahead—I would give some to my mother and Aunt Madge and take some to my teacher at school—my father, I knew, didn't like chocolates—and I'd give one each to all my friends, but there'd still be a lot left over for me. I'd eat them very slowly, just one a day, to make them last, and I'd hold tea-parties for my dolls and cut some of the chocolates up like cakes, into tiny pieces so they could all have a slice each. As I thought about them, I could almost taste the thick, dark chocolate, the delicious centres, the creams, the marzipans, the nuts and the cherries. I would eat the marzipans first, they were my favourites, I would ... .

'Ridiculous thing to give a child!' snapped my mother, shattering my daydream and twitching the box out of my hands as soon as the door closed behind the departing visitors. 'Fancy wasting their money on this—they must be barmy. Look at it,' she added tartly, as Aunt Madge came down the stairs. 'They brought this for Patty—did you ever hear the like?'

I looked desperately from one to the other as my aunt nodded in agreement.

'Yes, you're right—it must have cost a good few bob and no mistake,' she said slowly. 'Not suitable for Patty, at all—make her sick, all that chocolate. But it would be a really good Christmas present for somebody, that would ... .' Her voice trailed away, and her eyes met my mother's over my head. My heart sank as they both smiled, suddenly struck by the same thought.

'Miss Bellamy!' said my mother triumphantly. 'Of course, it'll be just the thing for her, Madge. Couldn't be better!'

I knew then it was useless to protest. Miss Bellamy, a tiny black-beetle of a woman, was our landlady. She owned all the houses on our side of Shelley Street, inherited from her father, who had built them at the turn of the century. Almost a recluse since, it was said, a disappointment in love half a century ago, she lived alone except for an elderly maid, in a Victorian mansion overlooking the park on the other side of the city. Occasionally she could be seen, still dressed in the fashions of her youth, being driven down the street in her ancient Daimler to rebuke an unsatisfactory tenant. Otherwise our rents were collected by her agent, a sharp-featured, weasely man whose name was Mr Pike. He was known to us as 'Lucy Locket', from the strong-smelling iodine locket he wore to protect himself from the germs that lurked in the unsavoury courts and alleys he had to visit. The nickname was so well-known that once my father had shouted out, 'Come in Lucy!' when he knocked at the back door, but luckily he hadn't seemed to notice, though we all had a job to keep our faces straight. Every Saturday he came, a leather satchel over his shoulder for the rent-money, scribbling his initials and the date in the rent book and rushing off again with hardly a word. But once a year, just before Christmas, Miss Bellamy herself held court in her house by the park, and her tenants were expected to fetch their rent-books for the New Year in person, at the same time presenting Miss Bellamy with an appropriate gift. And what could be more appropriate than a lavish box of 'King George' chocolates? It was so obvious I couldn't even begin to argue about it. I watched regretfully as my wonderful present was swathed in a clean tea-towel to keep off the dust, and put out of harm's way on top of the wardrobe in my parents' bedroom.

Bonfire Night came and went, with sparklers and Catherine wheels, and soon the shops were full of crackers and Christmas cakes. We practised carols at school, and I was given the part of the narrator in the Nativity play, having the best memory and loudest voice in the class. Then the Saturday came when Mr Pike for once paused briefly, to give us our orders.

'Next week—new rent-books ready. Call any day, ten till four.' The words were hardly out of his mouth when he was off through the door, looking annoyed at the delay. My mother turned to me.

'Break up from school on Wednesday, don't you, Patty?' she said thoughtfully. 'I'll go up Thursday afternoon, then, and you can come with me. Never been to Miss Bellamy's, have you? And you'll enjoy the ride on the tram.'

I nodded, realising that I was being offered this treat in compensation for unwillingly providing Miss Bellamy's Christmas present. Perhaps my mother thought she would open the box while we were still there, and give me one or two out of it, though from what I had heard of Miss Bellamy, this seemed unlikely.

We broke up from school, and the next afternoon, stiffly dressed in our best clothes, my mother and I set out, with the box of chocolates carefully wrapped in white tissue-paper in the bottom of my mother's shopping-basket. The tram rattled and clanged its way round the perimeter of the park, where the grass still sparkled with frost and the ducks pecked forlornly at the ice on the frozen pond. Now the shops, with their bright Christmas displays, were left behind, and large houses stood, each in splendid isolation, behind high hedges, looking to me like palaces with their huge windows and impressive entrances. When we got off the tram, we still had quite a way to walk before we reached Belleville, Miss Bellamy's home, a dark, gloomy house at the end of a long gravel drive. In spite of my woollen gloves and thick stockings, I was miserably cold and looked forward to warming up again in Miss Bellamy's parlour. Not that the house looked welcoming—heavy net curtains, none too clean, were draped across the downstairs windows to keep out prying eyes, and the panels of the front door were filled in with heavy stained glass in purple and bottle green. As we were calling on Miss Bellamy herself, we went to the front door, like proper visitors. On the rare occasions when Mr Pike was ill and the rent had to be delivered direct to Belleville, my father brought it up on his bicycle and went to the tradesmen's entrance round the back.

Miss Bellamy's maid, a tall, forbidding figure in cap and apron, answered the door and showed us into the chilly hall. Wide stairs disappeared into the darkness above and moth-eaten animals' heads decorated the walls. Even now, in the middle of the afternoon, the house was dim and full of shadows. Somehow the maid, grey-haired and bony, managed to convey contempt by the tilt of her eyebrows as she led the way into the parlour.

'Tenants, madam,' she announced curtly. 'From No. 99,' she added in response to my mother's whisper. 'For the rent-book, madam.'

A tiny fire flickered feebly in the enormous grate, and Miss Bellamy, wrapped in knitted shawls, huddled in an armchair in front of it, protected from draughts by a Victorian screen decorated with nursery scraps. A black lace cap covered her wispy grey hair and her long jet ear-rings glittered in the firelight. To me she looked ancient—a hundred years old at the very least—but shrewd dark eyes watched us suspiciously as we approached, missing nothing. Her feet, in tiny pointed button boots, rested on an embroidered footstool. Beside it on the faded rug, wheezing asthmatically, lay a black Pekinese dog, snuffling softly to himself. Miss Bellamy picked up a pile of green rent-books from a tiny papier-mâché table at her elbow, and silently shuffled through them till she came to ours. Our name must have been written on it already, for she peered sharply at us as we hovered nervously at the edge of the rug. When she finally spoke, her voice creaked like the wind in the winter branches of the trees outside the parlour window.

'Mrs Palmer, yes, that's right. You are Mrs Palmer,' she declared, glaring as if daring us to deny it.

'Yes, Miss Bellamy.' I could tell my mother could hardly get the words out by the gulp she gave and her timid smile.

The old woman held out the rent-book, the chain bracelets on her skinny wrist chinking. No one, I saw, had told Miss Bellamy it was rude to appear to be expecting a present, for her eyes were fixed greedily on my mother's basket as we edged forward to take the book.

'And this is ... ?' Miss Bellamy pointed the rent-book at me.

'Patty, Miss Bellamy. Our only one.' My mother hurriedly distanced herself from those of Miss Bellamy's tenants who fecklessly had broods of children to cause overcrowding and damage to her property. 'And,' she added quickly, 'she's got a little present for you, haven't you, Patty?' She slid the parcel out of the basket and into my hands. 'There, give it to Miss Bellamy and say, "A merry Christmas".'

'Merry Christmas, Miss Bellamy,' I croaked, as the claw-like hands seized the tissue-paper and tore it open. I picked up the rent-book which had fallen to the floor and handed it to my mother. As I bent down the black peke sniffed at my hand and I shuddered. His fur was matted in places and his eyes were sticky and sore.

Miss Bellamy, meanwhile, was clearly impressed by the size and quality of our gift. She shot a hard, questioning glance at my mother, and then nodded slowly to herself for a moment.

'Ah, yes, I remember now,' she announced. 'Knew your father, didn't I? A tailor—used to make my skirts for me when they sent me off to finishing-school. Sit down,' she continued graciously. 'We'll have a cup of tea. Ring the bell there, child. Harris won't like it, but it won't hurt her to make a pot of tea.'

I pulled the bell-rope hanging beside the fireplace while my mother, overwhelmed by this sudden mark of favour, perched herself on the edge of a chair opposite the old woman. A brief battle of wills, conducted by glares and counter-glares, was waged between Miss Bellamy and the maid Harris, but tea was finally brought, together with a very small plate of plain, stale finger-biscuits. After offering us one each—I accepted, my mother didn't—Miss Bellamy fed the rest to the peke, which gobbled them up with snuffles and growls. When they were all gone, Miss Bellamy turned to me.

'You take Chang out into the garden for a little run, while I talk to your mother,' she ordered, fumbling behind her in the chair and producing a lead. 'Don't let him go on the flower-beds. You can get into the garden by the back door. It's not locked,' she added, pointing down the corridor.

With Chang following reluctantly, I headed for the door that led into the garden, closing it carefully behind me. It was clear Chang had no intention of having a run—he shuffled along at a snail's pace behind me, sniffing at the flagstones of the path and stopping from time to time to wheeze and cough. Even for winter, the garden was a depressing place, with tall yew trees shutting out the sky and a lop-sided sundial leaning over a small square pond covered by green scum. Shivering in the bitter wind, I kept close to the wall of the house, passing a lighted window where Harris was munching buttered toast and reading the newspaper in front of a blazing fire, a cup of tea at her side. It was starting to snow as I trudged up and down, and I was glad when I heard my mother calling me at the back door. I hurried to her as fast as Chang would let me, relieved the ordeal was over.

'Oh, there you are!' My mother looked pleased to have got away from Miss Bellamy at last. Harris, appearing behind her, reached out and snatched the lead impatiently from my hand and led the dog away, leaving us to let ourselves out of the front door. I imagined Miss Bellamy tucking into my chocolates, perhaps even giving some of them to Chang, as we scrambled on board the tram and rattled home through the gathering darkness.

In the days that followed, as we got ready for Christmas, I forgot all about Miss Bellamy and Chang. It was only when my mother found half a dozen Christmas cards, addressed and stamped ready for posting but pushed behind the clock on the mantelpiece and forgotten, that Miss Bellamy's name came up again.

'Oh, lor, look what I've done now!' My mother was horror-stricken. It was Christmas Eve and anything posted today would be late in arriving. She flicked through them quickly. 'Let's see now ... most of these don't matter, thank goodness ... but this one's for Miss Bellamy. She's going to be offended if she doesn't get it, she is. Do you think you could take it up and push it through the door for me, Patty? Here's some pennies for your tram fare, and be sure to come straight back, won't you?'

Proud to be trusted out by myself for once, I set off, slipping the other forgotten cards into the pillar-box as I made my way to the tram. Once settled in my seat I watched the coloured lights of the shops dancing past till we came to the other side of the park and the secluded gardens of the big houses. Most of the windows were brightly lit and I caught a glimpse of Christmas trees and decorations, but when I descended from the tram and hurried towards Belleville I could see it was in darkness. I was glad—perhaps Miss Bellamy was out or upstairs having a nap. If so, I could put the card quickly through the letter-box and make my escape. But I had reckoned without the loud 'snap' of the old-fashioned letter-box. In the early evening air it rang out like gunfire. Almost instantly the light came on in the hall and the door swung open. To my astonishment, Miss Bellamy herself stood on the threshold, with Chang growling softly behind her.

'Here, little girl, I want you just a minute,' she called imperiously. She leaned forward and peered down at me in surprise. 'Why, you came the other day, didn't you? You're Patty Palmer. Good, you won't mind doing this for me. It's Harris's afternoon off, and Chang likes to walk round the garden before his supper. It's too cold for me to go out today, but you will manage nicely, I'm sure.'

So much for my mother's instructions to come straight back! I went reluctantly up the steps and took the lead she held out to me. As I passed the parlour door with Chang pattering along behind me, I saw my box of chocolates, open and half-eaten, on the table by Miss Bellamy's chair. Rebelliously I led Chang out into the shadowy garden, fuming to myself at this unexpected turn of events. Almost all the light had gone now and as we paraded up and down I could hardly see what lay ahead. Remembering the sinister, slimy waters of the pond I kept to the paths round the edge of the garden and for a time Chang seemed content to follow me. Then he began to tug on the lead, something he'd never done before. Perhaps some distant memories of puppyish behaviour were stirring, perhaps he was just as bored as I was. Suddenly, taking me unawares, he jerked the lead out of my hand and scampered off into the darkness, quickly vanishing from sight.

'Chang! Chang! Come back—good boy!' I was careful to keep my voice down for fear Miss Bellamy would hear me. 'Don't be silly—come here this minute. It's time for your supper,' I whispered craftily, hoping that greed would overcome Chang's yearning for freedom.

A noise at the back door made me stiffen in alarm, my heart sinking as I saw a figure outlined against the dim light of the hall. At first, of course, I thought it was Miss Bellamy come to call us in, but when I looked closer I could see it was someone much taller. Harris, home early? No, this person was burlier and moved in a way that seemed even at this distance to be furtive and cautious, shutting the door softly and moving silently forward, laden, apparently, by two heavy bags. A burglar, it must be—but what could I do about it? And if I tried to alert Miss Bellamy, there was nothing she could do, either—the man would be over the garden wall and off before the alarm could be raised. Holding my breath, I crept from bush to bush until I was only a few yards from the shadowy figure. He had a flat cap pulled well down and a scarf wrapped around his nose and mouth. If he got away now, I'd never recognise him again.

Then my nose began to twitch, as the breeze blew towards me a pungent smell, the heavy medicinal odour of iodine. The burglar was none other than Lucy Locket—Miss Bellamy's trusted agent, Mr Pike! Knowing Harris was away on her afternoon off, and Miss Bellamy dozing by the parlour fire, he had slipped in by the back door, never locked till nightfall, and now was making off with what he had stolen. But if I let him go now and accused him later, who would believe me? Somehow I had to stop him leaving the garden.

'Hallo, Mr Pike!' Suddenly I stepped out from behind the bush and spoke, just as the shadowy figure passed me. What happened next was pandemonium. Startled at hearing his name and realising he was recognised, Mr Pike spun round. Thrown off balance by the heavy bags, he slid backwards on the snowy grass and then gave a yelp of pain. Chang, quietly lapping at the dirty water in the pond and annoyed at being disturbed, had sunk his sharp little teeth into the intruder's ankle. There was a loud splash as Pike fell, swearing, into the mud and slime of the pond. The two bags went flying across the grass, scattering silver and jewellery over the snow, but Mr Pike made no attempt to pick them up as, covered in pond-weed and mud he scrambled out of the water, clambered over the garden wall and pelted off down the road.

Quickly I grabbed Chang's lead as Miss Bellamy and Harris, just returned from her visit to the cinema, came to the back door to see what the noise was. When I explained, Miss Bellamy nodded gravely.

'Gambling,' she said. 'That was Pike's trouble. I helped him out before, and he promised to give it up, but he must have got in a mess again. No, we won't bring the police into it.' For a moment her voice faltered. 'I knew his father, you see. That was why I employed him, for his father's sake.' She shivered, and led me into the house. 'Harris will pick everything up and make sure nothing's missing. You must get home to your mother, Patty. She'll be wondering where you are.'

While Chang gobbled up his supper and out in the garden Harris collected up the valuables, Miss Bellamy took me through the hall to the front door. As I turned to go, she pushed something into my hand, and to my amazement bent down and kissed my cheek.

'You've been a good girl, Patty,' she said. 'You won't be seeing Mr Pike again, but I know I can trust you not to gossip to anyone about what's happened here tonight. It'll be our secret. Now off you go—and a merry Christmas!'

'She gave you that, and said 'A merry Christmas'?' Back in the warm kitchen, my mother looked incredulously at the gold sovereign lying in my hand. 'Well, she's taken a fancy to you and no mistake! Who knows what might come of it? A gold sovereign—just for taking Chang for a walk!'

8

An Angel Unawares

When I decided to become a concert pianist, my mother took me to see Mr Haswell. Organist at Saint Martin's Church for over fifty years, he was chiefly famous for having seen an angel while practising at the organ there one winter evening. Very little was known about this—he never mentioned it now, and it was only spoken of in whispers.

'He saw an angel, you know,' people would murmur when his name came up in conversation. 'Never talks about it, of course, but at the time it was in all the papers. Unconscious, he was, when they found him. No wonder, really, with him all alone like that and then ... .' A shiver would run through the listeners as they imagined the scene—the dark, empty church, the fluttering of wings, the moan of the organ as Mr Haswell, blinded by a blaze of light, slipped senseless to the floor. A nine-days' wonder, and the years of silence, the vision never spoken of again, discretion so complete as to forestall any prying questions—it had become a local legend. When it came to piano lessons, Mr Haswell was the obvious choice—in fact, the only choice, since there were no other music teachers in our part of town. But if there had been twenty other teachers, my mother would still have chosen Mr Haswell. His odour of sanctity was irresistible.

'That's right, you take her to Mr Haswell,' the neighbours said, when she spoke about it. 'He'll give her lessons, tip-top lessons. He's getting on now, of course,' they added thoughtfully.

Mr Haswell was certainly getting on. Always, it seemed, an elderly man, he was now well over eighty, and I was eight. He lived some streets away, near the post office, and we walked there one evening after school, dressed in our best clothes, my mother like a grey mouse with her sharp pink nose and grey coat and hat, and me with my brown Melton overcoat tightly belted around me and my velour hat like a fur pudding-basin on my head. The brass plate by Mr Haswell's front door, polished till the copperplate letters had almost vanished, gave his name with the words, 'Piano Forte Instruction' still just faintly visible below. My mother rang the bell, and Mr Haswell's daughter Ada opened the door. I realised then that some preliminary arrangements had already been made, as she showed no surprise at seeing us on the doorstep. With a whispered greeting she ushered us into the dark hallway. I looked around nervously for any sign of angels, but saw nothing alarming until what I had taken to be a pair of moth-eaten fur gloves on the hallstand suddenly turned out to be a tabby cat, which hissed fiercely at us and then fled up the dusty staircase to the floor above. With Miss Ada going in front to turn up the gas, we shuffled into the parlour where, it seemed, the lessons were to take place.

Perhaps because of his disturbing encounter, Mr Haswell had married late in life. Ada was a tall, thin woman in her middle thirties with untidy dark hair and a sallow complexion, wearing a stringy cardigan and a print apron. This was her winter incarnation. In the summer season, resplendent in a black crepe dress with sequins, she played the violin in the quartet in the Cadena Café while visitors took afternoon tea. I had often dawdled on the pavement outside to listen to 'Pale Hands I Loved beside the Shalimar' and 'In a Persian Market', watching Miss Haswell as she swayed passionately to the music among the potted palms. Expecting a whiff of that glamour to cling to her at home, I was disappointed by the cardigan and the apron.

Then, as my eyes became accustomed to the gloom, I took in the room around us. Heavy lace curtains, obviously in need of a wash, kept out the last of the afternoon light and the gas spluttered feebly, but even so I could see that the room held unexpected treasures. Above the marble fireplace was a carved overmantel, and on its many shelves and on little tables and bamboo stands around the room was a collection of Victorian glass paperweights. I had no idea then what they were, but they were clearly 'ornaments'. So many useless objects in such profusion impressed me with a sense of untold wealth, and my faith in Miss Ada was restored. She was obviously an heiress of means.

She left us then, my mother sitting awkwardly on the edge of a chair with me standing behind her, both looking respectfully at the piano which, though not the 'grand' I had hoped to see, nevertheless shone in the reflected glory of the paperweights. We had an upright piano ourselves at home, once the property of a musical aunt, but it was rather battered and had a curious one-eyed appearance since in a house-move the left-hand brass candleholder had been snapped off. Mr Haswell's piano was of about the same vintage, but had both its candleholders and between them a panel of lighter wood inlaid to represent a bouquet of roses. I imagined myself playing it with immense panache, and Mr Haswell tearfully proclaiming me a genius.

After a few moments, during which my mother dabbed nervously at her nose with her clean handkerchief and I looked at the photographs on the walls—Mr Haswell seated at the organ—no sign of the angel!—a wedding group and several portraits, including one of Miss Ada in her teens—the door opened again and in came Mr Haswell himself, with his daughter hovering protectively behind him. I had expected him to look pale and spiritual, to have been marked out in some way from the rest of mankind by his experience, but as he tottered towards us with the aid of a stick, Mr Haswell looked more like an elderly Father Christmas, short, round, red-faced and whiskery, with watery blue eyes behind gold-rimmed spectacles. Miss Ada guided him to a high-backed armchair by the fireplace, where he sat looking from my mother to me and nodding gently. For a while it seemed we were all four of us going to sit there in silence for ever, but at last the old man spoke.

'She will come on Saturdays?' he said. His voice was thin and quavering. My mother nodded eagerly.

'Yes, if that suits you, Mr Haswell.'

'Between nine and ten, you said, Ada?' he went on, turning to his daughter. Miss Haswell nodded too.

'Starting this Saturday?' This time Mr Haswell looked at me, and the ghost of a smile passed over his face. Catching the habit, I nodded.

'Yes, please,' I murmured under my breath.

'I will give you some books.' He struggled to his feet and crossed over to the music stool by the piano. Lifting the seat he took out two small books, one with a red cover which said, 'The

On the way home I made up my mind to forget everything that had happened that morning. If I even started to think about it, my mother or Aunt Madge would know I was hiding something, and one way or another would get it out of me. They always did. But no, I thought, I won't tell them. I won't let Miss Ada down.

As it turned out, though, that was my last music lesson, after all. On Monday I got home from school to find my mother waiting for me with pursed lips, a cup of cocoa ready on the hob. I knew at once something was wrong.

'You won't be going to Mr Haswell's again, my duck,' she said solemnly, passing the cocoa to me when I'd taken off my coat. 'You mustn't be upset about it. It can't be helped.'

They've found out, I thought. They know he's deaf. Who told them? What will Miss Ada say?

Then I realised my mother was still speaking.

'He's dead, Patty, poor old chap. But he was a good age ... . Fell over and hit his head, according to all accounts. Mrs Fellowes told me when I went to the post office this morning. Everybody's talking about it. It is a shame, just when you were doing so well.'

It seemed that a chunk of broken glass, hidden in the matted tufts of the fur hearth-rug, had twisted under Mr Haswell's foot as he left the room after my lesson. Never very steady on his feet, he had pitched backwards on the sharp edge of the brass fender, hitting his head a fatal blow, and was dead when his daughter found him. The news, of course, spread like wildfire through the neighbourhood, and for a while I wondered whether, if the whole story came out, I would be held to blame. We sent flowers to the funeral, and my mother shed a few sentimental tears, but she made no attempt to find me another piano teacher, since to tell the truth my practising had got on her nerves and she was secretly glad it was at an end. Glowing reports of Mr Haswell's career appeared in the newspapers, with the story of the angel duly mentioned. His death was described as 'a tragic accident'.

Then, gradually, gossip began to reveal that things were looking up in the gloomy house by the park and that—except for Mr Haswell, naturally—in a curious way I might even be said to have done them a good turn. A visit of condolence by the cellist who played in the summer quartet at the Cadena Café became the beginning of a romance. Against all odds, Miss Ada appeared at Saint Martin's as a bride, radiant in white satin and orange blossom, swept off to a new home on the other side of town. Her mother, an invalid whom I had never met, recovered her health sufficiently to go and live with her married son in the North of England, and the house was left empty. What became of the Victorian glass paperweights I never knew, though I often wondered about them. Miss Hope said she quite understood when I explained that I wouldn't be taking part in the end-of-term concert after all. Some other time, perhaps, she said.

Rudiments of Music' and the other called 'Songs for the Young Pianist'. He opened the red book and stabbed at the first two pages with a gnarled finger. 'Read that before Saturday,' he said, watching me closely. 'You can read, can't you, young lady?'

'Yes!' I was the best reader in Miss Hope's class. I could read anything, and my pride was nettled, but he pushed the books into my hand and patted me kindly on the shoulder, unaware he had hurt my feelings.

'Good girl! Good girl! Then I'll see you on Saturday.' He turned and headed for the door, nodding to himself and pausing only to sketch a bow to my mother, who was in a huddle with Miss Ada. I heard the chink of money—clearly payment was too sordid a subject for Mr Haswell to discuss. 'Good evening, Mrs Er—er ... good evening,' he said as he reached the door. 'Till Saturday, then ... .' He vanished down the corridor.

Even Miss Ada seemed relieved the interview was over, and my mother's nervousness disappeared once the front door was shut behind us and we were out in the street. I clutched the dog-eared books closely to my chest as we hurried along under the street-lamps, and to celebrate my new career we took home roe and chips for tea.

I dreamt that night of paperweights and pianos, and next day at school I informed Miss Hope that I would give a solo recital for the end-of-term concert. I was sure by then I would have a whole repertoire of 'pieces' I could perform, probably most of the 'Songs for the Young Pianist' and more besides. Miss Hope thanked me gravely, and said she would put me on the list. I explained it had been arranged for my teacher to be the well-known organist, Mr Haswell.

'He saw an angel, you know,' I added automatically, and Miss Hope smiled gently, but said nothing. When Miss Cranstone, who had come in collecting for the Boot Fund, murmured something about a genie out of a bottle, Miss Hope shushed her quickly and sent me back to my place to get on with my sums.

After school, my mother took me round to the Thrift Shop on the corner of South Street, where everything was second-hand and cheap, and bought me a music-case for the books Mr Haswell had given me. We had the choice of two, one with the stitching coming undone and the other with a catch that locked, which impressed me though it had heavy scratches on the leather. To my disappointment, my mother put it aside and paid for the other.

'We can soon get your dad to stitch it up with his shoe-mending thread,' she said as we headed for home. 'There's no need for you to have a lock, anyway. Who's going to pinch piano books? They can't take the piano to go with them!'

I agreed wistfully, regretting the fancy lock, though I was intrigued by the way the case we had bought was fastened by looping the handle through a metal bar. My father, after some nagging, mended it neatly and polished it up with brown shoe-polish, so that it looked quite smart, and I was pleased with it when I put my books in it ready for Saturday. I had looked at the first chapter of the little red book and could read every one of the words in it, though I didn't know what they meant. My mother said Mr Haswell would explain it all to me when I went for my lesson. The book of tunes I looked through, too, reading all the titles, though how I was to change the black dots on the page into 'Home, Sweet Home' or 'The Bluebells of Scotland', I had no idea. I propped the book up on the music-stand of our piano and rattled away at the keys when my mother was out in the yard getting in the washing. But I could only manage my usual sweeping trills and discordant crashes. It didn't help that some of the notes came out as a dull thud—the piano badly needed an overhaul. My parents had agreed it was 'good enough to practise on' and that if I 'stuck at it' they would get it tuned.

On Saturday I set out for my first lesson, promising, like Little Red Riding Hood, to go straight there and not to speak to anyone on the way. I was so eager to see Mr Haswell again, I resisted all the tempting shop windows and crossed the road before I got to the park gates where I usually slipped in for a quick swing when I was running errands for my mother. I carried my music-case proudly, wondering if I was being noticed by the customers in the shops or by the postman emptying the pillar-box outside the post office. In no time, it seemed, I was standing once again on Mr Haswell's doorstep, and as I rang I heard the bell of Saint Martin's clock striking nine. It reminded me of the angel and I had a moment of panic. Luckily, just then Miss Ada opened the door, peering out anxiously, only to brighten up when she saw me standing there.

'Come along in, dear—Patty, isn't it?' she greeted me, letting me into the gloomy hall. She took my hat and coat and hung them on the hall-stand, admired my music-case and took my books out of it for me, and then led the way into the front room. The plush cover of the piano-stool felt hot and sticky under my bare legs and I wriggled to pull down my skirt while Miss Ada dragged a low armchair across the room so that her father could sit next to me. At home I had to use a kitchen chair when I 'played' the piano, and to sit on the stool, perched up in the air without any support, made me feel uneasy. The bad-tempered tabby had been asleep on the black fur hearth-rug in front of the brass fender and empty grate, but to my relief Miss Ada shooed it out in front of her as she left the room. Holding on to the sides of the stool, I gingerly looked over my shoulder at the ranks of glass paperweights, now gleaming softly in the morning light. In every colour of the rainbow they glowed and shone like precious jewels, all the brighter for their dingy setting, so many of them that I lost count. Then I heard a noise in the hall and began to wonder if I should stand up when Mr Haswell came in. We stood up for the headmaster at school, but not for the teachers. I decided to be on the safe side, and slid down off the stool.

As it turned out, it was the right decision, for when he came in Mr Haswell sat down himself on the piano stool, leaving me standing by his side. He smiled at me, said, 'Well, well!' a few times, and then spread his fingers out on the discoloured ivory keys and began to play. Whether, on that far-off night, he had seen an angel or not, Mr Haswell certainly played like one. I held my breath as the music flowed from his hands, and could have listened for ever. In the end, though, Miss Ada, who was fussing about in the background, sidled over to the piano and picked up the red book in a meaningful sort of way, and Mr Haswell brought his performance to a close. Then he moved across into the arm-chair, nodded me to sit on the stool, waited till Miss Ada had whisked quietly out of the room, and began my lesson. I learnt that Every Good Boy Deserves Favour, Mr Haswell's blunt forefinger sounding the appropriate keys, and copied him carefully as he spelled out F.A.C.E. The treble clef came next, and minims, crochets and quavers followed one after the other, so that I felt I was learning a new language. Mr Haswell's teaching method was to instruct—he rarely questioned except to say, watching me earnestly with his pale blue eyes, 'Do you understand? Is that clear to you, my dear?' nodding with satisfaction when I agreed. Once or twice I attempted a question of my own, but this he brushed airily aside with a reassuring wave of his hand, saying kindly, 'Early days yet, early days. We'll leave that till later, I think. We must walk before we can run, young lady. First things first!'

Each week I went home with a passage in the red book marked to study, and a line or two of music to commit to memory. Phrase by phrase I learned to stumble through 'Home, Sweet Home', and after one lesson Miss Ada told me on the doorstep to bring an extra sixpence next time to pay for a copy of a special piece called 'The Merry Reapers', its cover decorated by an illustration of frolicking peasants. This, I thought, would be ideal to perform at the school concert, and took it in on Monday for Miss Hope's approval. She glanced through it with an encouraging smile, and agreed it would be perfect as a finale for the concert, if I learnt it in time. Miss Cranstone, collecting this time for the Waifs and Strays, gave a sceptical sniff, but I pointedly ignored her. One day, when I was famous, she would be sorry.

Since every Saturday my lesson always began with a recital by Mr Haswell, I got into the habit of leaving the piano stool free for him. Once I was used to the eerie atmosphere of the silent room, I began to tiptoe around before he came in, peering at the faded photographs, dusting the leaves of the aspidistra with my handkerchief and trying in vain to count the paperweights, which continued to fascinate me. Finally, inevitably, I gave in to temptation, and picked one up. In the one I chose, my favourite, circular sections of glass rods in bright colours were arranged together to form a pattern, looking to me like chunks of fruit-flavoured seaside rock, orange, lemon, strawberry and lime green. It rested in the palm of my hand, heavier than I had expected but full of flashing lights when I crossed the room and lifted it up to the window. There was something magical about it and it held me entranced as I turned it this way and that, almost forgetting where I was and why I was there. Suddenly, the sound of the door opening brought me back to earth. To my alarm, before I could replace the paperweight, Mr Haswell shuffled into the room, waving his stick in greeting and seating himself at the piano. Overcome with guilt—'Don't touch *anything!*' my mother had warned me—I quickly hid the paperweight behind my back and crossed to the piano as Mr Haswell's music filled the room.

Somehow, I knew, I had to get rid of the paperweight before Mr Haswell ceased playing, for then I would be expected to take over with 'The Merry Reapers', my teacher watching every movement of my fingers like a hawk. I had no pocket to put it in, so I realised my only hope was to return it to its ledge before my turn came. Silently I began to move backwards an inch at a time, terrified that at any moment Mr Haswell might look up from the keys and discover that for once I wasn't listening admiringly to his playing. It was like our playground game of 'Grandmother's Footsteps' in reverse—instead of creeping cautiously forward, hoping to remain unseen by the child who was 'on', I was edging back on tiptoe towards the rickety little bamboo table, ready to set down the paperweight as soon as I was within reach. Then I could return stealthily to my place as if nothing had happened. I might have succeeded, but just as I had got to the table and, hardly daring to breathe, was reaching out with the paperweight, the door suddenly opened and Miss Ada came in. The horror and astonishment on her face as she saw me hovering by the fireplace made me start with alarm, the bamboo table rocked wildly and its contents fell pell-mell to the ground. Most of them landed harmlessly on the thick fur of the hearth-rug, but one—my favourite, the cause of all the trouble—tumbled askew into the tiled hearth and with an ear-splitting explosion shattered into a million coloured fragments. Miss Ada and I stared at each other in dismay, rooted to the spot. Then, after a few seconds, it gradually dawned on me that, incredibly, Mr Haswell himself was playing on undisturbed, unaware of the drama going on behind his back.

In two strides Miss Ada, her face grim, was across the room. She knelt down on the hearth-rug and began gathering up the jagged splinters of glass into her apron, as I watched in bewilderment.

'It's all right—go back to your lesson,' she hissed at me

urgently. 'Never mind about this—it was my fault for startling you. Don't worry about it—it doesn't matter.'

'But—but he didn't hear,' I blurted out. 'He went on playing. He didn't hear it break ... .'

She nodded impatiently. 'Yes, yes, he's deaf, stone-deaf. He didn't hear a thing. He's deaf as a post—has been for years.'

'But—he's been teaching me ... .'

Miss Ada sighed. 'We needed the money. And he can see if you make mistakes. Everything's so expensive now, and when your mother came round'—she shrugged and gave me a rueful smile. 'I should have known better, I suppose, but it was worth a try.'

My mind raced. This explained the time-wasting opening recital, the questions kindly brushed aside, the watchful stare as I played. But although, perhaps, I had been made a fool of, somehow her words filled me with pity—pity and a strange sort of pride. Miss Ada had spoken to me frankly, as an equal. Instead of trying to hide the truth, she had shared it, and this had never happened to me before. Determined to live up to her trust, I crept silently back to my place by the piano. Out of the corner of my eye I saw her leave the room with her apron full of broken glass, and the lesson continued.

When the hour was up, she was waiting for me by the hall-stand to help me on with my coat. Her eyes were red, but she opened the front door without a word, and as I bundled my books into my music-case I tried desperately to think what to say, how to let her know I would keep what I'd found out to myself, that I wouldn't give her away. I could just imagine the fuss there would be if I told tales at home—my father banging on the table and swearing—he liked nothing better than 'a good row'—my mother pleading with him to calm down, and Aunt Madge, shocked but privately delighted by all the excitement. Then, perhaps, angry demands for our money back, charges of fraud and false pretences, threats of 'taking her to court'—no wonder Miss Ada expected the worst. Somehow I had to set her mind at rest before I left. Edging past her into the busy street, I fell back on habit.

'See you next week, Miss Ada,' I said brightly as usual, and before I scurried off I saw her tense face relax in relief before she closed the door behind me.

On the way home I made up my mind to forget everything that had happened that morning. If I even started to think about it, my mother or Aunt Madge would know I was hiding something, and one way or another would get it out of me. They always did. But no, I thought, I won't tell them. I won't let Miss Ada down.

As it turned out, though, that was my last music lesson, after all. On Monday I got home from school to find my mother waiting for me with pursed lips, a cup of cocoa ready on the hob. I knew at once something was wrong.

'You won't be going to Mr Haswell's again, my duck,' she said solemnly, passing the cocoa to me when I'd taken off my coat. 'You mustn't be upset about it. It can't be helped.'

They've found out, I thought. They know he's deaf. Who told them? What will Miss Ada say?

Then I realised my mother was still speaking.

'He's dead, Patty, poor old chap. But he was a good age ... . Fell over and hit his head, according to all accounts. Mrs Fellowes told me when I went to the post office this morning. Everybody's talking about it. It is a shame, just when you were doing so well.'

It seemed that a chunk of broken glass, hidden in the matted tufts of the fur hearth-rug, had twisted under Mr Haswell's foot as he left the room after my lesson. Never very steady on his feet, he had pitched backwards on the sharp edge of the brass fender, hitting his head a fatal blow, and was dead when his daughter found him. The news, of course, spread like wildfire through the neighbourhood, and for a while I wondered whether, if the whole story came out, I would be held to blame. We sent flowers to the funeral, and my mother shed a few sentimental tears, but she made no attempt to find me another piano teacher, since to tell the truth my practising had got on her nerves and she was secretly glad it was at an end. Glowing reports of Mr Haswell's career appeared in the newspapers, with the story of the angel duly mentioned. His death was described as 'a tragic accident'.

Then, gradually, gossip began to reveal that things were looking up in the gloomy house by the park and that—except for Mr Haswell, naturally—in a curious way I might even be said to have done them a good turn. A visit of condolence by the cellist who played in the summer quartet at the Cadena Café became the beginning of a romance. Against all odds, Miss Ada appeared at Saint Martin's as a bride, radiant in white satin and orange blossom, swept off to a new home on the other side of town. Her mother, an invalid whom I had never met, recovered her health sufficiently to go and live with her married son in the North of England, and the house was left empty. What became of the Victorian glass paperweights I never knew, though I often wondered about them. Miss Hope said she quite understood when I explained that I wouldn't be taking part in the end-of-term concert after all. Some other time, perhaps, she said.

9

Fatty Patty and the World Walker

I don't suppose anyone else remembers the World Walker now. He was on his way to Banbury Cross when we met, and that was the last I ever heard of him, what with the war starting soon afterwards and being evacuated and everything. I was nine years old when I bumped into him, and I was in Miss Pumphrey's class. That was the worst class I was in in all my life—I was never out of trouble from the minute the bell rang in the morning till it was home-time. Like cat and dog we were, Miss Pumphrey and me. We fought from the day I went into her class till the day I left it. Except for the day the World Walker came to school.

My mother couldn't understand why I didn't get on with Miss Pumphrey. I'd got on well at Infant School, I'd got on well in Miss Hope's class, I'd even got on well in Miss Cranstone's class, and she was nearly as strict as Miss Pumphrey. At first my mother tried going up to school to sort things out, but Miss Pumphrey was so toffee-nosed and sarcastic my mother had to go home and lie down for an hour afterwards, so she gave up in the end.

'I can't go and see that woman again to save my life, Patty,' she told me. 'My nerves won't stand it. You'll just have to get on with her as best you can. Can't you keep out of her way?'

Keeping out of Miss Pumphrey's way wasn't easy. She used to warn us she'd got eyes in the back of her head, and I believed her. She didn't miss a thing that went on, even when she turned round to write on the blackboard. Some of the other children said she was a witch, and I could just imagine her riding on a broomstick when it was dark at night. I used to have nightmares about it.

I could see why she didn't like me. She was pin-neat and rake-thin, with black pleated skirts and white frilly blouses that never got dirty. Her iron-grey hair was scraped back in a bun and she had long, long finger-nails, shiny and dagger-sharp. She tapped with them on her desk while she waited for an answer.

'Come along, Trevor Simkins!' she'd say—tap, tap, tap—'Come along, we're waiting ... ,'—tap, tap, tap—then, her face red with fury, 'Are you a fool, boy?' she'd shout—tap, tap, tap—and poor old Trevor would blurt out 'Yes, miss,' and we'd all roar with laughter and get kept in at playtime.

Miss Pumphrey liked everything neat and tidy in her spotless little classroom, so no wonder she didn't like me. Somehow that year I couldn't keep tidy for two minutes put together, however hard I tried. I'd start off from home with clean shoes, clean socks, my dress washed and ironed and a clean handkerchief in my pocket, my face scrubbed and my hair just so, and before I got to school my shoes would be muddy, my socks wrinkled, my dress creased, my handkerchief lost forever, my face dirty and my hair all over the place. By playtime my fingers would be inky and my exercise-book covered with blots. 'Do it again!'—that was all I ever heard. Even if I got something right for once, Miss Pumphrey had to be nasty about it.

'The age of miracles is upon us,' she'd say, all cut-glass and hoity-toity. 'Wonders will never cease!'

It didn't help that, in those days, when anybody wanted to get my temper up, they'd call me 'Fatty Patty'. Practically every day I got into fights in the playground over it, and ended up looking more of a mess than ever. Mr Skelton, the headmaster—we called him the Skeleton, of course—had me in his office time and again, trying to persuade me it didn't matter what my nickname was, but I knew it did.

'I know what they call me, and I don't mind, Patty,' he said kindly. But they don't call it you to your face, I thought. They wouldn't dare—and that's the difference! But it was no use saying anything.

It had been an ordinary sort of morning, the day I met the World Walker—blots and scratches and slaps, and a row with Miss Pumphrey. I came down East Street hill carrying on the argument in my head, like you do, and thinking of all the smart-alec answers and excuses I hadn't been able to think of at the time, not looking where I was going, and I suddenly fell over this enormous pair of boots. Those boots! They had soles an inch thick and they looked as if they could walk to the ends of the earth and back all by themselves. I lay sprawled on the pavement with all the breath knocked out of me, and the stranger who was wearing the boots bent down and picked me up and set me on my feet again. He was standing on the corner outside the priests' house under the laburnum tree by the gate, next to the Catholic church opposite our house. While I was brushing myself down, I took a good look at him on the quiet, and I could see that the rest of him matched up to his boots. He had on khaki shorts like a Boy Scout and long woollen knee-socks, and across the front of his windcheater there were letters sewn on made out of tape which said, 'World Walker'. I couldn't think what it meant, then. There was a huge haversack on the pavement beside him, and he looked as if he'd put it down because he couldn't carry it a step further for all the tea in China. Never had I seen anybody look so tired, and when at last he spoke, even his voice was tired—tired, and hungry and ... Irish!

'The fathers are away at a conference,' he said. 'There's a note pinned to the door, saying so. Could you be after telling me where I could find a bite to eat around here, not too expensive? I have to get to Banbury Cross as soon as may be, but I need some food before I set off again, if I can get some.'

I was so excited I could hardly speak, and he looked pretty startled when I began tugging at his arm, but he picked up the haversack and followed me across the road to our front door. I hammered on the knocker and by the time my mother had come to see why I was at the front and not at the back as usual, I was able to speak again. She looked suspiciously at the over-grown Boy Scout by my side but before she could say anything, I began to explain as fast as I could.

'He wants a meal, mum,' I said, 'he's hungry and he went to the priests' house but they're away and he's got to go to Banbury and he's Irish!'

At the last word, the door swung right open, as I knew it would. My mother's own mother had been Irish, and since she had died when my mother was just a baby, anything to do with Ireland and the Irish was practically sacred to her. She believed that 'the ould country' was a place where all the people were quaint and kind and generous to strangers, and though she'd never been there she was always saving up odd coppers towards the fare to go, coppers that had to be spent on something else before they mounted up to more than a few shillings. So I was certain that if I turned up with a hungry Irishman on her doorstep, she'd be more than happy to find a meal for him in return for a few stories about the Emerald Isle, even if it meant my father would go short at teatime. The stranger clinched it when he reached out and shook hands with her, smiling down at her with all the charm in the world.

'To be sure, I hate to be troubling you, missus,' he said politely. 'This dear little girl of yours brought me over before I knew what was happening. If the holy fathers had been at home, I wouldn't have had any problem, for I've a letter in my haversack from his holiness the Pope commending me to their care, but they're away this very day and if you can spare a bite to eat ... .'

Sure enough, in next to no time, Michael MacMurphy the World Walker was sitting down in our front room eating bacon sandwiches and telling us how he'd come to set out on his travels. As he spoke, all the countries in the world seemed to come crowding into the room with him, and for once Miss Pumphrey, Trevor Simkins, Mr Skelton and all my troubles seemed to be a million miles away, and not worth worrying about.

Like a lot of these crazy things, Michael's great journey had begun as a bet. Back in Ireland he had an invalid little sister, Philomena—he showed us photos of her lying back in a wheelchair, smiling patiently, frail and thin as a fairy-child—Miss Pumphrey would have loved her!—and it was for her sake he'd started out on the longest walk in history. His parents, advised by the parish priest, had taken her to Dublin to see a specialist, who had said yes, there was an operation which would cure her, but it would cost a mint of money and there was no way the family could afford it. For the next few days they talked of nothing else, without hitting on any kind of a solution, till one evening Michael slipped out for an hour to have a drink at the village inn. There he got into conversation with an American tourist, a red-faced man in a loud tweed jacket with buttons as big as golf-balls. He listened to Michael's story with a jeering sort of a smile.

'Ten years of my life I'd give ... .' Michael was saying, when the American suddenly interrupted him.

'Aw, you Irish,' he drawled. 'All talk and no action, that's you guys. You've just said you'd give ten years of your life to cure your kid sister. Well, I tell you what—though I don't reckon you'll have the guts to do it! I'll give you the money for the operation, see? But to earn it you've got to walk right round the world first—and I want pictures to prove it from every country on the globe. Whadda you say, is it a deal?'

It didn't take long for Michael to decide—after all, he'd be seeing the world as well as helping Philomena—so it was fixed up legally with conditions and guarantees, and already he was well on the way to fulfilling his side of it. Out of his haversack he took dozens of newspaper cuttings and photos he'd collected, signed by mayors and bishops and politicians, and he spread them all out over the sofa for us to see. There were pictures of him on a camel in the desert, of him shaking hands with a Mountie outside a log cabin, of him being received by the Pope and dozens more. 'World Walker Hits Hollywood', 'World Walker on Everest', 'World Walker Down Under', the headlines screamed. And now he was sitting in our front room eating bacon sandwiches! I couldn't believe it. Then something happened that I remembered afterwards. It made me shiver then, and it makes me shiver now.

While Michael was telling us about the cuttings, another photograph fell out of his haversack, so I picked it up for him and looked at it. It showed a little man in a baggy uniform, with a sort of crooked cross on his sleeve. He had a black moustache and his hair fell down low over his forehead as he raised his arm straight up in a stiff salute. He was on a platform draped with flags and bunting, and there were thousands and thousands of people in front of him row upon row, all saluting back. Some of them were in uniform, with shiny black leather boots and metal helmets, some of them were in ordinary, everyday clothes, but their faces were all the same. They were staring up at the little man on the platform, every one of them, as if he was the most wonderful person in the entire world, and they would follow him to the ends of the earth and obey everything he ordered. I didn't know who it was—then.

'Him? Hitler, that is.' Michael MacMurphy looked at the

photograph grimly. Then he turned to my mother, and I could see she was worried, too.

'We'll be having trouble with that spaleen before long, missus, I can tell you. It's not healthy, so it's not, what he's up to in Germany. I stood right under the platform at one of his rallies and it made my blood run cold. Not a word of it could I understand, but I didn't need to. I could tell it was evil he was spouting, evil and wicked, and all those silly, stupid people listening to him like he was the saviour of the world. Hatred was pouring out of him, wave upon wave of it, and you can take my word for it I didn't need to speak the language to recognise it for what it was. Heaven help us all if he gets his way!'

He shook his head sadly, and pushed the photo out of sight. Then he carefully packed away all the rest of his cuttings and papers and fastened the straps of his haversack. Among them was a little needle-case I'd made at school which my mother was sending to Philomena. Goodness knows what she'd think of it—every stitch had been done and undone twenty times over to suit Miss Pumphrey. But Michael said it was something she'd treasure all her life long, and he'd give it to her on the grand day he was home again from his travels.

The needle-case reminded me of Miss Pumphrey and I realised I'd have to hurry to get back before the bell went for afternoon school. Michael said he would walk up the hill with me, since it would take him straight to the Banbury Road, where next day he was to be photographed with the mayor standing by Banbury Cross. I saw my mother slip some money into his hand as we went out of the door, and I guessed it was what she had saved up for her trip to Ireland. We must have looked an odd couple, the World Walker and me, as we set off up East Street hill, but there weren't many people about at that time of day, and I knew it was even later than I thought when I heard the school bell clanging just as we got to the pub on the corner. More trouble from Miss Pumphrey! I was going to start running when Michael put a hand on my shoulder.

'Woa up,' he said with a grin. 'I'll tell you what—I'll go in with you to see your teacher and make it right for you. I'm not having you in hot water when it's myself that's made you late with all my jawing on. You've been a Good Samaritan to me, Patty, old lady, to be sure you have, and I'm not one to let down a friend in need. I've got plenty of time meself, so I'll just have a word with this Miss Pumphrey of yours, and put the record straight.'

I didn't know what to say. I looked at his great big boots and his shorts and his haversack, and tried to imagine what Miss Pumphrey would think of him if he marched into her classroom as she was taking the register and started on about putting the record straight. The idea of Michael MacMurphy the World Walker having a word with Doris Pumphrey was a bit like St George having a friendly chat with the dragon, or David taking a cup of tea with Goliath, so in the end I said nothing and decided to see what would happen when they met. I led the way across the playground, empty now, of course, and cut past the milk crates, through the cloakroom and along the corridor to the door of our classroom. Then I let him go in first, and stood behind him out of Miss Pumphrey's line of fire. She had finished the register and was at the blackboard, just about to write up the next lesson.

She had the chalk-box in her hand and for a minute I thought she was going to drop it when she saw him, but before she could say a word Michael was across the room in two strides, seizing her other hand in his and shaking it while he talked away nineteen to the dozen. Somehow his Irish accent had got stronger than ever, and I don't know how much of it all Miss Pumphrey was taking in, but she just stood there with her mouth open while all the class sat grinning and nudging each other and giggling like mad. Michael took no notice of them—he was too busy gazing down into Miss Pumphrey's face as if he had crossed the world for this very moment.

'Ye'll excuse me barging into your classroom like this, ma'am,' he said warmly, holding on to her hand all the time. 'But I felt before I left this lovely little town of yours I had to come in and tell you what a real fine job you're doing in teaching these children not just reading and writing and that sort of thing, but genuine true Christian charity into the bargain. This little one here'—he brought me forward and Miss Pumphrey goggled more than ever when she saw who the 'little one' was—'she and her sainted mother have taken me in and fed me when I was on the point of dropping from hunger and exhaustion. Sure and I couldn't resist coming to meet you after little Patty here was telling me what a grand lady you are, so kind and patient and all. Now I see you with my own eyes, I know every word of what she says is true and more besides, for goodness and beauty shine out of your face like the faces of the blessed saints in the windows of our little church back home in Ireland. And I want you to know, ma'am, that it's an inspiration to me as I go on my long, long travels to meet real grand ladies like yourself who work day in, day out with all their loving hearts to make this poor old world a better place for us all.'

When I told my mother about this afterwards, she sniffed and said it sounded to her like a great big dose of Irish blarney, but whatever it was it did the trick with Miss Pumphrey all right. I couldn't believe my eyes—first she blushed—Miss Pumphrey blushing!—and then she simpered, all of a fluster like a girl at her first dance. She looked up at Michael and then looked away, and all the time she was trying to say something but she just couldn't get the words out.

'Well, I—er—I—you're very kind ... ' she stammered, going as red as a beetroot, knowing we were all listening as hard as we could. 'I must say—er—'

Goodness knows what would have happened next, but to Miss Pumphrey's relief the door opened and Mr Skelton walked in. He looked from Miss Pumphrey to Michael and from Michael to Miss Pumphrey and a smile of delight spread over his face.

'Why, Miss Pumphrey, what an absolutely splendid idea!' he cried. He turned to Michael and seized his hand, clapping him on the shoulder and beaming at him as he did so. 'You, of course, are that brave, noble young man I read about in the newspaper. I am so glad, so very glad, that a member of my staff had the forethought, the initiative, to invite you to our school today. It is a privilege to meet you, and I know these children here will remember this day for the rest of their lives, won't you, children?'

'Yes, Mr Skelton,' we chanted, and then he was off again as a new idea struck him.

'But why only these children—why not all the school?' he asked in excitement. 'That is, if it will fit in with your plans?' he added, turning to the World Walker. 'If you can spare the time, I'm sure all my staff would welcome the chance for their pupils to hear from you about your travels. It won't take a moment to get them all into the hall—this is something the whole school can share!'

Michael raised no objection, and in no time at all we were sitting in the hall listening spellbound as he told us about all the countries he had visited, the people he'd met and the wonderful sights he had seen. He showed them the photographs he'd shown to my mother and me—but not the one of Hitler, he kept that back—and ended up explaining how we had met outside the priests' house and how kind my mother had been to him. He even showed them my needlecase that he was taking back to Philomena, and when I looked round at Miss Pumphrey to see how she was taking it, she gave me a great big smile—Wonders will never cease! I thought to myself. Michael went right on till playtime, and all the while you could have heard a pin drop. When he finished, everyone clapped and cheered, and Mr Skelton stood up.

'There,' he said, 'that was something you'll never forget, wasn't it? But the thing I want you to remember most of all, children, is this. Out of the kindness of his heart, to help his poor little sister, Michael MacMurphy undertook this great journey. Out of the kindness of their hearts, people all over the world have done what they can to help him on his way. And I am proud to be able to say that out of the kindness of her heart, one of my pupils has played her part, too. Because she did, we have had this tremendous treat today, of meeting and listening to the World Walker. So I think she deserves a clap—thank you, Patty!'

I couldn't believe my ears, but they all clapped and cheered me too, even Miss Pumphrey, and when Mr Skelton had taken Michael off for a cup of tea in the staffroom before he started out for Banbury, I was a sort of heroine in the playground. All the children crowded round me asking questions about Michael MacMurphy and his invalid little sister, and nobody called me Fatty Patty at all.

After we got back into the classroom again, Miss Pumphrey seemed to have forgotten about me being late, and we all had a really good time, looking up the places Michael had been to and joining them up on a map of the world. Miss Pumphrey laddered her stocking climbing on a chair so that she could pin the map along the back wall of the classroom, but she didn't let it bother

her, and the map stayed up there for the rest of the term, till we went up into Class Seven in September.

That September the war began—the World Walker had been right about Hitler, I thought, as we huddled in the air-raid shelter with the bombs falling. Was there any chance Michael got home safely, I wondered, with so much trouble going on all over the world? Did he get trapped by the Germans in Norway? Had he joined the French Resistance in the mountains? Was he at Pearl Harbor when the Japanese bombed it? Was he fighting Rommel with the Desert Rats? I didn't worry too much, though—if he could deal with Miss Pumphrey, he could deal with anything.

As the years went by, I forgot about the World Walker, having other things on my mind, but last year, on holiday in Wales I came across something that reminded me of him, making me wonder again when and where he ended his journey. It seems that when their local tramp died, the people of the town had raised a memorial to him, paid for out of their own pockets. 'The great walker, let him rest forever,' it says. That goes for Michael MacMurphy too, wherever he is.

10

Meeting Madam Fallova

That summer was the last time we all went to the seaside together, my mother, my father, Aunt Madge and me. Once war broke out, 'the seaside' turned into 'the coast', festooned with barbed wire and dotted with concrete pill-boxes. It was suddenly a dangerous place to be, and we were glad, as we dodged the bombs, to be safe in the Midlands. We thought—at least, I did—of Mr and Mrs Parry, armed to the teeth, waiting daily to repel an invasion. Sometimes, as we huddled in the air-raid shelter, my mother and Aunt Madge would talk about them and wonder how they would make a living, now landladies were no longer in demand, seaside holidays being out of the question.

'War-work?' Aunt Madge suggested.

My mother shook her head. 'No factories.'

'Land-work, then. They'll have ploughed up the golf course,' said my aunt hopefully. 'Or maybe canteen work somewhere.'

I tried to picture Mrs Parry in land girl uniform, and failed. I had never seen her without a floral print overall, spotlessly clean and crackling with starch, her husband Willie hovering behind her, a dark little nut of a man, silent in her shadow. Nor, remembering her luscious rice puddings, flavoured with vanilla and topped with nutmeg, could I imagine her in a Naafi or a works canteen, serving out slabs of mashed potato and Spam fritters. Though with a war on, anything could happen ... .

For as long as I could remember, we had spent a week every year at Prestatyn with Mr and Mrs Willie Parry. Probably they were recommended to us by one of Aunt Madge's workmates at the box factory, since nearly everyone we knew went to North Wales for their holidays, travelling as we did in a taxi to the railway station and heading on the steam train for Rhyl or one of the small towns round about, set up, it seemed, specially to cater for Midlanders throughout the summer months. The taxi always smelled of leather and disinfectant, and on the station platform I munched Sun Maid raisins out of a miniature box from the slot-machine. My mother must have felt that taking holidays was the mark of a 'good' family, something that would favourably impress my teachers at school. Her father, she was fond of saying, always spoke of spending a month on the coast every year as a boy, the women and children installed with the maid at a seafront hotel, and the men joining them at weekends. Though we could only afford a week at a boarding-house—and that had to be scrimped and saved for all through the year—it was better than nothing. In fact, a deal had been struck with Mrs Parry which was an early form of self-catering holiday. Every morning we went shopping, just as if we were back at home, and bought food which Mrs Parry then cooked for our meals. She was a far better cook than my mother, a slipshod housekeeper, and transformed the cheap ingredients we took her into delicious stews and elaborate puddings. This was done, it was subtly implied, as a favour, a tactful acknowledgement that my mother and my aunt had unfortunately come down in the world, and in return we were expected to be equally obliging and take whatever rooms happened to be free. Other guests, who paid an overall fee for board as well as lodgings, had first pick of the accommodation. One memorable year my father, to his great indignation, found himself sleeping on a camp bed in the garden shed, but his complaints were quickly hushed for fear of offending Mrs Parry. That year he spent most of the daytime bedded down in the sandhills catching up on his sleep.

But it was that final summer when our unspoken agreement with Mrs Parry backfired. We arrived as usual at 'Bryn Gelli' and as usual Mrs Parry had a little weep when she saw me—she and Mr Parry had lost their only child, Megan, some years before, and had she lived she would have been exactly my age, so in a way in me they saw her ghost. This naturally always cast something of a damper over our arrival, as I was hugged tearfully to the print overall, but this particular year there seemed to be more to it than that. Mrs Parry's manner was flustered as she led the way upstairs to a room we'd never had before—the largest room in the house, with two double beds in it. She bridled a little as she threw open the door and stood back with a nervous smile for us to enter.

'I've had to put you all in the same room this year,' she announced, adopting a brisk, take-it-or-leave-it air. 'We're that full, this week, what with it being the height of the season and all, and I know you won't mind helping us out.'

My mother took an anxious glance at my aunt's outraged face, and avoiding my father's eye, she said faintly, 'The garden shed?'

But Mrs Parry was prepared for this.

'Mr and Mrs Pritchard's son, Dennis—he's too big now to sleep in his parents' room, see? He's going in the shed. Little Patty will be all right in with you, though, won't she? I'll leave you to unpack, then ... .'

She turned and retreated quickly down the stairs before anything else could be said, determined to gloss over the fact that it was my spinster aunt who was the problem, not me.

My father, who had clearly not fancied the idea of the garden shed again at all, shrugged complacently as he swung one of the suitcases on to the nearest bed.

'No help for it—we've got to keep in with her,' he said with a grin, slyly quoting my mother's words from the year of the garden shed. 'We'll manage—have to. But she's a crafty old beggar, isn't she? She didn't risk letting us know beforehand, so's we could go somewhere else, did she? Not likely, she didn't!'

I though, of course, that the objection was that we would all be too crowded by being in one room together instead of our usual two, my father and mother in one and Aunt Madge sharing with me, as we did at home. It was only when bedtime came that I realised there must be something else as well. We had taken our first walk down to the beach and back and eaten Mrs Parry's high tea—she had provided tinned peaches after the sardines on toast, perhaps as a peace offering—and then had sat for a little while in the municipal park opposite the war memorial, watching the bowls players, before returning again to go to bed. In the hall we hovered uncertainly, till my mother spoke.

'You go on upstairs first with Aunt Madge, Patty love,' she said finally, giving me a little push towards the stairs. 'We'll—er—come up soon. Try and get off to sleep like a good girl. We shan't be long,' she added, as I hesitated. Usually my mother always put me to bed.

Aunt Madge followed me up, with a face like thunder, and sent me to the bathroom while she put on her tent-like pink cotton night-dress. Then she helped me undress with shaking, impatient fingers and bundled me into the big double bed by the window, taking the place by the wall herself and pulling the eiderdown up round her ears. Tired by the journey and by the sea air, I would probably have fallen asleep as soon as my head touched the pillow, but something in the atmosphere kept me awake—disgusted glances exchanged between my mother and aunt that afternoon, sniffs and head-tossing behind my back, my father's sheepish smirk as he trailed along after us on the promenade. Whatever it was, I could tell he was the odd one out, as usual.

I felt my aunt flinch as the bedroom door opened, but it was only my mother. To my surprise she switched on the bedside lamp and turned off the centre light—usually my mother avoided touching light switches, being afraid of electricity, as we still had gas at home, and this added to my unease. In the darkened room she crept about as if trying not to wake us up, and finally climbed quietly into the other double bed without a word. But if she had hoped by this to spare my aunt's blushes, she was wasting her time. My father had obviously decided to brazen it out, and he entered noisily, shutting the door behind him with a bang and whistling defiantly between his teeth. There was a most peculiar frisson in the air as he began to take off his clothes.

'Look t'other way!' he cried, assuming a hideous kind of jovial modesty and waving his pyjama trousers in our direction. 'Look t'other way—no peeping!'

I heard my aunt, rigid with distaste, give a snort of exasperation, while I obediently turned my back. The bed-springs creaked as my father bounced into bed next to my mother, and I went to sleep puzzling over his peculiar behaviour. Why, I wondered, was he acting so silly? I couldn't understand it at all … .

Apart from the sleeping arrangements, our holiday went on normally. My aunt ignored my father, but there was nothing new in that. For a night or two he continued to make a fuss as he undressed—'I can see you peeping, our Patty!' though I wasn't—but at last he seemed to get over it, or more probably was told by my mother to 'Act your age!', her all-purpose put-down. In the mornings we did the shopping, and Mrs Parry went on making a special effort with the cooking, as if to repay us for the unsuitable quarters she had foisted on us. Most afternoons we went down to the beach, where I built sandcastles with my bucket and spade, and paddled while my father swam—not very well, considering all the years he'd been in the Navy—and my mother and aunt sheltered from the sea breezes in the hooded basket chairs that could be hired for a few coppers. A pony and trap plied between the town centre and the promenade and occasionally my father would pay for us to ride in it, leaning back in his seat with a lordly air as if he imagined he was driving in his own coach and four. Sometimes Aunt Madge would take me over to the patient, woolly donkeys that waited by the breakwater, and with the donkey-boy holding the bridle I jogged solemnly over the sand, clutching on to the leather pommel of the saddle for dear life.

Somehow, we always seemed to be eating at the seaside—ice-creams were fetched, dripping, from the other side of the promenade, getting covered if it was a windy day with a gritty coating of sand, tin trays were carried down from the Beach Kabin loaded with cups, a chipped brown pot of strong hot tea and buttered buns. During the week we spent a whole day in Rhyl, full of funfairs and amusement arcades, and considered 'common' by my mother and Aunt Madge, but I enjoyed the pier and the paddling pool and my father joined in loudly with the hymns played on the sands by the Salvation Army band. That day we never stopped eating, as candy floss was followed by toffee-apples, sticks of rock and a fish and chip tea. Another day we caught the bus to Dyserth, a famous beauty spot where a waterfall cascaded down the mountainside to foam among the mossy rocks below, next to the tea-garden where we drank lemonade and ate sponge cake before visiting the gift shop to buy fudge and slabs of pink and white nougat. The road to the waterfall was so steep that the bus tilted dangerously as it turned the corner and my mother, her eyes closed, clutched tightly at her seat, convinced the brakes would fail and we would plummet back into the valley below. My favourite day, though, came later in the week, when we always walked along the hot, dusty coastal road out of the town and past quiet bungalows hidden behind banks of fuchsia and red valerian. After a mile or so we turned off onto a narrow track leading uphill between high hedges, with brambles catching at our clothes and nettles stinging my bare legs. Shaded by trees which met overhead, even on the hottest day the tunnel beneath was cool and airy, but soon we emerged again into the blazing sunshine, the open hillside before us with smooth turf cropped short by rabbits. Bracken covered the lower slopes and in the distance the woods began, but we trudged up to the top of the hill where the white-washed coastguard station, now a tea-room, sparkled in the sun. Breathless after the long climb we entered the quiet parlour where a huge bay window overlooked the sea. In the ceiling a pointer swivelled to show the direction of the wind turning the weathervane on the roof, and through a telescope on the windowsill we could peer at ships on the horizon. A friendly waitress bustled in with biscuits and home-made ginger beer, and curled up half asleep on the cushions of the window-seat I listened drowsily to the creaking weathervane and the far-off sound of the sea. Home, with its dark, cramped rooms seemed a million miles away, and I wished I could stay there, drinking my ginger beer, for ever.

In the evenings, we went to see the Follies. A motley troupe of pierrots, they performed at a tiny open-air theatre alongside the beach. My father had theatrical pretensions himself, having belonged to a dramatic society in his village as a lad, and at the least encouragement would recount at length the plot of a play he'd been in, playing Gentleman Jim the cat-burglar. These memories made him regard the pierrots as his cronies, and he always spent a lot of time talking to them after the show. Sometimes we stood by the perimeter fence, which was crowded with holiday-makers ready to melt away when the wooden collecting-box came round, but more often my father would pay for tickets so that we could sit in the deckchairs set out in rows in front of the stage. It was the same troupe every year, and by now they were as familiar to us as Mr and Mrs Parry themselves. Led by a comedian called Sandy, with his wife Polly as soubrette, the rest of the team was made up of a pair of juveniles who sang romantic ballads, an older comedian called Simon and an over-worked pianist who was on stage most of the time. Photos of all the pierrots were displayed around the ticket kiosk, some of them obviously taken years ago, all smiling with a desperate brightness that I found almost frightening. The week's programme was pinned up on the noticeboard and promised an opening number called 'Meet the Stars'. This, we read, was to be followed by 'Polly and her Saucy Songs' and 'Millie and Billy on the Road to Romance'. Then the whole company would perform 'Our Play for Tonight, straight from the West End', after which we could watch 'Comical Capers from Sandy and Simon' and the show would close with the 'Grand Finale'.

'I hope they're a bit cleaner than last time, that's all,' sniffed Aunt Madge. This puzzled me, since though even to my eyes the baggy white costumes of the men and the matching short skirts of the women could often have done with a wash, I couldn't see why Aunt Madge let it bother her. What did the costumes matter, when everyone was so funny?

In fact the programme, a carefully worked out mixture of sentimental songs, noisy slapstick and smutty jokes, was aimed at a family audience with children, like me, too young to understand the double meanings that had my father guffawing loudly and my mother and aunt exchanging scandalised glances. The play, always a farce, involved the whole cast dashing frantically around the stage, bumping into each other and hiding behind the furniture. Usually it ended with Polly dressed in a scanty pair of pink satin cami-knickers posed coyly in centre stage as the curtains closed. Millie and Billy, the juveniles, neither of them by any means as young as they once had been, crooned familiar duets like 'If you were the only girl in the world' and 'You are my honey, honeysuckle, I am the bee', in which they encouraged the audience to join for the final chorus. I envied Millie the pale blue evening dress she wore for her turn, and wondered if she and Billy were planning to get married, though Aunt Madge said she didn't think so. Sandy and Simon's 'Comical Capers', of course, turned the air blue above my head, though I was careful to laugh along with everyone else so as not to be left out. In any case, I enjoyed every minute of it, ignoring the shabby costumes, the—to me—pointless jokes, the stray pom-poms held on by safety-pins and the layers of greasepaint hiding the wrinkles. Simon, in particular, seemed to me immensely funny with his bright orange hair, his rubbery face, his bushy eyebrows and his rueful air of perpetual surprise.

It was the custom on Friday evenings—the end of the holiday-makers' week—for the pierrots to put on an extra turn, a so-called 'Special Attraction' which sometimes took the form of a 'guest star', usually a performer from another troupe playing further along the coast, or from the local working men's club circuit. Advertised this year was 'Madame Fallova, the famous Russian Ballerina', and we made certain of good seats by booking ahead. At last the Friday performance arrived and took its usual course until, given a tremendous build-up by Sandy, the curtains opened on 'Madam Fallova'. Kissing her hands to either side, she advanced from the back of the stage to the footlights, her hair a mass of yellow curls, her eyes ringed with long black false eye-lashes, her cheeks rouged, her lips sticky with scarlet lipstick. She wore a green muslin tutu edged with tinsel, and when she performed an ungainly pirouette on her large pink satin pointe shoes she revealed frilly yellow knickers beneath her short skirts. In one hand she carried a flimsy wand topped with a tarnished silver star, while with the other she hitched up the straps of her massive bodice. After a few more simpering smiles at the grinning audience, she nodded to the waiting pianist and launched into a song. If her appearance was monstrous, her voice was equally bizarre. It wandered haphazardly between a shrill falsetto and a bass growl as she declared,

'Nobody loves a fairy when she's forty, Nobody loves a fairy when she's o—o—old ... .'

I knew there was something odd about Madame Fallova, something besides the extravagant costume and lewd gestures, but somehow I couldn't decide what it was. Her knobbly knees and hairy legs were ridiculous, but even they couldn't account for the braying laughter and the mocking catcalls from the boys around the fence. My mother and Aunt Madge, I saw, were tittering in spite of themselves, their eyes like saucers and their mouths agape with shocked delight. Tears of mirth ran down my father's cheeks as the ballerina ad libbed shamelessly, dropping her drooping wand and picking it up again in a flurry of frills. The applause when she sank into her final clumsy curtsey was thunderous. A bouquet of artificial flowers was handed up, and she coyly drew out a red carnation and flung it girlishly into the audience, hitting my father neatly on the ear. Not to be left out, I cheered and stamped with the rest. But I was puzzled—there was something eerily familiar about Madam Fallova.

'Is she really from Russia?' I whispered to Aunt Madge when the applause died down at last, and the pierrots swung into the Grand Finale.

'Don't be daft, pigeon, it's Simon.' She turned to my mother. 'Say what you like—and it was a bit near the knuckle—he's a good sport, fooling around like that at his age!'

I sank back in my seat hardly able to believe my ears, while on-stage the Follies sang that they were 'Sailing along on the crest of a wave'. So she—he—was only the podgy comedian after all. The grotesque appearance, the quavering pathos of the song, was all a fraud. And for some reason I couldn't fathom, everybody there seemed to think it was the funniest thing they'd ever seen. It was as if they knew something I didn't. A kind of jeering hysteria had seized hold of them, and I couldn't make out why. There was something frightening about it, like the baying of hounds. Coming on top of the unspoken peculiarity of the boarding-house bedroom, it made me shudder. What had gone wrong this year? Nothing was the same as it used to be.

The song had ended, and I clapped mechanically, but the show wasn't yet over. Besides the 'special attraction', another tradition was that on the last night fans of the pierrots would hand up cheap boxes of chocolates to the women and sometimes small cigars—Wills Whiffs—to the men. To do this seemed to my father the height of sophistication, a celebration of his patronage of the Follies, and he always scraped together all our remaining cash to buy gifts for the whole troupe. To my mother, of course, this was a wicked waste of money, and she sniffed scornfully throughout the presentation, managing only the sourest of smiles when Sandy, Polly and the rest mimed ecstasies of surprise and delight. Looking back, I think they probably returned the gifts to the woman at Beach Kabin and got the money instead, especially if they'd had a poor week at the box office. This time I watched carefully as my father handed up the gifts. Yes, Madame Fallova, who hadn't had time to change, got Wills Whiffs. That settled it.

After the show, Sandy and Polly kept my father talking, thanking him again and saying goodbye till next year, while my mother and Aunt Madge hovered uncertainly in the background. Suddenly, after all the excitement, I felt I wanted to go to the lavatories over on the other side of the promenade, and I tugged urgently at Aunt Madge's arm. Determined not to miss anything, she absent-mindedly pushed a penny into my hand and I scuttled away to the lavatories. Half-way there, though, a thought struck me. They'd be busy for at least ten minutes yet. With a hasty glance around—no-one was about—I dived into the sandhills and pulled down my knickers. Then, with my penny still intact, I swerved away to the ice-cream stall.

Keeping well out of sight with my penny cornet, I approached the theatre from the back, where a short flight of wooden stairs led up to the dressing-rooms. As I rounded the corner, to my dismay I became aware of Madam Fallova—Simon—sitting sprawled in an ungainly heap on the top step, smoking a Wills Whiff and drinking from a bottle. His blonde wig lay beside him and somehow this made his ambiguous appearance even more alarming. He leered at me, batting his false eyelashes in a suggestive wink. It was then I noticed that the green muslin frills were disarranged and from the centre of them protruded something I found repulsive and yet at the same time horribly fascinating. For a moment I couldn't move. Then suddenly the strange man-woman creature seemed about to lurch drunkenly towards me. With a cry of terror I struck out blindly with my only weapon, and for once my aim was true. There was a yowl of anguish and fury as the cornet hit its target among the tattered frills, and I took to my heels and fled. As I skidded over the sand, a bottle flew harmlessly past my ear and landed by the breakwater.

Luckily in the bustle of shaking the sand out of the damp towels so as not to annoy Mrs Parry and collecting up my bucket and spade, no-one noticed the state I was in, and I said nothing myself—how could I find the words? Back at 'Bryn Gelli' I had no appetite for Mrs Parry's farewell tea, till I remembered thankfully that we were taking the early train for home in the morning, to avoid the crowds.

For days I worried about what had happened. I knew I had done three wicked, unforgivable things—I'd been dirty, and used the sand-hills as a lavatory, I'd been greedy and spent Aunt Madge's penny on an ice-cream, and I'd been—I found it hard to sum up my assault on the nightmare figure behind the theatre—rude, I supposed, and if a complaint were made, all this would be found out. I watched to see if any letters came for my father, but none did. Gradually, I relaxed. Then I remembered—next year we'd go again to Prestatyn, next year I might well be exposed not as the good, quiet little girl I pretended to be, but as a dirty, greedy hoyden.

But we didn't go back—war broke out that September and seaside holidays were over for the duration. As we listened to Mr Chamberlain on the wireless—'This country is now at war with Germany ... ', the tension of the last few weeks broke, and I began to cry.

'Eh, what's up with her?' my father demanded in amazement.

'Switch that thing off—it's frightening her,' my mother snapped. 'Enough to frighten anybody, he is,' she added, dabbing at my face with her handkerchief. 'Him and his umbrella! Come on, my duck, there's a good girl. Stop crying, and I'll make you a nice cup of cocoa.'

11

The Silver Dancing Shoe

Cousin Ida had a lot to answer for—through her my father and mother had met. Ida, a waitress then at the Cadena Café, arranged to meet my mother after work one night on the steps of the Hippodrome, but she didn't turn up. Always flighty and unreliable, she had found something more exciting to do, as she usually did. Instead my father, on leave from the Navy, saw my mother standing there and got into conversation with her. Everything else followed from that, and Cousin Ida was always held to blame by my mother and Aunt Madge.

'Selfish little madam! If she hadn't let you down … .' Aunt Madge would say. 'But then, she always was selfish. We've said that over and over.'

'Yes, I've seen her sit eating a whole box of chocolates all to herself, and never offer one to anybody,' my mother would reply, implying that empty chocolate boxes and unsatisfactory husbands were on a par in her mind. 'No wonder she cleared off to London—everybody was fed up with her here.'

For a while, Cousin Ida came back home from time to time, full of far-fetched stories, but eventually she vanished altogether. I only saw her the once, and I hadn't thought about her for years. Then, when my mother died—six months after Aunt Madge, so there was nobody else left but me to tidy up—I went to empty the house before the landlord let it to another tenant. A house-clearance merchant took away all the furniture, but what he called 'family effects'—rubbish, in other words—he left for me to sort out, in my grandfather's old workroom at the back of the house. Above the kitchen and the pantry, with a window looking out over the garden, this was a long, narrow room where, years before, my grandfather had sat cross-legged on his tailoring bench, sewing uniforms for the men in the trenches of the Great War. He had stitched his life away on government contracts, working by gaslight far into the night, paid a pittance and desperate always to get his consignment completed before his next orders arrived in the post. Soon after the war he died, worn out from overwork, and the room fell into disuse. Damp rotted the floorboards and it was left, cluttered up with all kinds of lumber and thick with dust and cobwebs.

Now, treading warily over the broken boards, I crossed to a rusty tin trunk by the window and flung back the battered lid. Some old curtains, a few trumpery photograph frames with cracked glass in them, a cheap post-card album with faded seaside scenes and pictures of donkeys on the sands, a dented trophy won in some long-forgotten competition, programmes from the local rep—*The Ghost Train, Mother Knows Best, Peg o'My Heart*—a work-box with cotton reels spilling out of it, and finally, right in the corner of the trunk, a silver dancing shoe ... .

I sat for a time in a rickety basket chair, and cradled the shoe in my lap, thinking about it. With its splayed heel and diamanté buckle on the strap, it had never belonged to poor, plain Aunt Madge or to my narrow-minded mother. I knew the moment I saw it that it could only have been worn by Cousin Ida. Nobody else had ever come to our house who would have owned a shoe like that. Despite all the upheaval of her final appearance, I thought, all that remains of her in the end is this one silver shoe, relic of who knows what high jinks, left behind the sideboard or under the sofa and pushed hurriedly out of sight—till now. And once again I was wracked with guilt at the part, only half-understood, that I had played in sending her on her weary way. Where? And to what? I shall never know now. But I had been made the excuse, eagerly seized on and smugly trotted out, for cruelty and spite, revenge even, all those years ago, and as I looked at the shoe my eyes filled with useless tears, remembering that winter's day.

When I got home from school, I found Cousin Ida sitting by the fire in the kitchen, my mother and Aunt Madge exchanging angry glances behind her back. Aunt Madge, I gathered later, had been sent home early from the box factory because an exceptionally heavy fall of snow had stopped the buses from running by four o'clock. She arrived home cold and wet, only to find Ida already there, come half an hour earlier from the railway station, a shabby valise in her hand and desperation in her eyes. My mother, not knowing what else to do, invited her in, and now she looked like staying. My own arrival on the scene, apparently, added yet another complication, though I had no idea what it was.

That term, I was in Mr Jenkins's scholarship class and, along with five other children, I was to be entered for the eleven-plus exam in the spring. It had been a bad winter all through, with constant storms flooding the gutters, thick fog at night and frost in the morning, but my mother never let me miss a single day at school, even when I had to struggle there between banks of snow as high as my head. Sometimes only two or three children turned up in the classroom, but I was always one of them. At that time, I thought my mother the cruellest woman in the world. If I said I felt too ill to go to school, she would coax me over and over again to 'eat a bit of breakfast—just a Marie biscuit and a drop of tea', and when I did, she'd praise me for being a brave girl and pack me triumphantly off to school through the snow, however bad I felt. Sometimes, later on, I excused her, thinking she was simply keen for me to get on in the world, to have a profession, to be a success. This was behind, I thought, all her frantic efforts to curry favour with my teachers, whatever the cost. Only later still did I realise that to her and Aunt Madge I was a cast-iron insurance policy for their old age. If I became a teacher myself, they reckoned, I would never give it up, as teachers had to do in those days if they married, especially not after what I'd seen of my parents' own disastrous marriage. Then I'd stay at home to look after them for the rest of their lives. I'd have good pay and long holidays, wouldn't I? After all, what more could I want?

Even so, my mother didn't altogether trust Mr Jenkins, with his jokes and wisecracks—for her liking he was altogether too flippant for the serious task of getting me through the scholarship and into grammar school. She had once seen the *Racing Times* sticking out of his overcoat pocket, and I had told her, too, how occasionally, from boredom perhaps, he would take to carving the wooden handles of paintbrushes into elaborate patterns with his penknife, so that our minds wandered while we watched him. All this she felt, proved he was not nearly as dedicated as he should be to making sure we passed the examinations. The other five children she regarded anyway as deadly rivals—the pale, stodgy twins, Jack and Mary Rowbotham, Pamela Mullins, a plump girl with frizzy curls who had once beaten me for top place in the class, putting our whole house, as it were, into mourning, Mavis Tranter, a dark horse only recently come to the school, and one other boy, Gordon Stevens, who stuttered. Every night I was subjected to an inquisition, not only on how I myself had done in class but on how all the other five had done, too.

'They won't let you all pass,' my mother warned darkly.

I puzzled over this. Why not, if we were all clever enough? But as it turned out in the end, my mother was right, as usual. They didn't let us all pass—I was the only one who got through. But all that came later.

Now I stared at Ida big-eyed, conscious of my mother and Aunt Madge watching me as I took in her gaunt, chalk-white face and patches of rouge on her hollow cheeks, the cheap ear-rings and the shiny satin of her short skirt. Somehow I knew, without knowing how I knew, that there was something wrong, something alien, about the stranger sitting by the hearth, clearly ill at ease as she smiled a nervous greeting. With an awkward laugh, my mother broke the edgy silence.

'Here's little Patty, then, Ida,' she said brightly, unwinding the long woollen muffler from around my neck and pulling off my damp gloves. 'She was only a baby last time you came—she won't remember you. This is Cousin Ida, Patty, come from London to see us. You've heard me speak of Cousin Ida?'

What made me do it I don't know, but I hung my head and shuffled my feet, refusing to look at the garish figure by the fire.

'Oh, come along, you're not shy.' My mother gave me a push towards the stool where I always sat to take off my wellingtons, and shot a meaning glance at Aunt Madge. 'She's not used to strangers, Ida,' she went on. 'And I expect she's tired after school. They work them very hard, because of the scholarship exams after Christmas.'

While I ate my tea, I watched as my mother and my aunt continued their silent conversation, shrugs, sniffs and raised eyebrows making clear that the visitor was unwelcome, and the sooner she was gone, the better. Later, when Ida left them alone to go round to the back of the house for the outside lavatory, they began at once to whisper together, forgetting that I was sitting in the shadows at the foot of the stairs with my dolls, blonde Rosie with her pink china face and black Ragdoll Topsy. The stairs, which led up to the bedrooms, were enclosed in a sort of cupboard, and a door at the bottom closed them off from the kitchen. Hidden by the half-open door, I could pretend I was in a little house of my own—and I could hear, too, what was said in the kitchen. Now I listened with all my ears as Aunt Madge and my mother discussed Cousin Ida. To me their voices sounded excited, scandalised and cross but in an odd way somehow enjoying it.

'Funny, isn't it, how children *know*? She senses, poor little thing. Ida will simply have to go, there's no two ways about it.' That was Aunt Madge, bridling with indignation.

Then my mother, pleased as Punch to be able to say it: 'Yes, we can't have her fretting, just before the scholarship. It's not fair, Ida turning up like this. She's made her bed'—a stifled titter—'and she'll have to lie on it, that's all there is to it!'

'Chambermaid, indeed—some chambermaid,' continued Aunt Madge scornfully. 'And the cheek of it, coming here boasting of the toffs she's met. Wouldn't get up in the morning till she'd smacked his bottom, and him a Lord Somebody. Disgusting! Not fit to be in the same house as a young child. She ought to be ashamed of herself, coming here where she's not wanted. She's caused more than enough trouble for us already, leaving you standing on those Hippodrome steps!'

'She can sleep on the sofa tonight and in the morning she must go.' My mother got up and began to clear the table with an angry rattle of teacups. 'She's got friends, bound to have. Ill? Not her—it's the drink and all the late nights and the fast living. Hush!' —spotting me—'The child's listening. That settles it—she goes tomorrow. She's only got herself to blame.'

I can remember now how I played up to it, peeping timidly at Ida from behind my book as she sat staring into the fire, and then avoiding her eye if she smiled at me. She shivered from time to time and once she rummaged in her bag and took out some tablets, looking round quickly to make sure nobody was noticing before she swallowed them. My father came in soon afterwards and gave

Ida a noisy, jovial greeting, but even he quietened down as he sensed the disapproval hanging heavy in the room. Later, out in the back kitchen to have my face wiped before bed, I whined peevishly to Aunt Madge that I didn't like Cousin Ida, she wasn't going to stay long, was she? She frightened me—making sure Ida's fate was sealed when Madge, triumphant, repeated all this to my mother in a whisper. Meanwhile, my father and Ida sat at the kitchen table eating fish and chips brought in from the chip shop down the road. Ida, warmed by the food and by the bottle of stout she'd asked my father to fetch her from the Ring o'Bells, was recovering now from the strain of the journey. As I came in to say goodnight, they were exchanging silly banter about drinking, my father swearing loudly that he'd never touched beer since he signed the Pledge years ago in the Navy. He believed, it seemed, that the Pledge of Abstinence, intended as a promise to be teetotal, applied only to beer and not to spirits and other forms of alcohol, and Ida was flirtatiously teasing him about it.

'But, listen, our Ronnie, you do drink—I've seen you!' She slapped him coyly on the arm. 'I've seen you drink whisky, I've seen you drink rum—you're an old fraud, that's what you are, you and your Pledge!'

'Ah, but you ain't never seen me drink beer, you cheeky young monkey,' he contradicted her, grinning. 'The Pledge is for giving up beer, and I've never drunk beer and I never will—I can't stand the stuff.'

'No, no, it's alco—alcohooo—hoooo ... .' Laughing and spilling her stout on the tablecloth, Ida suddenly began to hiccup loudly, red in the face and gasping like a fish. My mother tossed her head in disgust, but my father jumped up and began to maul Ida about, banging her on the back with a heavy hand and shouting in amusement to my mother.

'Look what you've done now with your sauce, Ida—get us the doorkey, Annie,' he bellowed. 'Put it down the back of her blouse—a cold doorkey stops 'iccups in no time!'

But Ida, remembering perhaps that for her at present discretion had to be the better part of valour, hastily gulped down her squeaks and settled back demurely to her supper. My father went on holding forth about his Navy days, nudging Ida affably from time to time in the ribs and taking no notice of my mother's sniffs or my aunt's stony face. In the end, my mother stood up and struck a match to light my bedtime candle, bristling crossly.

'I'm taking Patty up to bed now, Ida,' she announced, steering me towards the door at the bottom of the stairs. 'And I'm not coming down again either—I've got a splitting headache and I'm going to bed myself. Madge will get out the pillows and the blankets for you. You'll find the sofa's quite comfy—just for the one night,' she added pointedly.

Bending down, she picked up Rosie from the bottom step and pushed her into my arms.

'Take your dolly up with you, Patty, there's a good girl,' she continued. 'You mustn't leave her lying there for folks to fall over. Now, off you go—it's long past your bedtime.'

Holding my doll I went obediently ahead of her up the dark stairs and along the narrow corridor to the bedroom I shared with Aunt Madge. Now I was even more puzzled about Cousin Ida—my mother and aunt didn't like her, that was clear, but my father seemed friendly enough towards her, smirking and winking at her, as excited in his way as they had been in theirs. As I lay in bed I could hear his voice rumbling on, and at first I thought Aunt Madge would soon come up to bed herself. After a while, though, I realised she was staying down, silently reading *Peg's Paper* by the fire while the others went on talking. Perhaps, I thought, she's staying up to help Cousin Ida with her makeshift bed. Yes, that must be it—she won't be up for ages, and I decided to do what I often did when I couldn't sleep. I slipped quietly out of bed and crept into the room next door, my grandfather's old workroom.

Lit eerily by the moonlight sparkling on the snow, it seemed as always in a different world from the hot, stuffy kitchen below. I edged between the broken chairs and empty boxes to the window where a cracked pane let in the chilly night air, and perched on the end of the dusty tailoring bench, peeping out at the stars.

My grandfather had died years before I was born, but I'd heard tales of him from my mother and my aunt. He had been married twice, and his first wife, Fitzy, was our family legend. All families cherish stories of aristocratic connections, and Fitzy, rumoured to be the illegitimate child of an Irish housemaid and the son of the rich family for which she worked, was ours. Graceful and golden-haired, she had charmed my grandfather from the moment they met, married him and given him two little daughters, dying all too soon when my own mother was a tiny baby. Not for twelve years did he marry again, this time to the local girl he had jilted to marry Fitzy, dying himself only six years later. Now, as I thought drowsily about these long-ago love stories, I was suddenly brought back to earth by the sound of voices and the clatter of crockery. Aunt Madge and Cousin Ida had begun to wash up in the back kitchen below, and because the window was ajar to let out the steam of the boiling kettle, I could hear what they were saying.

'It's because of the child, you see, Ida. It's upsetting her. We don't often have visitors and Patty's not used to it. Annie's afraid it'll put her off her lessons at school and spoil her chances of the scholarship. I'm sorry you've been having a rotten time of it, but there's nothing we can do, I'm afraid.' Her next words were drowned by water swilling down the sink and then I heard her speaking sharply to my father. 'You go on up now, Ron, and I'll find Ida the bedclothes. No, I don't need any help. And mind you don't wake Patty—she'll be asleep by now.'

Hurriedly I crept back to my bed and curled up under the blankets. A few minutes later my father came upstairs on tiptoe and closed the front bedroom door behind him. As he did so, I heard my mother snoring softly. Soon Aunt Madge, sighing wearily, followed him up, and as I dropped off to sleep, I heard the sofa springs creaking. Cousin Ida had made her bed, I thought, just like my mother had said, and now she was lying on it ... .

It seemed to me the middle of the night, but probably only an hour or so had gone by when a sudden loud crash woke us up, followed by an outburst of angry swearing, joined a moment later by hysterical screams from Cousin Ida. Burglars! I thought in alarm, and jumped out of bed as Aunt Madge struggled to her feet and groped for her dressing-gown. A beam of light fell on the wash-stand, and with a vague idea of repelling the intruders I seized the big jug of cold water put ready for Aunt Madge's morning wash and staggered with it to the door. Scuttling along the corridor to the top of the stairs, I flung it with all my might at the figure, dimly seen in the dying light of the kitchen range, sprawled across the bottom steps. There was a roar of fury as the jug hit home, drenching the shadowy figure with icy water.

'What—what the devil ... ? Good Lord deliver us, what's going on?' Only when I heard the voice did I realise that the 'burglar' was wearing pyjamas and was none other than my father, now soaked to the skin. Aunt Madge joined me a few seconds later and the light of her candle showed me that I was right. Creeping back downstairs for some mysterious reason of his own, my father had twisted his ankle on Ragdoll Topsy, left forgotten at the foot of the stairs and providing the perfect booby-trap for prowlers. As he staggered up from the puddle of water and the pieces of broken crockery, my father gave a yelp of pain when he tried to put his weight on his twisted ankle. My mother, a blanket over her shoulders, joined us on the landing.

'Oh, Madge, whatever's up?' she asked nervously. 'What's Ron doing downstairs at this time of night? And why's Ida screaming?'

'Well may you ask.' Her face grim, Aunt Madge began to descend the stairs and, determined not to be left out, I followed close behind her. By now my father had lit the kitchen gas and was rummaging in the washing basket to find some dry clothes, while Ida huddled on the sofa, her face ashen. Seeing Aunt Madge appear, she broke into a gabble of guilty explanation.

'I don't know anything about all this, Madge, honest I don't,' she protested. 'I was asleep till just a minute ago, and there was this awful crash, and I didn't know who it was—I never dreamed it was Ron.' An idea seemed to strike her. 'Sleep-walking, was he?' she ended innocently.

'Sleep-walking, you brazen hussy?' Aunt Madge rounded on Ida, her eyes blazing. 'You know well enough why he came sneaking down here in the dead of night. You'd fixed it up between you, I shouldn't wonder, behind my back. I wasn't born yesterday!'

'Now hold on, Madge, 'tweren't like that at all ... .' Clutching his wet pyjamas across his chest, my father tried sheepishly to interrupt, but my aunt cut him short.

'I don't want to hear anything from you, neither,' she snapped. 'You get back upstairs where you belong and put some dry things on before you catch your death.' She caught sight of me, goggle-eyed on the bottom step.

'Look at poor little Patty—she'll be fit for nothing in the morning, and just when she needs all her wits about her at school!'

'I'll take her back to bed—come along, my duck.' My mother ushered me upstairs in the wake of my father hobbling ahead. 'I'll be down in a minute, Madge, to help you clear the mess up. And Ida'd better get off to sleep, she's got a journey ahead of her tomorrow.'

Bundled back into bed, I puzzled over what had happened. I'd left my ragdoll carelessly on the stairs and tripped up my father—but no-one had been cross with me. I'd made an awful mistake, and thrown a jug of water at him and wet him through—but still no-one had been cross with me. Cousin Ida had stayed in bed good as gold, but everybody was cross with her. My father was cold and wet and had hurt his foot, but instead of being sorry for him, everybody was cross with him, too. It didn't seem to make much sense, but then things often didn't. I lay still as Aunt Madge crept back into the room and settled down to sleep. I could hear the rumble of angry voices along the corridor, and when they finally died down at last, I fell asleep.

Next morning the kitchen was full of the smell of wintergreen ointment as my father massaged his swollen ankle. Cousin Ida was packing her valise as Aunt Madge bundled away the spare bedclothes from the sofa. When I went to wash in the back kitchen, I looked at myself in the speckled mirror over the sink and saw I looked pale and heavy-eyed, but I knew it was no use saying I was too tired to go to school. I ate my breakfast and set off through the snow, knowing that when I got back, Cousin Ida would be gone, for good. Somehow I knew I would never see her again.

In the years that followed, I seldom thought of her, though when I did, I gradually realised what had really gone on that night. And now, as the light faded, I got up with my eyes still full of tears to go on clearing out the rubbish. When they found me, hours later, on the floor of my grandfather's workroom, there was blood on the corner of the trunk where I must—mustn't I?—have hit my head when I fell.

'No permanent damage,' the doctor in Casualty said cheerfully. But you can still see a faint scar on my forehead.

Oddly enough, it's shaped like the heel of a shoe.

12

Lottie Craxton's Crowning Glory

'There was a terrible shortage of ink, see?' Cousin Bert watched me closely, in between the letters he was forming slowly and carefully on the paper in front of him. 'So instead of writing our name C-R-A-C-K-S-T-O-N, like that, we began to write it with an 'X', C-R-A-X-T-O-N, like this. Saved ever such a lot of ink, it did. Well, stands to reason, dunnit?' he added, nudging me with his elbow.

I nodded solemnly, though as usual I hardly knew whether to believe him or not. More than twenty years ago, long before I was born, Cousin Bert had come back from the Great War 'not quite the ticket', as my mother said, and now another war was raging in Europe. But to me Bert was always kind, and I loved to watch him doing the embroidery he'd learnt to do in the Army hospital—cross stitch, chain stitch, lazy daisy and satin stitch. Aunt Dot's house was full of chair-backs, cushion covers and tray-cloths, all decorated with crinoline ladies in cottage gardens. When Christmas or a birthday came round, he gave us tea-cosies, nightdress cases and handkerchief sachets with our names on, garlanded by butterflies and flowers.

Cousin Lil, though, was definitely odd. I knew this was nothing to do with the Great War since Lil never left the family smallholding at all, except for a day trip to the Whitsun Crock Fair. Pasty and pale, with bare, flabby white arms and a round moon face, she listened to Bert now with a gap-toothed grin as she tore the feathers from the goose she was plucking ready for the oven. We were all sitting in the big, untidy kitchen, which somehow managed to look cluttered and barren at the same time. A sulky, smoking fire, damped down with tea-leaves, flickered feebly in the grate, while a pan full of pig-swill or hen-mash simmered on the hob. An open door led through a stone-flagged passage into the yard, where two ducks hung on a nail, their necks wrung but still twitching. I hoped they'd be still before I had to carry them home on the bus.

On each side of the door two long, narrow pictures showed children in Victorian dress stepping heedlessly into mortal danger. In one, a little girl reached to pick flowers over the edge of a perilous ravine. In the other, a small boy in a sailor suit carrying a butterfly net was just about to step on to a broken bridge above a raging torrent. Behind the children guardian angels with snowy wings hovered, smiling tenderly, ready to snatch them from the jaws of death. I avoided looking at the pictures as far as I could, but from time to time the vivid reds and blues, the sickly pinks and greens, caught my unwilling eye. Hurriedly, I turned instead to the dresser, piled high with an assortment of articles which could well have come straight from a jumble-sale—a cracked jug, some balls of wool, a bundle of stiff collars, a hammer and a rusty mouse-trap. Among them stood half a dozen jars of shop-bought jam. These I looked at sadly.

The jam was our month's ration, sacrificed to our Craxton cousins in return for poultry, eggs and some fresh farm butter. With four hefty farm-hand sons to feed, Aunt Dot needed all the jam she could get, so she and my mother had hit on this country-cousin-town-cousin barter to supplement the rations of their two families. It was really the butter my mother was after. She still did errands for a teacher who had taught me at infants' school, a thin, vinegary cat-faced spinster who claimed her digestion was so delicate she 'couldn't touch margarine'. So all our butter ration, and any extra she could scrounge from Aunt Dot, was taken over regularly to Miss Minchin's pin-neat house on the other side of the city. In return, Miss Minchin gave advice about my education and the best way to get me into grammar school. It seems unlikely to me now that she could have had any influence at all on my chances, but my parents were convinced she could pull the right strings if they kept her 'sweet'.

'You go on buttering her up,' my father said, snorting with laughter. My mother glared. Education was no joking matter as far as she was concerned.

Just as Bert finished his ink-saving demonstration, the door opened and my cousin Charlotte came in. The youngest of Aunt Dot's children, she was the family beauty, her skin flawless, her dark eyes fringed with thick, curling lashes, her hair a rich chestnut piled up in a bunch of ringlets at the back of her head. To me, a dumpy ten-year-old, Lottie, as she was always known, was the princess of every fairy-tale, the heroine of every story-book. She seemed to enjoy my shy admiration, for she always made a fuss of me, while her brothers, apart from Bert, either ignored me or made jeering comments about 'book-learning'. She came straight over to me now, gave me a hug and turned on Bert in mock indignation.

'Has he been teasing you again, my lovey?' she demanded, flashing her bright eyes at him. 'You don't want to take no notice of him—he'll say anything but his prayers, and them he whistles!' Leaving Bert no chance to reply, she took my hand. 'Come on, pet, I'll take you down to see Tom's ferrets!'

Though I had no wish at all to see the ferrets, which I privately thought to be dirty, vicious little beasts, I followed Lottie down the path between the rows of lettuces and beans to the wooden cages ranged along the side of the tool-shed. From behind the wire netting, the ferrets glared out at us, their angry red eyes gleaming as they scampered to and fro in a flurry of yellow fur, and a sweetish, fetid smell wafted over to us, mingled with the heavier odour from the pig-pen beyond the shed.

'Now whatever you do, don't put your hand near the wire,' Lottie cautioned me. 'Have your finger through to the bone, they would, in next to no time, the little devils.' Leaning against the blistered paint of the shed door, she heaved a sigh. 'Oh, Patty, I dunno what to do. That old Tom, he keeps on at me to go and work for Mrs Pearson at the Roadhouse, and I don't want to. But she needs a waitress, he says, and she's got him right under her thumb. Waitress—I know the sort of waitress she's got in mind.' she added darkly.

All this meant little to me, though I was flattered that Lottie was confiding in me. I remembered hearing my mother and Aunt Madge talking about Mrs Pearson, who was, it appeared, 'no better than she should be', whatever that implied, while Tom Craxton, Aunt Dot's eldest, was 'old enough to know better'. Well over forty, Tom like his brothers had never married. Recently, it seemed, he'd taken to spending all his evenings at the Roadhouse, a kind of sleazy hotel on the edge of the village, much to his mother's annoyance, coming home after midnight with empty pockets and smelling of drink. Now Mrs Pearson wanted to get her claws into Lottie as well. In my imagination, she loomed over her like the Wicked Queen in 'Snow-white'. Taking on the role of the Good Fairy, I looked up at Lottie encouragingly.

'So—what would you really like to do, Lottie?' I asked, wishing I had a magic wand in my hand to wave as I said it.

Lottie flushed, and a shy smile came and went.

'I'd like to be a hairdresser, Patty,' she whispered, dropping her voice as if the ferrets might tell tales to Tom. 'I could be apprenticed to Mr Errol at Maison Beauty in the High Street, but ... .' She gave a rueful shrug.

'Well, then?' To me it seemed the perfect solution. Mr Errol, though he was something of a figure of fun as he minced about his tiny beauty parlour, was harmless enough compared with the sinister Mrs Pearson.

'It's the premium, see?' Lottie sighed. 'Fifty pounds it costs, and where would I get money like that? I told Ma about it, but she says apprentices don't get no wages to speak of, and I'd best take the job Tom's got for me. She reckons Mrs Pearson'll pay well if I work hard, and I can keep an eye on Tom when he goes to the Roadhouse. But I don't want to be Tom's nursemaid, do I?'

As she spoke, Aunt Dot appeared at the back door. A tall, gaunt figure, she wore as always a man's cap and boots, with a huge water-proof apron covering her print overall. She yelled and waved, and Lottie dashed off obediently, leaving me to wander away to see the hens in their ramshackle enclosure at the end of the garden.

This was the part of our country day I enjoyed the most, when I was alone and could pretend to myself that I was a farmer's wife living there all the time. There were fields all around, and though I was nervous of cows I loved the placid sheep with their baby lambs. As I poked chickweed through the wire the hens came running up in excitement. Usually I stayed there, talking to them and making sure they all got a share of the chickweed, till I was called in to tea, but today Lottie's problems were on my mind, and

I went instead to see the pig. Before I got there, though, I had to pass a broken-down greenhouse, and what I saw inside it made me stop short in surprise.

Through the dirty glass I could see Lil, an expression of concentrated venom on her face, busy with a pair of scissors cutting something into tiny pieces. I could tell she hadn't seen me, and her furtive air made me curious. I slipped quietly in at the greenhouse door before I spoke.

'Hallo, Lily. What are you doing, then?'

Lil jumped guiltily, and tried to hide the scissors. In doing so, she dropped what she was holding in her other hand, and I pounced on them quickly. I saw they were photographs, photographs of Lottie. Lil had already cut one of them up and it lay in shreds on the ground around the shabby galoshes she wore on her bare feet. Glancing at the rest, I saw that they had been skilfully tinted, so that Lottie's rosy cheeks rivalled the apple-blossom she was holding up to her face. Used as I was to Lottie's beauty, I couldn't help a gasp of admiration.

'Oh, these are lovely! Who took them, Lil?'

To my astonishment, Lil suddenly coloured up like a boiled beetroot, and she half-turned from me as she muttered her reply.

'Timmy Rachet took 'em, him down at the chemist's. He's sweet on our Lottie,' she snapped spitefully. 'And she won't get him to take none of me, so I'm cutting 'em up, and serve her right, the mean little madam.'

'What a shame, Lily!' My thoughts raced ahead, and I put on a sympathetic smile. 'Here, look—tell you what. I'll get my mum to let me bring our Brownie next time we come, and I'll take some photos of you. How would that be?'

Lil nodded, still sulky.

'But don't cut up any more of these pictures', I went on, 'or you'll get into trouble with Aunt Dot. Let me take them up to the house and I'll slip them on the dresser when nobody's looking. Aye, aye, sailor?' I added, using the catchphrase that Lil, for some reason, always thought hilariously funny. To my relief, it worked, and her face cleared.

'Aye, aye captain!' she cackled in reply, following docilely as I led the way back to the house. Letting her go ahead of me into the kitchen, I hung back in the narrow passage—the ducks, I was glad to see, were still now—and I quickly slipped one of the photographs into my satchel, which hung on a peg with my coat. I had to bring my school books with me every time we came, for Aunt Dot to marvel over. Then I hurried into the kitchen after Lil. Luckily, in the bustle of sitting down to the huge farm tea set out on the table, nobody noticed me slip the rest of the photos behind a pile of *Farmer's Weekly* on the dresser.

We made our way home on the bus, my mother with a dozen eggs and the precious butter hidden in her shopping-bag and me with the ducks carefully disguised in a brown paper parcel. The next hurdle was to get hold of the copy of our local newspaper with the entry form I wanted. It was too late when we got home that night, and I hid Lottie's photograph in my atlas, but I knew I would find the coupon for the competition among the pile of newspapers my father kept for lighting the fire. All I needed was a chance to rummage through them.

Next evening when my father had gone out and my mother was in the back kitchen washing up—'You get on with your studying, Patty,' she'd said as usual—I found the page and tore it out, telling myself if any questions were asked I could always say I'd needed some paper for the outside lavatory. I waited till my mother came in and settled down by the fire to read the latest *Peg's Paper*. Then with a beating heart I stood up, picking up a comic from the sideboard.

'I'm going to do a competition, mum.'

This was a weekly ritual. I regularly sent in competition entries to Enid Blyton's *Sunny Stories*, *Chick's Own* and *The Rainbow*, and just as regularly got back 'Certificates of Commendation', sometimes the prize of a children's book and, very occasionally, a half-crown postal order. My mother nodded.

'Mind how you put the gas on. The ink's in the chiffonnière with the mapping pen.'

The front room was cold as ice. Apart from my occasional activities in there, it was used only at Christmas, when a fire was lit. Cautiously I stood on the settee to pull down the arm of the gas fitting, wobbling a little as I struck the match. My mother had been adamant in refusing to have electricity laid on in the house when the landlord offered it, regarding it as certain and agonising death to the unwary. As the gas mantel flared, then glowed steadily, I clambered down and went over to the mahogany chiffonnière. In it were kept the bottle of Stephenson's blue-black ink, a wad of pink blotting paper and the mapping pen, which enabled me to fill in neatly the narrow lines of my competition entries. Working quickly, I completed the form in the comic—'What did Little Boy Blue blow? Who sat by Little Miss Muffet?'—cut it out and addressed the envelope. Then, ready to use my atlas as a cover, I read through the other competition, the one in the newspaper.

'Are you the Forces' Pin-Up Queen of the Midlands?' demanded the headline. 'Send us your photograph for consideration by our panel, made up of ENSA's leading show-business personalities. The lucky winner will receive a cheque for £100 (one hundred pounds) and the four runners-up will win £25 (twenty-five pounds each). Don't delay—send today.'

Various rules followed, but none of these seemed to prevent my plan to send in Lottie's photograph, so I wrote her name and address on the coupon, stuck it neatly on the back of the photo with Seccotine, and found an envelope among my store big enough to take it. Luckily, my mother always kept stamps in the cupboard for my competition entries, and I suppose we more or less broke even with my occasional postal orders. I stamped Lottie's entry along with my own, ready to post next day on the way to school. As I slipped it into the pillar box on the corner, I breathed a sign of relief. Lottie's troubles, perhaps, were over, and I had been a Good Fairy after all.

But over the next week or so, though I kept watch on the paper every day, my hopes began to fade. Nothing more appeared about the contest, and before long it would be time to take the jam again to Aunt Dot. Then, incredibly, it was Miss Minchin who broke the news to us of Lottie's success. We had missed seeing the paper that morning, having set out early to take some lumps of coal we were 'sparing' for Miss Minchin's fire, and at first we were at a loss to know why we were so coldly received. Behind Miss Minchin's back we exchanged puzzled looks while she tipped the coal out of our bags into her coal-scuttle with barely a thank-you. It was clear something was wrong, but what could it be?

At last, unable to keep it to herself any longer, Miss Minchin picked up her copy of the day's newspaper, sniffing as she gave it a disapproving shake.

'I see your young relation's been getting herself in the news,' she commented icily. 'Not the sort of thing I would have expected, not at all, though of course a hundred pounds is a lot of money, but even so ... to make yourself cheap like that ... . I must say it's most unsuitable in my opinion, most unsuitable. I take it you hadn't heard?'

'Heard? Heard what?' My mother took the paper with trembling hands, and gave a little moan of dismay as she goggled at the banner headline, 'Lovely Lottie's Lucky Win'. Below was an enlargement of Lottie's photo, followed by a dramatic account of Lottie's amazement at her success and her bewilderment over the 'mystery friend' who had secretly entered her picture in the contest and won her the title of the Forces' Pin-Up Queen of the Midlands. The 'warm-hearted country lass', it went on, had generously agreed to sign copies of her photo for every regiment or ship whose brave lads wanted to make her their 'very own pin-up'. On an inside page, the four runners-up smiled out under the headline, 'The Gallant Losers', and they, too, it seemed, were equally willing to allow their pictures to be sent worldwide to cheer up 'our boys on every front'. 'With girls like this to come home to,' the story concluded, 'we can be sure that our soldiers, sailors and airmen will soon have Hitler on the run!'

Dazed by my success, I hardly listened as my mother stammered out her excuses, assuring Miss Minchin that she personally had known nothing at all about this, and would have advised strongly against it had her opinion been asked. Miss Minchin huffily accepted the apology, and we left earlier than usual, and hurried away conscious that we remained under a cloud.

'Silly old cat,' said my father when we told him. 'What harm's it done? Good for Lottie, I say.'

But my mother and Aunt Madge ignored him, as usual, agreeing with Miss Minchin that Lottie's apparent good fortune might well prove to be the first step on the primrose path of dalliance. We waited eagerly for our next visit to the Craxtons to hear all the details of 'Lovely Lottie's Lucky Win'.

Within a week the jam ration came due, and laden with it we set off on the bus that would take us to the village. When we got to the house, to my disappointment Lottie was nowhere to be seen. Instead, a large framed copy of the famous photograph hung in the place of honour over the mantelpiece. Alone in the kitchen, Aunt Dot was mixing up pastry, and she greeted the jars of jam with relief. Nothing was said as she rolled out the pastry and slid the first batch of tarts into the oven. Then she boiled up the kettle for tea, poured it out and as she passed it to us, nodded with a mixture of pride and defiance to the photograph.

'You've heard about our Lottie, I suppose, Annie?'

My mother gave a wintry smile.

'It's a lot of money for a young girl, Dot,' she replied cautiously. ''tis to be hoped she won't let it go to her head.'

'Go to her head? Go to her head?' Aunt Dot's voice was shrill with indignation. 'I tell you straight, Annie, our Lottie's got her head screwed on right, that she has, and if anybody says different, I say it's nothing but jealousy!'

Before my mother could respond, I interrupted, unable to bear it any longer.

'Is Lottie going to learn hairdressing with Mr Errol at Maison Beauty, Aunt Dot?' I burst out.

They both looked at me in astonishment.

'Learn hairdressing? That she is not!' Aunt Dot's tone was scornful. 'Whatever gave you that idea? She's getting married.'

This time my mother was as surprised as I was.

'Getting married, Dot? But—but who to?'

'Why, to Timmy Rachet, him as took the photograph.' To Aunt Dot, it apparently seemed obvious. 'He won't admit it, but I reckon it was him as sent that photo in to the paper. Anyway, seeing our Lottie with the newspaper people and the forces lot all hanging around her, it made him pluck his ideas up and ask her. He's going to be called up in a week or two, so they're getting married right away, soon as the banns are called. And Lottie's going out to work so they can save up for a house when the war's over.'

Horrified, I threw caution to the winds.

'Not to Mrs Pearson's? Not to the Roadhouse?' I begged.

Once again, Aunt Dot looked at me with scorn.

'The Roadhouse? Of course she ain't going to work there—Timmy Rachet soon told our Tom where to go when he suggested it. Said he wasn't having no wife of his working in a place like that.' She smiled complacently. 'They had a row about it, and then Tom had a row with Mrs Pearson over it, so he don't go to the Roadhouse no longer neither.'

'Then where is she going to work, Dot?' asked my mother. 'There's not much for a girl around here.''

'There is now.' retorted Aunt Dot smugly. 'She's going to work at the munitions factory, along with all her pals. They pay good money there, and there's a bus from the village every morning and back again at night. Like I said, our Lottie's got her head screwed on right, and no mistake!'

Tactfully, my mother changed the subject by offering to squeeze a few clothing coupons for Lottie's wedding dress, and I slipped away down the garden to share my secret sorrows with the hens. But before I got there, I bumped into Lil, hidden behind the pig-pen. When I saw what she was doing, I gave a shudder. Her face contorted with murderous fury, she was stabbing a blunt kitchen knife into the body of a battered rag doll. As the knife rose and fell again and again, I felt like running away as hard as I could go, but screwing up my courage I strolled on along the path. Careful to make my voice nonchalant, at last I spoke.

'Hallo, Lily. What are you doing with that doll, then? Won't be much good when you've finished with it at that rate, will it?'

Lil turned her pale eyes on me and grinned.

'I'm getting my own back on our Lottie,' she answered slyly. 'She's pinched Timmy Rachet off me, she has. I wanted to marry him, but he's sweet on her. So I've called this doll Lottie, and I'm carving her up. I can't do it to Lottie,' she explained with a matter of fact air, ''cos if I do the blood'll all come out, and I can't stand the sight of blood nohow. But I'm getting my own back anyway, 'cos this used to be Lottie's doll, see?'

I thought for a minute. Then I bent confidentially towards Lil, and spoke as convincingly as I could.

'You don't want to be jealous of Lottie, Lil.' I said earnestly. 'Why, I think you're much prettier than she is, and I bet Timmy Rachet thinks so too, really. He's just marrying her for her money—the hundred pounds she won. He's nothing but a rotten fortune-hunter, so he's not worth bothering about either, is he?'

The doll forgotten, Lil was listening with her head on one side, her mouth open as she took this in. Slowly she nodded in agreement.

'So don't you give it another thought, Lily,' I went on. 'You're the best off—anybody would tell you that.' I forced a bright smile on to my face. 'Aye, aye, sailor?'

To my relief, as always it worked. Lil's face lit up in a triumphant smile.

'Aye, aye, captain!' she chortled happily, as Aunt Dot called us in to tea.

13

Judgement Day

It was a nightmare journey.

The 'All Clear' sounded just after six o'clock and we set out almost straight away, my mother finally being convinced it was time for us to go. The raid had gone on all night, starting so early we had no time to get to the Anderson shelter at the bottom of the garden which we shared with our neighbours, the Peakes. Instead, we huddled in the cupboard under the stairs as the planes passed over and the bombs rained down. While my mother and Aunt Madge whispered together—'That sounds like the BTH got hit!' 'No, it was further away,'—I read my 'William' book by the light of my torch. I liked being under the stairs better than in the shelter. The Peakes wouldn't let me use my torch, for fear I gave away our hiding-place to the German planes, so we sat in pitch darkness, listening to old Mr Peake snoring and Mrs Peake whimpering with fear every time a bomb fell near us. In the cupboard, though, we were on our own and could please ourselves, drinking tea from a flask and nibbling biscuits. When the steady tones of the 'All Clear' rang out at last, we came out into the kitchen, brushing off crumbs and the flakes of whitewash dislodged by the jarring of the explosions. The raid, I realised, had lasted for eleven hours.

'Doreen,' said Aunt Madge. 'We'll go to Doreen. She'll have a room, perhaps, and if she hasn't, she's sure to know somebody who has. The sooner we get off, the better, or they'll all be full up after this.'

I can remember now the smell of burning as we locked the front door behind us, the smuts of ash and the rubble under our feet. We passed several houses on fire, for many families were already 'sleeping out', as we said, travelling each night to lodgings in the countryside to escape the raids, and no-one was home to tackle the incendiary bombs before the fire caught hold. We took a roundabout way, avoiding the city centre, and there was no chance of transport—the railway station was out of action, the tramlines buckled up, half the buses destroyed and the rest requisitioned by the emergency services—but at last we came to the Kenilworth Road. There we joined a procession of families trudging into the darkness, the sky red behind us from the light of the fires. Most of the crowd carried bundles, but some had suitcases neatly packed—like going to the seaside, I thought. For the most part they were quiet and orderly, except when a child wailed and was coaxed into silence. I remembered newsreels I'd seen at the cinema of refugees in Europe. Now we were refugees, too, I supposed, in a way. I had my satchel slung on my shoulder, full of school books, and a brown paper carrier bag in my hand, with our spare shoes. My aunt had wrapped her few treasures up in newspaper—her father's gold watch-chain, two old five-shilling pieces and a silver locket—and poked them down into the toes of the shoes before she put them inside the carrier. Sneak-thieves would hardly suspect me of being given anything valuable to look after ... .

My mother's face was grim. We had left my father behind in the ruined city, on duty with the Police War Reserve. In uniform, he was in his element, ordering civilians about and arresting looters. She hardly gave him a second thought, but what she hated was the idea of going among strangers. All their lives, she and Aunt Madge had 'kept themselves to themselves', as they said, and now she feared the worst. The raids had been going on for days, until this final night of devastation, and we were all worn out from lack of sleep. Aunt Madge stumbled along with the heaviest bag, her eyes red-rimmed and wide with alarm. Doreen Phelps, a workmate in the box factory, lived in Kenilworth, five miles away. Like my mother, my aunt prided herself on never asking favours, but now there was no choice. It was time to leave, while we were all still alive.

The November night was clear and cold, with hoar-frost covering the woods where the summer before we had picknicked among the bluebells. My legs ached, and we seemed to have been walking for hours. At last relief workers met us on the outskirts of the town, with a mobile canteen set up at the side of the road, handing out tea and buns. To my disappointment, my mother gave a faint smile and shook her head, so we plodded on. Before long we met up with air raid wardens handing out maps to show where the rest centres were, Scout huts and church halls hastily prepared to cope with the new influx of evacuees. My mother ignored them, too, but Aunt Madge took a map and peered at it anxiously in the dim light outside the ARP post.

'Annie,' she said wearily, 'we've got to tidy ourselves up a bit before we go to Doreen's. We can't turn up there like this. Anyway, Patty needs a rest—we all do. Come on, we'll go to the reception centre at the library. That'll be all right.'

Luckily, the library was in the part of town where Doreen lived with her widowed mother. Its windows were shrouded in blackout curtains and criss-crossed with wide sticky tape, but there was a chink of light from the doorway as we made our way over the frosty grass. Inside, camp beds lined the walls, and I sat bolt upright on one of them between my mother and my aunt, who had no intention of lying down in a strange place. There were plenty of blankets piled up on tables at the end of the room, and I looked at them longingly, but my mother shook her head.

'Fleas!' she hissed, and that, I knew, was that. Again, she refused even a cup of tea till Aunt Madge insisted, giving me a few sips as well, once the rim had been carefully wiped with her handkerchief.

Around us, most of our companions slept in sheer exhaustion, some whimpering as if they were dreaming of the relentless rain of bombs. Others, like us, were tense and wakeful, checking their bags and bundles to make sure nothing had got lost or stolen on the trek from the city. A few with blisters after the long walk were patched up by the Red Cross, while others, weeping and shaking, were given a sedative and eventually lulled off to sleep. By now it was getting light outside and Aunt Madge led the way to the cloakroom. I flinched as she scrubbed at my face with the icy cold water, but it woke me up and I felt better afterwards. My mother tidied her hair and straightened her hat in the mirror. Outside, we rubbed our shoes on the grass to get rid of the dust, and set off down the quiet suburban street.

A dog ran up to us, barking, as we crossed the town centre, and a greengrocer was taking down his shutters as we passed. Soon we reached Doreen's house, where she spotted us as she drew back the front curtains, and rushed out with cries of dismay. In no time there was tea and toast on the table, and now my mother accepted it gratefully. Doreen, after all, had been to our house for meals often enough, and everything here was clean and spotless.

While we ate, Doreen and Mrs Phelps began to discuss lodgings.

'You'd have been more than welcome here, Madge, you know that.' Doreen sighed and shook her head. 'But Uncle Brian and Aunt Rhoda turned up with young Bobby only last Sunday, and asked us to take them in till the raids eased off. And the neighbours both sides have got evacuees, so they're full up. There's Mr Robins down the road—he lives on his own … .' Her voice trailed off uncertainly.

'They can't go there!' Mrs Phelps was scandalised. 'Filthy, his place is, and him drunk half the time. And the Battersons are full up with their own kids, one every year and left to run riot,' she added with a sniff. 'There's just nobody in this street, Doreen.'

Doreen frowned. Then suddenly her face cleared.

'Mrs Roke,' she said triumphantly. 'I knew I'd think of somebody. Mrs Roke's got plenty of empty rooms. I'll take you along there, Madge, as soon as I've had a wash. It's not very far—one of those big houses down by the castle'.

Mrs Phelps nodded.

'Yes, you could be right, Doreen,' she agreed. 'That great big house, with only the two of them in it, apart from Paulette in the attics. It's certainly worth a try. Any port in a storm, eh?' she chuckled, patting my mother on the shoulder.

But my mother still looked worried.

'Surely, though, if they're posh people with a big house, they won't want to take in lodgers?' she objected. 'Won't they think it a cheek, us going round there? What makes you think they'd take us in?'

'Posh? Old Mother Roke?' Mrs Phelps shook her head. 'No, you've got hold of the wrong end of the stick there, I can tell you. She was housekeeper to poor Mrs Finch as died last year of a heart attack. They found out afterwards that Mrs Finch had made a will and left the house and everything in it to Lizzie Roke. As for Jim, he was nothing but the handyman, he was. You don't need to feel shy of going to see them, my dear. They're no better than the rest of us, by a long chalk.'

'And if he was paying her money, she'd take in King Kong himself,' joked Doreen, coming in with her hat and coat on. 'Why, she and Jim still live in the servants' quarters, to save on the heating. So there's plenty of room, don't you worry. We'll get you fixed up in no time.'

Reassured by the news that Mrs Roke, far from being a wealthy householder, was in fact no more than a former servant, my mother and Aunt Madge set off down the road with Doreen and I followed along behind. 'Afton' turned out to be a large, detached Victorian villa set in a rambling garden at the end of a quiet cul-de-sac. The night's frost was dripping dismally off the leaves of a ragged laurel hedge by the front door as Doreen rang the bell. A few moments later shuffling footsteps could be heard and the door opened a crack. An old woman with whispy white hair peered out suspiciously, and on recognising Doreen ushered us grudgingly into the hall. The air inside struck chill and dank, and the old woman herself was swathed in a tattered woollen shawl. She eyed us narrowly as Doreen brightly explained our plight, careful to repeat several times that we would, of course, be only too happy to pay for our lodgings if Mrs Roke would oblige us.

Her eyes on me, Mrs Roke muttered something. I heard the words, 'the child' and 'noise'.

In reply, Doreen laughed airily.

'Little Patty? You wouldn't know she was in the house, Mrs Roke,' she assured the old woman. 'Quiet as a mouse she is, always reading her books and doing jigsaw puzzles. An only one, see, and never allowed to be troublesome, take it from me.'

At this, Mrs Roke seemed to relent, and Doreen felt able to leave us to sort out the details for ourselves. We were to go back to her house later on, for a meal. One of the first things Mrs Roke spelled out was that no cooking or eating was to go on under her roof. A sittingroom and a bedroom she would provide, available to us between the hours of six in the evening and eight in the morning only. For the rest of the time, she implied, we could go to the devil for all she cared. She showed us first into the vast front room with its chilly marble fireplace and hard slippery chairs. Then she led us up a gloomy staircase covered with worn matting to see the bedroom. This was also at the front of the house, along a cold corridor with closed doors on either side and a further flight of stairs up to the attics, where Mrs Roke's niece, Paulette, had made herself a flat.

'You won't see nothing of her, though—out till all hours, she is,' Mrs Roke grumbled. 'Still, only young once, aren't you?' she added with a leer, throwing open our bedroom door.

It contained a lumpy double bed, a huge wardrobe and a horsehair couch on castors. The couch, Mrs Roke indicated, would do for me, and she pulled some moth-eaten blankets and a stained pillow out of the wardrobe for me to use. On the floor, marooned on the pale green linoleum, were several peculiar fur rugs, the pelts of strange, rough-haired animals, and I knew I would never dare to tread on them. Framed bible texts hung round the walls and I read these while my mother, Aunt Madge and the old woman discussed terms and rules. 'Wait upon the Lord'—no laundry provided. 'Thou, God, Seest Me'—no food in either of the rooms. 'Vengeance is Mine, saith the Lord'—no pets, no wireless, no noise of any kind ... .

'You'll be back at six, then?' Mrs Roke concluded briskly. 'Pay now, shall you? Never know these days,' she added with gloomy relish as money changed hands.

When we left the house, I noticed a hall-stand apparently composed entirely of reindeer antlers, and a grandfather clock topped by a brass eagle in full flight, heavily festooned with cobwebs. There was something sinister about the house, though I couldn't make out just what it was—the bleak rooms, the low wattage bulbs giving out their dim, watery light, perhaps, or the spiteful black cat I spotted lurking in a doorway, hissing and spitting as we passed. I was puzzled by a soldier's forage cap which hung from an antler, greasy and stained. Our own home wasn't cosy, but I found 'Afton' distinctly chilly. I shivered when the door was safely closed behind us, partly from cold but also from foreboding.

'I don't like her much,' I ventured, as I tagged along behind my mother and Aunt Madge.

'Who said anything about liking her? Beggars can't be

choosers,' snapped my mother. 'At least we've got a roof over our heads,' she added as we set off to wander round the town till it was time to go to Doreen's.

We settled in, and crept about the stairs and corridors, talking in whispers and walking on tiptoe. We got round the 'no food' rule with flasks of tea and sandwiches, packets of biscuits and precooked sausages toasted at the gas fire, brushing the crumbs through a crack in the floorboards. Our laundry—bed-linen and towels—we had to carry home a few at a time to wash in Shelley Street, and though the horsehair sofa was uncomfortable, I stopped slipping off it every night once I turned it round so that the back-rail prevented me from falling on to the floor. It was a bizarre, makeshift sort of life, but we made the best of it. I still felt uneasy about our new lodgings, but I enjoyed reading by torchlight under the blankets every night till my mother and aunt came to bed. Some parts of the house were out of bounds—once I took a forgotten bottle of milk through to the dusty, untidy kitchen where Mrs Roke and Jim, the former handyman, still lived, and met with such an icy stare from Mrs Roke's pale blue eyes I was careful never to go there again. Equally forbidden were the attics, where Paulette had her flat. She had come from London at the outbreak of war to stay with her aunt and was, according to Doreen's genteel whispers, 'no better than she should be,' hence the forage-cap in the hall.

'I expect her name's really Pauline,' sniffed my mother nastily, but I was intrigued by our mysterious fellow-lodger, and hung about on the upstairs landing hoping to catch sight of her. But, as Mrs Roke had said, Pauline was seldom home before midnight, often spending quite a while on the doorstep before she ran upstairs. I had just slipped my book and torch away one night when my mother and aunt came in, whispering together, thinking I was asleep.

'She's down there again, the brazen hussy,' hissed my mother indignantly. 'Kissing and cuddling on the doorstep—it's disgusting!'

'Yes—and worse!' added Aunt Madge vindictively. 'And Mrs Roke turns a blind eye to her goings on, instead of stopping it.'

My mother's reply was lost as the bedsprings creaked, and I lay wide-eyed in the dark. 'Kissing and cuddling'—'Yes, and worse!' But what *could* be worse than kissing and cuddling? I drifted off to sleep, trying in vain to imagine what was going on down below on the doorstep in the shelter of the laurel bushes.

Before long, life in the ruined city settled down to what, in wartime, passed for normal, and soon we were travelling in by train each morning, my mother to keep the house and get the rations in for my father, while my aunt along with Doreen headed for the box factory and I caught the school bus. At the end of the day we all met up again to return on the train to our bleak refuge at Mrs Roke's. I had never got over my first uneasiness, and it still lurked, like Tinker the cat, at the back of my mind, something I tried to ignore for the sake of peace. To confront it head on, I felt, would be unwise ... .

The horsehair sofa, with its pile of scratchy blankets, was uncomfortable, and late one night, unable to sleep, I suddenly realised I had forgotten to put my homework books into my satchel, which hung on a peg in the downstairs lobby along with our outdoor coats. Glad of an excuse to prowl around the empty corridors, I slipped on my dressing-gown and picked up the books from under the sofa, telling myself I was sure to forget them if I left them till morning. My mother and Aunt Madge in the double bed continued to snore gently as I crept from the room and edged silently down the stairs to the hall. Unbuckling my satchel, I slipped the books safely inside and fastened it up again with a sigh of relief. Then, as I turned to go, I froze with alarm. The kitchen door on the other side of the lobby was open a crack, and I could hear the voice of old Jim. A gnarled, silent little gnome of a man, he could occasionally be seen in the wilderness of a garden behind the house. But usually he only glared malevolently—I had never heard his voice before. Now, he seemed to be finding fault with Paulette.

'Staying out till all hours,' he grumbled. 'She wants telling, she does, the little madam. And them chaps from the Army base, they're just as bad ... .'

But Mrs Roke cut him short.

'You didn't say that this time last year, did you?' she jeered. 'Glad enough of Pete and Harry, we were, weren't we, when we wanted them to witness the will, before they left for France? Don't reckon as you've got any cause to grumble about Paulette's pals. Here today and gone tomorrer, and best of luck to 'em I say. They did us a good turn, and no questions asked. So just you shut up about Paulette, d'you hear?'

I stood rooted to the spot. Clearly I was hearing more than I should, and if Mrs Roke found out I was there, she might well throw us all out, probably at a minute's notice. On tiptoe I turned and headed for the stairs—only to find that by now the front door was open. Paulette, heavily entwined with her latest boyfriend, was installed under the antlers. In the moonlight from the front garden, I saw a flurry of green silk frills and khaki uniform. Trapped, I shrank back among the coats in the lobby. By now the old man was wheezing with laughter, choking with amusement at some recollection from the past.

''Pon my soul, I'll never forget the way as you got ole Elsie Finch to sign that will, Lizzie,' he spluttered. 'Got it all worked out as right as ninepence, you had, me ole beauty. Locking her up in the attic for four days, starving, and then taking her up a chicken dinner with all the trimmings, so's she could smell it. That got her signing all right, that did.' Again he broke off, chuckling and choking with glee. 'Her face,' he went on. 'Her face when you put the chicken dinner down on the floor for the cat after all—and offered her the dish of catfood instead! I can see it now—and then she called on the Lord to strike you dead with her dying breath. Fat lot you cared—you'd got what you wanted.'

More raucous laughter shook him, drowning Mrs Roke's reply. Then he went on, slapping his hand on the table as he spoke.

'Do you know, old girl, I reckon as it was the shock of seeing old Tinker wolfing down her dinner as killed her, no matter what the doctor said about a weak heart. 'Course, he only saw her back in the best bed, all tidied up nice and proper, and you crying your eyes out. You're a right one, Lizzie, you are, I'll say that for yer, and no mistake!'

By now, I was stone cold with horror, and to my relief I heard Paulette scurrying upstairs. Giving her time to reach the attics, I followed, thankful that the way was clear at last. Then, just as I reached the front hall, a black shape darted out in front of me, and

I fell full length with a resounding crash—I had forgotten Tinker's habit of skulking in the shadows. Hearing the kitchen door flung open, I scrambled desperately to my feet, but I was only halfway up the stairs when Mrs Roke switched the light full on.

'And what might you be doing, young lady?' she demanded in a fierce whisper.

Knowing what I did now, I could only shake my head, terrified. The old woman advanced to the bottom of the stairs, scowling. Unable to move, I clutched desperately at the bannisters.

'I think you've got some explaining to do, you spying little toad,' she began. 'Ho, yes, you're not getting away with'—but she broke off, as an enormous explosion rent the air, and the whole house seemed to shake.

I watched in horror as the grandfather clock appeared to leap into the air. It crashed forward, twisting so that the brass eagle struck Mrs Roke a murderous blow with its outstretched wing, pinning her lifeless to the ground. At the same moment, all the lights went out. Shaking, I crouched on the stairs till my mother, Aunt Madge and Paulette arrived, Paulette carrying a candle stuck in a wine bottle. None of them realised I had witnessed the whole scene and, if Jim knew, he said nothing. Emerging from the kitchen, he took one look at Mrs Roke's body and went out into the street to fetch help. We could hear fire engines and ambulances in the distance, and the pavement glittered with the glass from broken windows.

Since it seemed obvious what had happened to Mrs Roke, no further questions were asked. She was only one of a number of people killed that night by the landmine jettisoned over Kenilworth by a German bomber wandering off course. Eventually we got back to bed, and I lay awake till morning.

When everything was finally sorted out, Paulette inherited the house, since her aunt and Jim had never been formally married. She pressed my mother and Aunt Madge to say on at 'Afton', but they declined. 'Sleeping out' had made a change, but now it seemed safe to return to the city. We heard from Doreen that before long, of course, just about the whole of the Army base made Paulette's house their second home, putting to flight forever the ghosts of Mrs Roke and her secret victim.

Old Jim was sometimes seen trudging about the town after Paulette turned him out, but he was the only reminder of Mrs Roke, apart from the bomb-site in the town centre where the landmine had fallen, destroying several shops and damaging a row of houses. It was all an accident, but some of the evacuees, indignant at the high prices they were being charged, saw it as a judgement on the town's rent racketeers. But I was uneasily aware of a more precise act of revenge that had taken place that night, and I remembered a text on the wall of our bedroom. 'Vengeance is Mine, saith the Lord', I thought, as I saw again the eagle falling.

14

Miss Miranda and the Ring o'Bells Romance

'He sang *Sweet Genevieve* and then he proposed to me!'

'Must have been drunk,' said Aunt Madge, hardly bothering to keep her voice down.

'When was this, then?' asked my mother, trying to smile admiringly at Josie Peake's ring and glare at Aunt Madge at the same time.

'Outside the Ring o'Bells,' replied Josie with an excited giggle. 'Just after closing time.'

'Told you so,' snapped my aunt, delighted to be proved right. She glared back at my mother, who was peeling potatoes at the scullery door, and I hovered behind Aunt Madge near the mangle, wondering if there was any chance at all I would be asked to be a bridesmaid. On the whole, it seemed unlikely. We were never very friendly with the Peakes, though we'd lived next door to them for years.

'We're getting married when he comes home again on leave next month,' Josie went on. 'We'll be able to have a bit of a honeymoon before he goes overseas.' She looked down with a simper at her ring, and sighed sentimentally. Her mother, red-faced and portly, leered suggestively at me.

'Your turn next, Patty,' she sniggered. 'Before you can say Jack Robinson you'll have a ring on your finger, too. Getting a proper big wench, ain't she?' she tittered coarsely, turning to my mother. 'Grown up and gone, they are, these days before you know it, you mark my words!'

'Oh no, not Patty!' Now my mother turned her glare on Mrs Peake. This was something to be squashed right away, before I began getting any ideas into my head. 'Patty's not interested in boys—she's too busy studying. She'll be going away to college in a year or two. Anyway, she's not old enough for any of that sort of nonsense. She's only twelve.'

Mrs Peake, though, was not taken in. She knew well enough that I would be thirteen in a few weeks, and I was, as always, big for my age. Already I could have made two of Josie, who at seventeen was whey-faced and scrawny.

'Ah well, you never know.' As she turned to go, Mrs Peake, offended, couldn't resist a parting shot. 'If you arsk me, it's the quiet ones you have to watch. Come on, Josie, your father'll be wondering where we are.'

Bristling indignantly—after all, she'd only been trying to spread the excitement around a bit, in a neighbourly way—she waddled off across the yard with Josie at her heels, and shut her back door behind them with a bang. My mother and Aunt Madge exchanged a sour smile.

'Took the pug, didn't she?' said Aunt Madge in satisfaction. 'You put her peg out and no mistake, Annie. And as for having to watch anybody, well, the way Josie's been carrying on just lately at the bottom of the entry ... .' A sudden thought seemed to strike her. 'As far as that goes, you don't think ... ?' She broke off as my mother shook her head with a warning glance at me. 'Oh well, if she's planning on a white wedding,' she continued thoughtfully, veering off on another, not entirely unconnected, tack, 'she'll be after us before long to borrow some clothing coupons. That's unless Charlie Fisher can get some on the black market off those dodgy pals of his. Proper lot of spivs they are. Anybody with half an eye can see that.'

As I sat down at the kitchen table to do my homework, I wistfully imagined Josie in a gleaming white wedding dress, a lace veil covering her stringy yellow hair. Charlie Fisher, or Chuck as we all called him, would wear his Army uniform for the ceremony, his untidy red curls plastered down with Brylcreem. The eldest of a whole crowd of brothers and sisters, he had been courting Josie ever since they both left school. The Fishers lived in a squalid alley off East Street, and apart from Charlie the whole family had been in and out of trouble with the police for years. Mrs Fisher was famous in the neighbourhood for having once tried to get her layabout husband summonsed for keeping a dangerous dog. The story went that he'd rashly accepted a vicious Alsatian bitch in payment for a gambling debt, but before long, after it had bitten the dustman, the rent collector and the policeman who came to make enquiries, it had quietly disappeared. Just before the war began, Chuck had joined the Army as a boy soldier, mainly, it was supposed, to get away from home.

On one of his early leaves he had helped my father to build the Anderson shelter at the end of our garden, ready to share with the Peakes when air-raids started. Mr Peake, elderly and lame, couldn't be expected to do the heavy digging that was required, but Chuck and my father soon got the deep hole dug in the sticky clay soil in time for the delivery of the corrugated iron for the shelter itself. This was supplied free by the Government, the sheets bent ready to shape, to be sunk into the hole and bolted together to form a small underground room, with a hillock of earth piled on top and sandbags stacked up to protect the entrance. From the start, Mrs Peake as usual had looked on the gloomy side.

'Smells like a grave, don't it?' she said, wrinkling up her pudgy nose when we all went down the garden to inspect the finished shelter. 'Mind you, that's what it will be once Jerry starts his tricks. Never get out alive, we wouldn't. Just you wait and see!'

But when the air-raids finally began, somehow we had coped well enough, huddling together on makeshift benches as the planes droned overhead and the bombs fell. Only an occasional bright beam flashed through a chink in the doorway as searchlights swept the sky, showing Mr Peake snoring with his mouth open, Mrs Peake taking a nip from her bottle of brandy and Josie curled up in a corner. When the 'All Clear' wailed, we scrambled out, thankful to go back to our beds for an hour or two before morning. Luckily my father, who even in peacetime lived in a state of constant warfare with the Peakes, had managed to get himself taken on to the Police War Reserve and had volunteered for permanent night-duty, so he was never there to share the shelter with us.

We also had air-raid practice at school, in case of daytime raids, though most of the bombing happened at night. Glad of a break from lessons, we filed with our gas masks into the dimly-lit passages dug below a piece of waste ground behind the school building. Once down, the registers were called and we all filed out again, pleased to be back in the fresh air. By now I was at the all-girls grammar school on the outskirts of the city, travelling there every day on the bus. I must have looked strangely out of place as I hurried through the shabby backstreets to the bus-stop in my school uniform, with my black velour pudding-basin hat trimmed with a cockade of blue and gold ribbon, my navy raincoat and my long, Ovaltine-coloured stockings, lugging my heavy satchel full of books.

Most of the other girls at the school lived in the quiet, tree-lined avenues nearby, and walked to school or rode there on their bicycles. I was the only one who came by bus.

Now, as I filled in the Cinque Ports on my outline map, I thought enviously about Josie's wedding. I might not be interested in boys—I never met any—but I was interested in weddings. Sometimes the girls at school talked of being bridesmaids to their elder sisters. They described their special dresses, restricted by clothes rationing to plain styles suitable to be cut down later for everyday wear, but still far prettier than anything I ever had myself. I knew in my heart there was no chance Josie would ask me to be her bridesmaid, since if she wanted any she could pick half a dozen from among Chuck's sisters, but I let myself daydream a little as I shaded in the sea on my map. Peach-coloured satin, I decided, with a basket of rose-petals ... .

A raucous voice jerked me rudely back to reality.

'It's That Man Again, It's That Man Again ... .'

On the sideboard the wireless, a misnomer if ever there was one, with its tangle of wires and acid-filled accumulator batteries, sprang into life as my father switched it on. He never missed *ITMA*, a popular comedy programme starring the comedian Tommy Handley along with a mixture of comical Cockney chars—'Can I do yer now, Sir?'—and choleric colonels. Intended to boost wartime morale, its mixture of broad humour and double entendre always put him in a good mood, though it was a struggle for me to do my homework against its racket. It was too cold, even in summer, to work anywhere else in the house, so I had to make the best of it. Now, as she cut his sandwiches, my mother told him Josie Peake's news, shouting at the top of her voice to make herself heard.

'Reckons they're getting married on his next leave—can't you turn that thing down a bit?—and going off on honeymoon,' she bawled. 'Pleased as Punch, Mrs Peake is, and Josie's like a dog with two tails. Looking forward to the money coming in from the Army, I suppose. Do you want corned beef or cheese? There's not much of either.'

'Good Lord deliver us, they'll mek a bright couple, they will, the pair on 'em.' My father paused as he filled up his Thermos flask of tea. 'A babby every year, I'll be bound. Still, he'll be off at the front till the war's over, and who's to say what state he'll be in when he comes back? If he ever does come back', he added grimly, screwing the top on his flask and picking up his helmet.

That night I dreamed of weddings, with Josie marrying Colonel Chinstrap from *ITMA* and my father marrying Mrs Fisher. I was their bridesmaid, but instead of a peach-coloured satin dress I was wearing my school uniform and searching frantically for my gas mask, so I woke in the morning with a sigh of relief. That day I had to stay late after school, as for the first time I was to join in the elocution classes. These were an 'extra' and cost my parents half a guinea a term. Miss Minchin, my old infants' school teacher, had talked them into paying for it, on top of the regular three guineas school fees, suggesting with a mixture of genteel tact and devastating candour that my Shelley Street accent needed ironing out. She had discovered that every week a visiting teacher came after school hours to take a group of girls for special lessons, to get rid of stammers, lisps and shyness. My own little geographical problem, Miss Minchin was sure, would be child's play to such an expert. It would be an investment in my future, a guarantee that, later on, I would be able to hold my own at college. If she had ever actually met Miss Miranda Lafontaine, she might not have been quite so keen. Miss Miranda, as we were told to call her, would not have been at all Miss Minchin's cup of tea.

A former actress, she had been brought out of retirement by the wartime teacher shortage, and now she poured upon her classes all the intensity she had once given to her dramatic performances. Tall and thin, with her faded auburn hair swept up into an enormous Grecian knot on top of her head, she was draped with long Liberty scarves and tinkling chains, her dangling ear-rings flashing as she swooped and swayed among the sinks and Bunsen burners of the science lab where the lessons took place, in order to be out of the way of the cleaners busy in the main part of the school. The other half-dozen girls who took the lessons had had time to get used to Miss Miranda's peculiarities, but as a newcomer I was stunned by her extravagant gestures, her outlandish clothes and above all by her voice which trilled at the top of the scale one moment and the next sank down to a deep bass growl. Coming from a home where, for everyday purposes, all emotion was drained out of life, I couldn't believe my eyes and ears. All the other teachers at the grammar school were more or less what I had expected from the schoolgirl stories I had read—the jolly, blue-eyed English teacher, the fussy French mistress, the elderly history specialist and the hearty games mistress in her short gym-slip and long stockings who scolded us for slacking. But Miss Miranda was an exotic creature I had never met up with between the pages of a book or anywhere else. Her cry of greeting made me turn scarlet with embarrassment while the other girls collapsed into giggles.

'Ah, you must be our new little companion, Patty. Do you know you have a grrreat name to live up to, my deah? Yes, a vurry, vurry grrreat singer was called Adelina Patti. Perhaps one day you will be famous too, just like her.'

She beamed upon me, nodding and smiling in delight, as her voice soared and fell, trembling with emotion. Then, to my relief, she remembered the rest of the class, and the lesson began. I quite enjoyed the bizarre mixture of speech training rhymes—'Bobby had blue buttons on his new blue coat, funny little buttons, shaped like a boat,'—breathing exercises, poetry and scenes from Shakespeare. Most of all I enjoyed watching Miss Miranda as she fluttered about like a rare tropical butterfly. I tried to imagine what Aunt Madge would make of her, and failed. When the action-packed session ended, I was already looking forward to next week.

Then, half an hour later—'A *parachute?*'

It was my mother's voice. As I arrived home, I heard her repeat incredulously, 'A parachute? Go on, Louisa, she's pulling your leg. You can't mean it—it's too daft to laugh at. A parachute for a wedding dress? Get away with you!'

'No, honest to God, Annie, I'm not making it up.' As I came

into the kitchen I found Miss Plumb sitting by the range with a cup of tea and telling her news to my mother and Aunt Madge, who had just arrived home from work herself. 'Charlie Fisher's got this friend of his in the stores of an RAF camp,' she explained, 'and he's getting him a parachute for Josie to have cut up into a wedding dress. I've got to make it up for her, that's how I know. It's all very hush-hush, of course, so don't tell anybody, will you? If anything's said, they'll make out it was a faulty one, I suppose. Anyway, that's got the dress settled, and no coupons needed neither. All I've got to do is to make sure I finish it in time for the wedding, so I'd better go off home and get started!'

It was something of a relief that Josie wouldn't after all be asking us to lend her some of our precious clothing coupons. Most of ours went on my school uniform in any case, and we only got 24 each every six months. A winter coat cost 18 at one blow, so there weren't any to spare, even though my father's police uniform was provided free of charge and free of coupons. While I ate my tea, Aunt Madge and my mother discussed Miss Plumb's news. Though they agreed it wasn't quite like buying black market coupons to get material for a wedding dress, using a parachute smuggled out of RAF stores seemed like getting it 'under the counter', as we said about the treats that shop-keepers saved for their favourite customers. Miss Plumb, who did all the sewing jobs in the neighbourhood, had taken on no easy task. She had got to turn the crumpled, damp-smelling folds of white cloth into a beautiful wedding gown, somehow getting rid of the ribbing and cords that gave away the parachute's original purpose. At last, however, the dress was ready and one night, as I sat by the fire drinking my bedtime cocoa, Josie and Mrs Peake came in with Miss Plumb hovering protectively behind them. My mother put down her copy of *Peg's Paper* and my aunt stopped knitting. I looked up wide-eyed and even my mother gave a gasp of amazement.

'Oh, Josie, it's lovely. Louisa, you've done a wonderful job,' she exclaimed as Josie spread out the full skirt of the long white dress. Tight narrow sleeves ended in ruffled frills at the wrist and more frills edged the sweetheart neckline of the fitted bodice. Josie smiled happily as she turned to display the row of tiny pearl buttons down the back. Nothing about the dress now suggested the word 'parachute', and Miss Plumb allowed a gleam of satisfaction to pass across her tired old face. Meanwhile I looked on, hardly able to believe my eyes. Josie, pale, skinny, boring Josie Peake was, for the moment anyway, the equal of any Hollywood film star I had ever seen at the pictures.

Everything seemed all set for a happy ending to Josie's romance, but unfortunately just at that minute old Mr Peake decided to give Dinkie, their three-legged mongrel, his evening run. Normally Dinkie, chained up by his kennel 24 hours a day, made the most of his five minutes of freedom by tearing off up the garden at top speed to hide among the overgrown bushes while Mr Peake, cursing, tried to drive him back to his kennel. Tonight, though, Dinkie spotted our open back door, and before anyone knew what was happening he hurtled into the kitchen and flung himself joyously on me, hoping perhaps that I would go out into the garden to play, as I sometimes did. Taken unawares, I let the mug of hot cocoa fly out of my hands into the air, showering to my dismay all over Josie's white dress. The mug itself smashed on the hearth, scattering more drops of sticky cocoa over the hem of the dress, as I burst into frantic tears. After a horrified look at the damage, Josie followed suit, and the two of us wailed in concert while Dinkie was banished outside, Aunt Madge began to pick up the pieces of broken crockery and Miss Plumb, Mrs Peake and my mother snatched up tea-towels and face-cloths to dab desperately at the spreading cocoa stains.

'It'll wash, Josie, it'll wash,' my mother kept saying consolingly. 'Don't cry, Patty, you couldn't help it. That wretched dog ... .'

Eventually Josie tottered out to try to wash the dress, my mother pushing a packet of Rinso into her hands as she went by way of reparation. I stumbled up to bed to sob myself to sleep, praying that in the morning when the dress was dry the stains would have vanished completely.

But of course they hadn't. Either the material was particularly prone to staining or my cocoa the night before had been made stronger than usual—both, perhaps—but even after several washings the whole front of the dress was covered with ugly brown blotches. In desperation, Mrs Peake dabbed on some household bleach, only to watch the fabric dissolve into tatters under her sponge. Josie, seeing her vision of a fairytale wedding dissolving too, had hysterics and took to her bed. That day I went to school weighed down with guilt. I felt an outcast, a pariah. Before long, I knew, the whole of Shelley Street would know what had happened, and I was sure they would all blame me. After all, I blamed myself. If only I had held tight to the mug. If only I had drunk up my cocoa quicker. If only ... if only ... if only ... .

As it happened, it was the day of my elocution lesson again. I had seen Miss Miranda several times since that first occasion, and I was getting used to her. I liked her better than any of the more conventional teachers and looked forward to her lessons. As we waited for her in the science lab after school, I wondered what excitements lay in store this week, and for a few moments I was almost able to forget the catastrophe that had happened at home.

Not knowing the other girls in the group very well—they came from forms up and down the school and none was from my own particular class—I sat quietly looking through the poetry book which Miss Miranda had lent me the week before to learn a poem for today's session. It was some time before it dawned on me that time was passing and there was no sign so far of Miss Miranda herself. Gradually the other girls, who had been sitting talking among themselves, fell silent and finally a pale, shy girl from the sixth form looked at her watch.

'I don't think Miss Miranda's coming,' she said anxiously. 'Perhaps we'd better go home. The cleaners will be wanting to lock up the school soon. We can't stay much longer.'

She began packing her books away in her satchel and soon she and the other girls had gone. Reluctantly I started to collect my own books together, and as I did so Miss Miranda's poetry book fell to the floor. When I picked it up I noticed a faintly pencilled address on the fly-leaf—'M.F., Kendall Lodge, Kendall Avenue', it said, which I recognised as the name of a gloomy old house some distance from the school which I passed on my way to get the bus home. A plan began to form in my mind. I could call there and see if Miss Miranda was all right. After all, there must be some reason why she hadn't turned up for our lesson, and it would be the perfect way to find out more about her. At the very least, it would delay returning to Shelley Street. I wasn't at all anxious to face Josie or Mrs Peake again. With the wedding now only a day or two away, I felt it was best to avoid them at all costs.

I set off down the empty, echoing corridors and out of the school gates, my satchel on my shoulder and the poetry book in my hand. That would be the excuse for my call, and I rehearsed the words in my head as I hurried along. 'Please, Miss Miranda, I've brought your poetry book back. Please, Miss Miranda, I hope you don't mind but ... .'

I was so busy trying to find the right words, I almost passed Kendall Lodge when I came to it. It stood back from the road behind a sooty privet hedge, and dingy curtains hid the windows. I could hardly believe that the flamboyant Miss Miranda lived in such a dreary place. It seemed incongruous to think of her in a setting like this, as depressing in its way as where I lived myself. Puzzled, I went up to the front door and rang the bell. I waited, but there was no reply. Greatly daring, I gave the door a push, and to my mingled alarm and delight, it swung open a crack.

'Miss Miranda?' I called, but again I was met with silence. I pushed the door further open, looking into a dark, narrow hallway with a flight of uncarpeted stairs leading upwards. Surely, I thought, Miss Miranda must be at home, or she would have locked the front door behind her when she went out. I moved cautiously forward, passing a shadowy sitting room on one side and a bleak, dusty dining room on the other. Then I heard a muffled groan, which seemed to come from a doorway immediately ahead of me. I hurried through it, to find myself in a bare, high-ceilinged kitchen, with an assortment of groceries scattered across the quarry-tiled floor. In the middle of them, near an over-turned chair, lay Miss Miranda.

But not the Miss Miranda I knew at school. Without her colourful make-up, her face was pale and lined, and her hair hung down now in a long, untidy plait. She was wearing a shabby dark green velvet dressing gown, and on one foot was a worn bedroom slipper. Her other foot was bare, and the ankle above it was horribly swollen. It was obvious what had happened. Standing on a chair to reach into a cupboard, Miss Miranda had slipped, fallen and twisted her ankle. To my relief, her eyes were open, dark and flashing as ever, and when she spoke it was with her familiar voice, perhaps a little weaker than usual but still vibrating with emotion.

'Why, Patty, dear, dear child ... how kind of you to come.' With a struggle she propped herself up on her elbow, wincing with pain. 'So silly of me—I slipped off the chair. Do you think you could run the tap on that cloth over there to make me a cold compress? Then perhaps I can get upstairs and lie down. If you hadn't come, I shudder to think what I'd have done. I've been lying here for simply hours!'

With cold bandages swathed round her injured ankle, and leaning heavily on my shoulder, Miss Miranda hauled herself upstairs to her bedroom, an eerie cavern of a place cluttered with photographs of her stage triumphs. Downstairs again I tidied away the jumble of groceries and made her a cup of tea. When I took it up to her she was already looking much better.

'No need for the doctor, I think, Patty. No bones broken, after all.' She beamed at me gratefully. 'What a Good Samaritan you've been to me, child. And I'm sure I can rely on you, can't I, not to gossip with the other girls at school? Things haven't been easy since I left the stage and came back to live here, in my parents' old house. But I mustn't keep you chattering. Your poor mamma will be wondering where you are. You really must go home.'

At the word 'home' all my worries came flooding back. Something of this must have shown in my face, for she gave a cry of dismay and clutched at my hand.

'Oh, good gracious, whatever is it? Patty, you are happy at home, aren't you? They're not—not cruel to you, are they? They won't beat you for being late? Do please tell me if there's anything wrong!'

Suddenly it all came pouring out—the parachute, the wedding dress, Dinkie and the cocoa. Miss Miranda listened, with not the least flicker of a smile on her face, though it must have sounded a comical story the way I told it. When I finished, she patted my hand gently and pointed to the huge old wardrobe that filled one wall of the room.

'Look in there, child. See if there's anything that will do—my Ophelia gown, perhaps, or my Juliet.' She sighed. 'So long ago, and I shall never wear them again. It would be a small recompense for all your kindness to lend one to your friend for her wedding.'

I opened the heavy doors, to find the wardrobe crammed with silks, satins, velvets, furs and yes, a beautiful white lace-trimmed gown. With trembling hands I lifted it out, hardly able to believe my luck, and half an hour later I watched as Josie tried it on in her bedroom.

'It fits perfectly! Oh, Patty, how wonderful ... and your teacher just lent it to you for me, when you told her what had happened?' Josie hugged me, her eyes full of happy tears. 'It's like a dream come true. Chuck will be ever so pleased. You're coming to the wedding, aren't you? Do you think your teacher would like to come, too?'

I tried to picture Miss Miranda as a wedding guest along with all the Peakes and the Fishers and the rest of Shelley Street at the Ring o'Bells reception on Saturday. Perhaps I was wrong, but my imagination boggled and my courage failed. Discretion, I decided, would be the better part of valour. Hastily I explained about Miss Miranda's injured ankle which, still very painful, would make it impossible for her to be present.

'She won't be better in time, Josie,' I said regretfully. 'But she'll be really delighted when I tell her you like that dress so much.' A sudden thought struck me. 'I know what,' I said happily. 'Why don't you send her a slice of wedding cake?'

15

A Good Send-Off

'I'm signing nowt!'

The roar made us all jump, and my father followed it up by banging his fist on the table in time to his words.

'I'm signing nowt,' he repeated, bellowing above the rattle of the crockery, 'and that's an end on it. Now give over, will yer, and stop moithering me. I've 'ad enough of it, see? I ain't signing.'

My mother tossed her head in exasperation, her lips pressed grimly together. Eyes wide with alarm, she looked across at Aunt Madge, who was frozen with astonishment. They had both been so busy all these years currying favour with my teachers and keeping me hard at work, they had never imagined that, at the end of the day, my father might refuse to sign the forms for me to go to college. It was as unexpected as if the kitchen table had suddenly walked out into the yard, or the next-door dog started to talk instead of barking.

A smirk of satisfaction creeping over his flushed red face, my father picked up his newspaper again and turned to the sports page. As he pretended to spell out the captions, we could see him watching us out of the corner of his eye. Next to his plate lay the forms, ready for signing. For once in his life he held the whip hand, and he was enjoying it.

By now my parents' feud had waned, but the bitterness still smouldered, flaring up from time to time. My father, sullen and moody, resented Aunt Madge for preventing him from ruling the roost, but we depended too much on the money she brought in for him to get rid of her. My mother, forever ill with imaginary ailments, treated him like a lodger, and I was kept out of his way as much as possible. Now here was his chance to get his own back on the lot of us. To take up my provisional college place, once my exams were safely passed, I had to apply for funding. If he went on refusing to sign, we could do nothing. There was an ugly whiff of blackmail in the air.

'It's that crowd he's got in with at the factory,' my mother said angrily, after he had slammed out of the house, still grinning unpleasantly to himself, later that evening. 'They've put this daft idea into his head, I bet you anything. He'd never have thought of it off his own bat.'

'Daft or not, it's thrown a spanner in the works and no mistake,' replied Aunt Madge gloomily, putting the forms on the mantelpiece behind the clock. 'Still, don't worry, Annie. He'll give in soon enough—he always does.'

But I wasn't so sure. Like a lot of people, my father had been changed by the war years. When peace came, he was furious to find himself obliged to hand in his police uniform, too old now to stay on in the force when younger men were demobbed and available again. Instead, he had found himself a labouring job on the factory floor, a come-down after all his wartime adventures. Probably my mother was right, and it was his new cronies at the factory, eager to cause mischief, who had egged him on to dig his heels in over the forms. 'Why should you dance to their tune all the time? Mek 'em dance to yourn for once—teach 'em a lesson!'—it was easy to imagine them in the works canteen, winking at each other behind his back.

For the moment nothing more was said, and the forms gathered dust on the mantelpiece. But secretly my mother and Aunt Madge arranged to consult my old infants teacher, Miss Minchin, as they always did in a family crisis. On Saturday afternoon, when my father was at the football match, we set out for her house on the other side of the city. With us we took gifts, to make sure of a warm welcome—farm butter from Aunt Dot in the country, a bunch of bananas Mrs Peake had let us have 'under the counter', and a bag full of cardboard offcuts smuggled out of the box factory by Aunt Madge, for Miss Minchin to use at school. Though the war had been over now for several years, everything was still in short supply. When the parcels had been examined and put away, we were ushered at last into the chilly front parlour and told to sit down.

'I got your postcard, Annie,' said Miss Minchin briskly when we were all seated. 'Now what's this about a little difficulty?'

Patty's not having trouble at school, is she?' Despite her air of concern, I could see she was agog with curiosity.

'Oh, no, never in this world. She's getting on fine,' my mother replied hastily. 'It's not that, Miss Minchin. It's Patty's father. He's turned awkward.'

With Aunt Madge chipping in from time to time, my mother explained about the forms and the need to bring my father back to heel. From her sceptical expression and the occasional questions she asked, it was clear Miss Minchin found it hard to believe that two grown women were being thwarted by a mere man, especially one who, not to put too fine a point on it, could hardly be described as the brightest of the bright by a very long chalk.

'Can you not trick him into signing?' she suggested at last. 'Give him a pile of papers to sign, and put Patty's form among them? Just slip it in, somehow, without him noticing?'

I thought of all the palaver that went on in our house when any kind of writing was to be done—the bottle of Stephenson's blue-black ink to be fetched from the front room chiffonière, the new nib to be fitted to the pen when the old one was found to be crossed, the tattered sheet of pink blotting-paper brought in to be leaned on, and wondered how all this could be done without my father noticing. With something of the sort at the back of her own mind, perhaps, Aunt Madge shook her head sadly.

'I'm afraid not, Miss Minchin,' she replied apologetically. 'He's on his guard, you see, and if signing's so much as mentioned, it's like a red rag to a bull. You—er—you don't think you could have a word with him yourself, do you? We'd be ever so grateful, wouldn't we, Annie?'

As my mother nodded eagerly, Miss Minchin's pale, pinched face turned paler than ever at the thought.

'Much as I'd like to help you, Miss Fennel, no,' she answered firmly. 'I simply couldn't risk it—my heart condition, you know. Any kind of argument, any altercation ... .' Then a sudden thought seemed to strike her. 'But wait—I've just had a wonderful idea!' She leaned forward confidentially. 'After her exams, Patty has some time off school, doesn't she, before our own end of term? Well then, if she came up to help me in my classroom, she'd get to know Mr Winter, our headmaster. Now if he took an interest in

Patty, and had a word himself with her father ... .'

She left the sentence unfinished, but it was clear that a word from Mr Winter was more than enough to settle the hash of Genghis Khan, Napoleon Boneparte and Adolf Hitler combined. My mother and Aunt Madge gave a gasp of relief.

'Yes, yes, of course—and she'd love to come and help you, wouldn't you, Patty?' My mother gave me a sharp nudge and I joined in the chorus of agreement, smiling brightly despite my misgivings. When the details were settled, we started off on our way home, hurrying to get back before my father returned from the match wanting to know where we'd been. Now we felt far more hopeful of getting the forms signed on time after all, and the only drawback to the plan was that I had committed myself to being Miss Minchin's henchwoman when my exams were over. Memories from the past began to stir, and I couldn't help feeling uneasy.

But it was only when the time finally came that I realised just what I had let myself in for. There were no two ways about it—in spite of her prim and proper appearance, Miss Minchin was a sadist. She taught now at a large modern school near the city centre, and she ruled her class with a rod of iron. Compared with her, Miss Pumphrey, who had made my own life a misery years ago, was the merest amateur. Though Miss Minchin seldom raised her voice, her sinister purr was far more chilling than the loudest roar of rage. In the staffroom her sarcastic comments had made her so unpopular with the other teachers that she now kept very much to herself, having her coffee brought to her classroom by one of the older girls and eating her sandwiches at her desk at dinnertime. She expected me to do the same, of course, so I hardly ever went over to the main part of the school, Miss Minchin's classroom being in one of the temporary huts on the far side of the playground.

At first I was nervous of bumping into the legendary Mr Winter, but I soon discovered that he too spent most of the day in his own cosy room. The only time he emerged was at the end of the morning, when he trotted over to the dining hall and returned with a laden tray. A tubby little man with glasses and a mild expression, he hardly looked a match for my burly, belligerent father, but I consoled myself with the thought that appearances could often be deceptive. When aroused, Mr Winter might turn out to be a tiger.

Though my mother and Aunt Madge were delighted to think I was getting classroom experience as Miss Minchin's teaching assistant, in fact she herself saw my role very differently, more that of an unpaid charlady. I spent my first few days sorting out the stockroom, which looked as if it hadn't been cleaned and tidied for years. Chalk dust lay thick on the shelves and I found it difficult to muffle my sneezes as I dusted and stacked the piles of dog-eared cards and boxes of coloured counters that lay scattered everywhere. Behind me in the classroom itself all I could hear was the scratching of pencils, broken from time to time by an outburst of sharp slapping. The sobs and snuffles that followed were hurriedly stifled as Miss Minchin purred silkily, 'Oh, look, Class Five, we've got a dear little cry-baby at school today!'

Apart from a few quiet, tidy children, mainly girls, whose mothers had, like my own, had the sense to get on the right side of Miss Minchin with gifts and flattery, she picked on her victims more or less at random. Some of the rougher, tougher boys boasted between themselves that they 'weren't afeard of ole Minnie,' but I saw that even they had tears in their eyes when their turn came round to be slapped and poked and ridiculed. After the stockroom was finished, she set me to clear out the cupboards and shelves in the classroom itself, so that now I could see as well as hear what was going on, the bullying, the spite and the mockery.

Most of the children had been in Class Five long enough to have learnt to avoid, as far as they could, drawing attention to themselves, but one timid, pale little boy named Alfie Jellings had only recently arrived and as yet he hadn't got used to Miss Minchin's ways. He would wander out of his seat to ask a question or to sharpen his pencil, and no matter how often Miss Minchin sent him scuttling back to his place, before long he would get up and trail out again. At last, in the middle of one dreary afternoon, her patience finally snapped and she rounded on him in fury. While he goggled at her like a frightened rabbit, the rest of the class listened with bated breath. What was she going to do to old Smelly Jelly this time? If she had turned into a dragon and swallowed him whole, they would hardly have been surprised.

As she raised the lid of her desk, they exchanged excited

glances. They knew she kept a cane in there. It was only for show, since she wasn't allowed to use it, but they thought she could. It wasn't the cane she took out now, though, but something she kept hidden in the palm of her hand. She bent down so that her face was level with Alfie's, and he backed away, almost falling into the wastepaper basket. The class tittered, and she swung round to glare at them, before turning back to Alfie.

'Are—you—here—again?' she demanded, spacing her words out as she poked him with her bony finger. 'Well, then, I'll just have to use—this!' With a melodramatic flourish, she held up under his nose the enormous safety-pin she had taken from her desk. 'I'm going to pin you to my skirt, Alfie Jellings, that's what I'm going to do.' Pursing up her thin lips in a tight smile, she quickly seized the cuff of his grubby shirt-sleeve and pinned it to a fold of her long tweed skirt. 'There—that will teach you to stay in your seat in future, won't it? Wandering about all day like a lost sheep, indeed—I won't have it! And,' she added, snatching up an empty jam-jar from the painting-table, 'if you want to "leave the room", you'll have to use this!'

Alfie, forced to scurry after her as she strode about the classroom, burst into floods of tears while the children watched in sniggering delight. Sickened, I turned away, my cheeks burning, but what could I do? I was as much under Miss Minchin's thumb as Alfie.

Luckily Class Five were due soon for country dancing in the hall, and even Miss Minchin must have realised that she couldn't risk being seen in public with Alfie pinned to her skirt, clutching his jam-jar and his eyes red and sore with weeping. She lined the class up at the door and then turned to me, unfastening the pin as she spoke and tossing it back into her desk.

'This horrid little boy doesn't deserve to go to dancing, Miss Palmer,' she said contemptuously, pushing him roughly into his seat. 'I'm going to leave him here with you while you get on with your work. Just ignore him completely,' she added sharply as she led the other children out, perhaps detecting the sympathy in my eyes as I looked at Alfie.

As soon as the door was safely closed behind them, he put his head down on the desk, sobbing quietly to himself. I went over to him and patted him gently on the shoulder.

'There, there, Alfie, don't upset yourself,' I said softly. 'You'll make yourself ill if you go on like this.'

Alfie looked up, his face grimy with tears and sweat. 'But—but I feel poorly now, Miss,' he gulped. 'I bin feeling bad all the week, but me mam has to go to work so I couldn't stay 'ome. I dunno why Miss keeps picking on me. 'Taint fair, is it?'

'Never mind—you'll be going up to Class Six after the holidays,' I said, trying desperately to sound cheerful. I wiped his face with my handkerchief and tidied his hair with my hand. 'That's better. Now read your book, there's a good boy, while I dust these shelves. It's nearly hometime, anyway.'

When the class came back, it was time for Miss Minchin to lead them in their evening hymn, 'God Whose Name is Love', and she took no more notice of Alfie. The next day, Friday, there was no sign of him, and I was glad to see he had stayed off school. Meanwhile at home the stalemate with my father continued and so far we seemed no nearer the promised confrontation with Mr Winter. I had begun to suspect that Miss Minchin by now had no intention of arranging it, and even my mother and Aunt Madge were getting worried.

'Surely she won't let us down?' my mother said plaintively to my aunt, but I was afraid that was just what she was going to do. But then what happened on Saturday made us all forget all about Mr Winter.

I got up that morning with a sore throat and a headache, and by the afternoon I had developed a rash on my neck and chest, quickly spreading to my arms in thick, rough patches. When the doctor came and, at a glance, diagnosed scarlet fever, remembering Alfie's flushed face and sore eyes I knew exactly how I had caught it. My mother, of course, backing away in panic, laid the blame at once on my father.

'It's his fault,' she wept. 'If he hadn't been so pig-headed, you'd never have gone near that awful school, full of germs and things. Now what can we do? We might all catch it. It can be fatal, can't it, doctor? If she dies, it'll be down to him. And I might easily catch it myself, in my state of health. Oh, this is terrible—terrible!'

'Steady on now, Mrs Palmer. There's no need to talk about

dying.' The doctor exchanged a look of dismay with Aunt Madge, who was watching anxiously. 'We'll get this young lady off to the isolation hospital ... .'

'The fever hospital? Oh, no, doctor, we can't let her go there,' my mother interrupted in horror. 'I can't bear hospitals, and Patty's never been to hospital in her life either. Oh, whatever shall we do?'

'I'll look after her.' Aunt Madge spoke at last. 'Annie can't do it—she's not strong and her nerves are too bad. But you tell me what to do, doctor, and I can cope by myself. That way Patty can stay at home with us. You'd like that, wouldn't you, my duck?' she added with a comforting smile.

I nodded wearily. My temperature was soaring and I was soaked with perspiration. My mother had disappeared downstairs and the doctor stayed only long enough to impress on my aunt the need for every precaution to stop the infection from spreading. Then we two entered into a twilight isolation of our own, the room stripped bare, the curtains drawn and a sheet soaked in disinfectant hanging over the doorway. I can remember now the grey, gritty taste of Gulson's Fever Powder used to bring down my temperature and the chill of damp cloths on my forehead.

For days I lay tossing and turning, my limbs aching and my head too heavy to lift from the pillow. Aunt Madge crept silently about, changing the damp bedclothes and taking them down to the kitchen copper to boil them herself so that my mother ran no risk at all of catching the fever. At times I was delirious and when I slept at last I dreamed muddled dreams, waking to find my aunt dozing in a chair by the bed and ready at once to give me my medicine. Two weeks had gone by before the doctor agreed I was, against all the odds, finally on the mend, and praised Aunt Madge for her skilful nursing. At this my mother gingerly climbed up one of my father's old window-cleaning ladders to wave to me through the bedroom window. It was only to please Aunt Madge that I waved back in return.

Slowly I grew stronger, though I was still infectious and would be for another fortnight. I began to take an interest again in what was going on downstairs, and my aunt told me that my father and Charlie Fisher, the Peakes' son-in-law, had decided to dismantle the old air-raid shelter at the bottom of the garden, leaking now and full of evil-smelling water, for fear the stench from it had anything to do with my illness. My mother, she said, had been over to Aunt Dot's to get some new-laid eggs for when my appetite returned, and while I was ill my exam results had come through and were good. Once my father signed the forms, my college place was secure.

'So don't you worry any more about that, Patty,' she said as she shook up my pillows. 'He'll come round now, you'll see. It gave him a nasty fright, you being so ill. He won't have the heart to let you down.'

But for once Aunt Madge was wrong. I began to hear the familiar rumble of quarrelling downstairs, and soon I could see she was beginning to despair, though she tried to hide it from me. When my father was out of the house I could hear my mother crying and my aunt's voice growing more and more despondent. I could tell matters were coming to a head, and I was thankful to be alone upstairs, out of the way.

Then one night as I lay reading I heard the clang of a spade at the far end of the garden, and realised that work had begun on the air-raid shelter. Putting aside my book, I slipped out of bed and across to the window. Still shaky from my illness I held on to the window-frame as I looked out into the darkening garden. In the distance I could see my father swinging his spade among the elderberry bushes that had grown over the shelter, almost hiding it from view. Probably Chuck Fisher would be along to help as soon as he got home from work. While I watched, a pale shadow seemed to move forward slowly by the garden wall—Aunt Madge, was it, taking him a cup of tea? I knew my mother was lying down in the other bedroom with a headache, so it could only be my aunt, unless it was just a trick of the light. Before I could be sure, I suddenly felt dizzy and my head swam as I sank to the floor.

When the banging of the entry door roused me again, I was cold and stiff from lying on the bedroom lino, and I knew some time must have passed. Shivering, I scrambled back into bed, while down in the yard below I heard Chuck's voice as he called out to my father. I was just getting warm again when there was a commotion under the window, voices shouting, lights flashing and footsteps rushing down the entry. Everything went quiet for a while, but then there was more shouting, more footsteps and what seemed to be the banging of a car door in the street outside. Soon after that I heard the voice of old Father Desmond from the priests' house opposite—but why would he be visiting at this time of night? It was pitch dark now, and I began to be afraid.

Much later Aunt Madge finally came upstairs to tell me there had been a horrific accident, and my father was dead, drowned in the air-raid shelter. It seemed he had slipped in the mud, hitting his head on a jagged piece of corrugated iron that formed the shelter wall, before plunging unconscious into the stagnant water. Charlie Fisher had found him, far too late to revive him, and had sent for the police. Father Desmond had come across as soon as he heard, and was downstairs with my mother now. My aunt, shuddering and sobbing from time to time, patted my hand while I wept quietly, feeling chilled to the bone by the dreadful news. Though I had never been close to my father—my mother and Aunt Madge had seen to that—it seemed impossible that I would never see or speak to him again. But even as I wept, at the back of my mind, though I felt ashamed to think it even to myself, was the thought that now there was nothing to stand in the way of my going to college. And I tried, and failed, to remember exactly what I had seen earlier that evening ... .

There was an inquest, of course, which helped to scotch the rumours going around the neighbourhood that my father and Charlie Fisher had quarrelled that night, and fought. The police, it turned out, had found a half-empty bottle of rum in the pocket of my father's jacket, hung up on a tree near the shelter. This helped to explain, along with the mud and his ill-fitting Wellingtons, why he was so strangely unsteady on his feet. No blame, the coroner said, was attached to anyone, and he commended Charlie for his prompt action. A tragic accident, he concluded, particularly sad since the deceased had come unscathed through all the hazards of the war years.

The funeral could now be held, but the doctor thought it best for me to avoid the stress of going to the cemetery with my mother and Aunt Madge. Miss Plumb offered to stay at home with me and help get ready the food for the visitors. As we cut the sandwiches and arranged the cakes, I remembered how I used to play in the cemetery all those years ago, while my mother poured out her troubles at her aunt's grave. I thought of the night I had gone back there to find my lost dolls, returning home on Billy Weatherby's bicycle.

'Do you remember … ?' I began, but Miss Plumb had heard the noise of the funeral cars outside, and was gone to open the front door.

My mother, in deepest mourning, was ushered in first and sank down into the armchair by the front-room window. Her eyes were red with weeping but, perhaps unjustly, I felt there was something mechanical about the way she occasionally remembered to dab them with her handkerchief. Aunt Madge, too, bustled briskly into the kitchen to put the kettle on, as if the funeral had been a strictly routine affair and the sooner the guests were fed and sent on their way, the better. But my Birmingham aunts and uncles were clearly determined to make more of it than that. They had provided a lavish supply of bottles 'to give our Ronnie a reely good send-off'. At first my mother would take nothing stronger than a cup of tea, but when Mr Sephton came in to offer his condolences, she agreed to take a glass of sherry with him, for old times' sake. Soon Father Desmond joined them, full of the news that Father Con was about to go back to 'the ould country' to a parish of his own. Would he, I wondered, meet up with Maggie O'Shea, perhaps, or even with the World Walker? By now the room was filling up with relatives and neighbours, all crowded together and spilling out into the kitchen and the yard. As so often happens, once the ice was broken, what had begun as a melancholy event turned into an enjoyable party, as if the dead were only remembered in order to make those left behind more glad to be alive.

'And you're off to college now, Patty,' said Ivy Salter, taking one of the sandwiches I was handing round. 'Bunty sends her love, and says she's sorry she couldn't be here today, but she's playing the lead in *Naughty Marietta* in Bradford at the minute.'

'I'm glad your mother's bearing up so well,' Mrs Salter added, nodding across the room to where my mother was talking now to Aunt Dot and Cousin Lottie. 'Must have been a narsty shock for you all, what happened. And after you'd been at death's door yourself, too, in a manner of speaking.'